I0609867

INDEPENDENCE

STARSHIP JERICHO
BOOK 5

TOBY NEIGHBORS

MYTHIC
adventure
PUBLISHING

Indepence (Starship Jericho Book 5)

Copyright © 2025 by Toby Neighbors

ISBN: 978-1-952260-94-0 ebook

978-1-952260-95-7 print

Mythic Adventure Publishing, LLC

Idaho, USA

CHAPTER 1

HE WAS THERE FOR ANSWERS. Captain Zeke Darius, formerly of the SDF ship *Jericho* and, more recently, of the Arodoni ship *Renegade,* had a Medical Bay full of humans that were not from Earth or even the Sol system.

"GIGI is improving the translation app, sir," Master Sergeant Remmy Steel explained. "But it's a primitive language, and there are still some hiccups."

"We'll have to do our best, Master Sergeant," Darius said.

The extraterrestrial humans had been slaves on a space station that trafficked in trading people. Slavery was alive and well in the galaxy and the emaciated figures on the medical beds were proof that it was just as horrible an institution as he had always surmised. Several of the humans were barely alive. But there were a few who were strong enough to answer his questions. Food, IV fluids and vitamins had worked wonders for a handful of the former slaves.

"I've learned some names," Doctor Vivek Lanski said. "This is Malah, Gidri, and I think you know Anki, Master Sergeant."

Anki sat up on her bed, holding a flashlight. She offered it to Remmy, but he shook his head.

"You keep it," he said. Their language device translated the words and she smiled. "Anki, that's a beautiful name. I'm Remmy."

"Rem...ee," she said slowly.

"This is Captain Darius," the Master Sergeant explained. "He's in command of our ship."

The girl did not meet Zeke's steady gaze. She looked to be only fifteen or sixteen years old, painfully thin and dirty. Her hair was one thick tangle. It was brown with streaks of a lighter color. Her teeth were yellow and she had long hands with tapering fingers, that looked as though they belonged to a pianist.

"It's a pleasure to meet you, Anki, and your friends," Darius said.

Her friends were boys. They looked to be about her age and just as starved as she was. But the three of them did not seem to be upset or frightened. In fact, they had what Darius thought of as youthful optimism.

"You're like us," the boy named Malah said.

"Humans," Doctor Lanski said. "We are all humans."

The word obviously meant nothing to the trio of former slaves. Darius wondered how it was translated into their language.

"I'd like to know how you got to be slaves on that space station," Darius said. "Do any of you know?"

"Dura is the memory keeper," Anki said.

"I suppose that's a title for historian," Remmy said.

"We'll need to speak to her," Darius said. "In the meantime, what can you tell me about your life."

"I will be a mother," Anki said proudly.

Darius turned to Doctor Lanski.

"No," he said. "The scans did not show pregnancy. She's just a child."

"But old enough to get pregnant," Remmy said.

"I suppose," Lanski said, clearly uncomfortable at the thought of such a young girl having children.

"The pregnant women had more food," Remmy said. "They were honored if you can call it that."

"What about you boys?" Darius said. "Will you be fathers?"

They shook their heads. "We'll be taken," Malah said.

"I don't want to leave," the boy named Gidri said. "Can we go back?"

"Shut it!" Malah snapped at him.

Darius saw tears in the boy's eyes. It made him seem younger than Darius had first thought.

"No one is going to take you from us," Darius said. "You are safe here and you'll be able to stay together."

"In the light up top?" Anki asked.

"Yes," Darius said. "No more toiling in the darkness. You are on a spaceship now. We have food, lots of it. We have apartments and clothing. There is hot water and soap. When you're strong enough, we'll let you choose where you want to live on the ship and what you want to do. No one is going to force you to do anything you don't want."

Master Sergeant Steel gave the captain a sidelong look but didn't say anything. Darius knew he was making a promise he might not be able to keep. The *Renegade* was still in enemy space. They could be captured or killed. But as long as Darius was in charge, he wouldn't let anyone force the former slaves to do anything.

Darius turned to Doctor Lanski. "Who is Dura?"

"I don't know," he said. "The rest of the refugees have either been too weak or too reluctant to talk. More than half were pushed to the point of total exhaustion just getting off the slaveholder facility."

"It was a climb," Remmy said. "Several stories and things got dicey."

"Understood," Darius replied. He had just gotten the first block of real sleep in several days himself. "Are any of them in danger?"

"There are a few of advanced age," the doctor explained. "They are all malnourished and suffering from a variety of ailments that were the result of their poor diet."

"What were the slavers feeding them?" Darius asked the Master Sergeant.

"Nothing," Remmy said. "From what we saw, they ate garbage and rodents. It couldn't have been easy keeping that many people alive eating bugs and the occasional rat."

Darius shook his head in disgust. "Make sure they have everything they need," he ordered. "Including the opportunity to get cleaned up. I want them in real clothing as soon as possible. And when this Dura wakes up, I need to know at once."

"Aye, Captain," the doctor said.

"Master Sergeant, with me," Darius said as he headed back toward the main doorway.

In the concourse he stopped and watched the activity. The ship was in hyperspace, which was, in many ways, the safest place it could be. Darius still didn't understand it completely, but the ship passed from normal space into a hyperdimension that cut travel time down to a tiny fraction of what could be achieved via conventional means. Until they returned to normal space, they were safe from attack. And with their laser cannons still out of commission, Darius was relishing any sort of safety they could manage.

"Look at them," Darius said to his friend, Master Sergeant Remmy Steel. "So many innocent lives."

The concourse was a busy place. The *Renegade* had taken on volunteers from the Casa system. They were Casians and Dudonus, but Remmy's commando team had freed dozens of alien races from the slaver space station. Unlike the humans, they were in decent health. The volunteers were busy getting names, stories, and, generally, as much information as they could from the freed slaves.

"What do you plan to do with them?" Remmy asked.

Darius shrugged. "Once we get to the free worlds, they can choose their own future."

"What if they want to go back to where they came from?"

"I suppose they'll be able to find transport," Darius said. "We're a warship, Master Sergeant, not a taxi service."

"Yes, sir," Remmy said.

"Tell me what exactly you found in the space station?"

"It was a trade center," Remmy explained. "A place for the slavers to spend their ill-gotten gains."

"And these beings?"

"They were just locked in holding cells," Remmy said. "It was impossible to tell if they were being traded or sold. To be honest, sir, I didn't free them out of principle."

"What?"

"We needed cover, Captain," Remmy said. "I freed the captives so that if we were fired on, they might offer some protection for the humans we were there to retrieve."

It was a grim thought. Darius was both appalled at his friend's confession and surprised by the Master Sergeant's tactical genius.

"Maybe we don't tell them that," Darius said.

"No, sir," Remmy concurred.

"Tell me about the humans."

"They were scavengers," Remmy said. "They separated the garbage that came down chutes from the higher levels of the station."

"With no oversight?"

"None that we could detect, sir," Remmy explained. "There might have been some sort of surveillance, but when I say it was dark down there, I'm talking pitch black. It was like being in a cave."

"There were no lights at all?"

"Not in the sorting chamber. It was big, like a hangar, with huge pits where inorganic material was either recycled or, more likely, burned for fuel. It's a miracle that anyone could survive in that place."

"Our race has an indomitable will to live, Master Sergeant."

"Yes, sir, we absolutely do. There were a couple of smaller areas beyond the big sorting facility, Captain. One was where the majority of the humans slept right on the deck and kept their belongings. I can't say for certain, but it looked like a blanket would be worth a fortune in that place. Attached to that was a room with real beds - cots really - but still a step up from the other place. That's where the pregnant women were kept."

"Any idea how the breeding program worked?"

"No, sir. That's not clear. But my guess is they let the males stick around long enough to impregnate the women, then shipped them off as laborers for the slave ships. Beyond the room with beds was a small chamber with no doors. That's where they kept the children."

"It's a wonder they aren't born blind down in the darkness," Captain Darius said. "You did an excellent job getting them out."

"Two casualties is too many, sir," Remmy said.

"Doctor Lanski tells me Corporal Fry and Corporal Berry will both make full recoveries."

"That's good, but in the meantime, we need the new recruits to pick up the slack. I'm going to the armory now to inspect the new weapons harness for the Casians."

"Very good. I look forward to your report on their progress."

Remmy snapped to attention and saluted. Captain Darius returned the salute and then watched his friend join the crowd in the concourse. It felt strange to think that such a beautiful place could be filled with so many sad people. Not that the aliens looked sad. If he were guessing, they seemed overjoyed to no longer be captives, but to Captain Darius, they represented innocent beings who were ripped from their families and homes.

"Good morning to you, Captain," Commander Lori Lee said as she approached from the busy Administration Center that was directly across from the Medical Bay.

"To you as well, Commander. How are the new additions to our ship getting along?"

"They seem to be thriving, Captain. And the Dudonus are only too happy to welcome them aboard and see to their every need."

"The Dudonus volunteers aren't put off that we have incarcerated their leader?"

He was referring to the alien called Nurek, who had served

the imperial family as a slave for many years. Darius was keeping him isolated after the alien had murdered Emperor Vang. Not that the heinous act wasn't justified to some degree. Nurek had been held against his will for most of his life and forced to serve with no compensation. Darius couldn't begin to imagine what horrors the slaves across the galaxy were facing. A jury of Nurek's peers might not see his actions as a crime, but Darius was the absolute law on the *Renegade*. Warships were not democracies and there was no higher authority than the ship's captain. In Darius' view, Emperor Vang was a prisoner and it was the ship crew's responsibility to keep him as healthy as possible. Nurek had sidestepped their obligation and executed the prisoner, which was not only an ethical violation of their sworn duty but also kept Darius from being able to leverage the emperor in negotiations with the Imperial forces.

"I don't think they see Nurek as their leader," Commander Lee said. "None have complained to me."

"Maybe they think he's getting what he deserves," Darius said, although Nurek wasn't suffering. He was kept isolated in one of the unused crew cabins in the Command Section of the ship.

"I doubt that's true," Lori Lee said. "None of them speak well of their captivity. And from what I can tell from their stories, they were all abducted and kept on the slave ship for only a few weeks at the most. But the Dudonus live in fear of capture all their lives. They long for freedom."

"And they deserve it," Darius said. "I only hope our small contribution to their struggle is enough to make a difference."

His comlink beeped and then Ensign Alex Stanislaus spoke via the tiny device in the captain's ear.

"Captain Darius, this is Ensign Stanislaus. I've found something on the ship's computer. Do you have the time to come and take a look at this?"

Darius tapped the device, then replied, "I'll be right there, Ensign."

"Trouble?" Commander Lee asked.

"I hope not," Darius replied. "Something's up with the ship's computer. Do you have the time to join us?"

"Yes, sir, Captain," Commander Lee said.

They made their way back to the Command Section of the ship, which had multiple levels and included the Systems Control room. It was a large, wide chamber with computer stations that made up what appeared to be a long console. There were several holographic projectors that showed the *Renegade* from various angles and included readings on the various life support systems. Darius was thrilled as he walked into the chamber. It was one of the many places on board the alien ship that was so technically advanced that he felt as though he were suddenly thousands of years into the future. The human space fleet certainly had nothing like the Systems Control room on their ships.

There were three enlisted crew members at various places on the long central console. Their hands worked controls that caused the holograms to change. Ensign Stanislaus was at the far end of the room. He looked up as the captain entered.

"Captain on deck!" He shouted.

The three enlisted personnel all snapped to attention.

"As you were," Darius said as he strode across the room. "What have you got for us, Ensign?"

"Actually, Captain, I don't have it. That's the problem. There are firewalls around certain parts of the ship's computer logs."

"Firewalls? Are you saying that part of the ship's computer is restricted?"

"It is, Captain," Stanislaus replied.

"That's not all that unusual," Commander Lori Lee said. "There is restricted information on the computers of every ship in the fleet."

"Yes, Commander, I'm aware of that. But this is different," Alex Stanislaus said before lowering his voice and stepping closer to his superior officers. "This appears to have been added recently, sir. Just within the time we've been on board."

"By whom?" Darius asked.

Stanislaus shrugged. "If you think about it, there is only one person it could be."

"GIGI," Commander Lori Lee whispered the name so softly Darius barely heard her.

Alex nodded. A cold sense of dread filled Zeke Darius. He was the captain of the ship, but the alien artifact who called herself GIGI, or the Galactic Information and Guidance Instrument, was a super powerful artificial intelligence. Upon being brought on board the *Jericho,* GIGI had synced to the ship's computer. It seemed to enhance the computer exponentially, but until that moment, they had no reason to fear the alien artifact had done anything nefarious. When they found the *Renegade* and woke up the Arodoni ship's computer system, GIGI had synced to it as well. Ultimately, the alien device, or entity, had control of the ship and could lock them out at any time. She had proven what she was capable of on the slave ship when it was hijacked. The alien artifact had pumped all of the air out of the ship, killing the aliens who had stolen it. Darius knew she could do the same thing on the *Renegade* if she wanted to.

"What is being restricted?" Darius asked in a whisper.

"Ship's log and something to do with the ship's propulsion system," Stanislaus replied. "I can try to hack my way in."

"No," Darius said. "Don't do that. Just leave it alone, for now, Ensign. And good job. You've done excellent work here."

"Thank you, Captain," Alex said.

"Best not to speak of it, either," Commander Lori Lee said softly.

"She's right," Darius said.

Stanislaus nodded. They had a saboteur on board. Perhaps the alien artifact wasn't working against them, but it appeared that she wasn't giving them the full story either. Darius knew that was a dangerous place to be for a ship of war in enemy territory.

CHAPTER 2

REMMY STEELE MADE his way through the crowd that was gathered in the commerce section of the huge starship. The *Renegade* was divided into sections, so they could keep track of where things were. The massive, fish-shaped vessel had a Command section, an Industrial section, an Agricultural section with hundreds of lavish apartments overlooking it and a massive Technological section, complete with laboratories and classrooms. The Commerce section of the ship was like an indoor, multi-level shopping complex. The crew had laid claim to several of the vacant compartments. They were like storefronts that looked out over a gleaming concourse that was made of polished stone tiles and incredible accent pieces, some of which made of huge diamonds. It was a lavish part of the ship.

Remmy passed two bars and a dance club with throbbing music that had been set up by the human members of the crew. There was a wide compartment that looked to Remmy like the interior of a barn, complete with large bales of hay and huge troughs of water. There were big bins full of green vegetation that was the staple of the Casian diet. The six-legged pachyderms were social aliens. The barn, as most of the human crew referred to the Casian storefront, was their version of a tavern.

The Dudonus had their own storefront. It was similar to what the humans had done but less flashy. They had comfortable seating areas, shelves of books and strange but appealing artwork on the walls. There were even rugs and brightly colored pillows that were part of their culture. At least, that was what Remmy had been told. He was glad to see the volunteers making the ship their own. It allowed the different species to learn more about one another and, even with the former captives his team had liberated on the slaver space station, all of these occupants of the massive ship barely occupied a fraction of the alien vessel.

As he made his way through the park, he could see more aliens strolling along the grassy fields and taking in the sights of the incredible Agri section of the ship. It was still the most appealing part of the *Renegade* to Remmy. A person could completely forget they were even on a spaceship while relaxing in the park. There were wide fields with exotic grasses growing, strange trees, streams and flowering plants. Hovering or slowly drifting were elevated platforms with different flora, most likely cultivated from alien worlds. There were living creatures, too; herds of small to medium-sized animals grazed the wide pastures. Insects buzzed around the flowers and fish could be seen in the clear waters that flowed through the park. It was a stunning agricultural achievement that was far beyond the capabilities of the human race.

Remmy had been on dozens of space ships and space stations built by man. They were all claustrophobic vessels made for function, not form. He vividly remembered the narrow hallways, low ceilings and thick, heavy doors. They were built from metal that seemed crude in comparison to the elegant materials used in the alien ship. Remmy knew there were probably luxury vessels that were much nicer than the Space Defense Force ships he had traveled and served on, but nothing could come close to the technological superiority of the Arodoni.

Remmy reached the gravity lift and stepped out into nothing.

He passed easily from regular gravity to zero gravity, and it only took a small push to send his body drifting downward. He passed several levels on his way to the Space Marine armory. He knew there were hundreds of workshops, artist studios and what had probably been offices in the past. The entire ship had been abandoned by the Arodoni. It was a mystery that still plagued Remmy's logical mind. There had been no record of what happened to the former occupants and builders of the incredible ship. They had vanished, leaving behind a priceless treasure which the crew of the S.D.F. *Jericho* had taken possession of. And Remmy didn't like the feeling that he was missing something, maybe something important.

"Hello, stranger," Laila McPherson said as he reached the lowest level and stepped out of the lift. "How are things up in the Officer's domain?"

She was the Marine Staff Sergeant and Remmy's secret lover. She was in baggy fatigues, her short hair pulled into a ponytail. The sides of her head were shaved, which made her prominent cheekbones stand out all the more. But it wasn't just her good looks that appealed to Remmy. Laila McPherson was a combat veteran and very capable Marine. She took her job seriously and was deadly with a long rifle. Maybe the most appealing part of her nature was her never-quit attitude. Remmy had the same compulsion.

"Quiet for the moment," he replied. "Tex and Izzy are recovering."

"I stayed until they were out of surgery," Laila replied. "I'm so glad we didn't lose them."

"Me too," Remmy said.

She turned and walked with him toward the armory.

"Any idea where we're headed?"

"Not really," Remmy said. "I was told, but it didn't mean anything to me. Some part of space where several hyperspace lanes meet, I think. We'll be traveling in another forty hours or so."

"Wow, a couple of days with no mortal danger? What a pleasant surprise," she teased.

"Don't knock it," Remmy said. "There's no telling what's waiting for us on the other side."

"Maybe nothing," she said.

"With our luck, I doubt it," Remmy said. "How are the combat harnesses for the Casians coming?"

"They turned out pretty good, even if I say so myself."

Remmy knew that Laila had taken charge of the design process. The Casian volunteers were willing to help defend the ship, but their anatomy didn't lend itself to traditional weapons. Fortunately, the three-dimensional printers and maintenance droids could create just about anything the crew could imagine. The Casians were six-legged beings with big skulls and a tactile, articulating trunk. Remmy thought they looked a lot like elephants.

Inside the armory, a group of the Casians were gathered. Hugo McManus and Leigh Ann Poh were securing a contraption onto one of the aliens. They were calling it a battle harness and it consisted of a pair of rotating machine guns that could extend up over their head and were controlled by voice commands. The Marines had also developed a type of battle helmet that was based on the human space suit design. The Casians weren't built for special operations and couldn't carry out missions in space. They could be very useful in terrestrial combat where they would carry out artillery functions. On board the *Renegade*, they helped move heavy equipment and joined the humans in policing the spacecraft.

"How's it going?" Remmy asked.

"Fits," Hugo replied.

"It's a good design," Leigh Ann Poh said. "They've got ammunition, electrical power, and weapons without overloading the Casians."

The alien in the battle harness made a low grunting sound, which Remmy's language device translated into words.

"Fits like a glove, Master Sergeant," the alien said.

"You look pretty mean in that rig, Gawff," Remmy replied. "Can you control it?"

"Yes, Master Sergeant," the alien said.

"The guns are made of titanium," Laila explained. "Air-cooled and loaded with tracer rounds. The Casian helmet has a targeting app, too. They should be good to go once they've gotten some experience with the weapons."

"They're all anxious to get started," Hugo said. "I've had one of the computer guys working out a simulation program. They won't have full movement in the sims yet, but we'll get them started."

"Excellent work," Remmy said. "Where is Thompson and Sergeant Oliver?"

"On security patrol," Laila said.

It wasn't an optimal situation. Even if the Marine platoon were at full strength the *Renegade* was so big they couldn't patrol it properly. All they could hope for was a show of force to let the crew know there was a law enforcement presence on board, although policing wasn't what his platoon was trained for. They were special forces commandos, the best of the best at crossing enemy lines, disrupting enemy operations and carrying out combat engagements against superior enemy forces. They weren't police, and if things got out of hand on board the ship, Remmy wasn't sure if his people would make it better or worse.

"What about live-fire drills in the shooting range?" Remmy asked, referring to the live fire shooting facility they had set up in the hangar adjoining the armory.

"One at a time," Leigh Ann said. "We'll test the weapons and get the recruits used to the sound and fury of these guns."

"Plus, we can swap the machine guns out for just about any heavy weapons systems," Laila said. "Surface to surface missiles, surface to air, mortars, you name it. The Casians can get the job done."

"We won't let you down, Master Sergeant," Gawff proclaimed with a blast of air through his trunk.

"I have no doubt," Remmy said. "Carry on."

He and Laila left the armory and started back up the zero-gravity lift.

"Any word on how the humans got on board that space

station?" She asked as they drifted upward toward the park together.

"Not yet," Remmy said. "Captain Darius is asking questions, but the younger ones don't know anything. The older ones are still recovering from the long trek out of that station."

"I don't feel bad about shutting that place down," Laila said. "I think it may be the first operation I've carried out with zero regrets about it. Of course, that would be different if you hadn't come back."

"I'll admit, it wasn't as smooth as I would have liked."

They were almost to the park level, and she reached out. Remmy looked down; there was no one behind them, no one to see. Laila grabbed his arm and pulled him close. Their kiss was fierce but short. Remmy ran his hand down her shoulder and gave her hand a squeeze, then they pushed apart. It was as much affection as they could risk in public.

"No more close calls," she said.

"Agreed," he told her. "The Captain mentioned going home once we get the refugees and volunteers to the free worlds. That happens; we'll probably be locked up in different facilities for who knows how long."

"We should have stayed on Casasil," Laila said.

"Whatever happens," Remmy said. "I'm going to wait for you, Laila. I'm no choir boy but I've had my heart set on finding someone special. That's you."

"You're going to make me blush, Master Sergeant."

"I hope so," he said. "I love you."

The words were said quietly. There was a moment of silence as they reached the park and maneuvered themselves out of the gravity lift. Then Laila turned and looked at Remmy. It was intense. Her eyes were locked on his and he understood that she was being as vulnerable as she could be at that moment.

"I love you, too."

CHAPTER 3

SHEIKA KAHN WAS FURIOUS. They had been so close, yet the enemy had slipped away. He didn't know how, but it seemed the big alien ship had jumped into hyperspace. He had scout ships searching the area for a portal, but there was nothing on the navigation charts. As his generals linked their ships to the *Retribution*, forming a cluster that allowed them to join him in person, he prepared for what he knew was coming.

"Lord, I have news," the shipmaster said from just outside the open door to the Kahn's private quarters.

"Speak," Ulrech Sheika commanded.

"Scouts have found a portal. It's not on any navigation map, Lord Kahn. We have no idea where it goes."

A hidden hyperspace portal wasn't exactly news. The Imperium knew that portals existed throughout the galaxy. What they didn't know was how they were created. Most were marked and mapped via the ever-growing navigation system that was shared by all Imperial spacecraft. But it had long been suspected that felonious ships used unmarked hyperspace lanes to escape the Imperium after carrying out their criminal enterprises.

"Send in a scout," Sheika Kahn ordered. "I want to know everything."

"As you wish, Lord Kahn," the shipmaster said with a bow.

Sheika Kahn looked at himself in the full-length mirror. His ship, the *Retribution*, was a combat vessel, but as his flagship, it was built with luxury and style. His quarters consisted of a grand salon, an office, his bed chamber and a private armory. He was already wearing ornamental armor, but he was about to parley with his generals. They were the highest-ranking military commanders in the Ashi Fleet. As such, they held the loyalty of thousands of Ashi who would always prefer to see a powerful warlord as their emperor rather than a politician. But Sheika Kahn knew that politics could be just as savage and as dangerous as combat. He was past his prime as a warrior. In fact, he had grown fat, serving as the emperor's envoy for many years. In a fair contest of strength and martial abilities, he would lose. But in mastering politics, Sheika Kahn had learned never to fight fair.

He replaced his ornamental armor with stylish military-grade protective gear. The stomach was the weakest spot on any Ashi. Sheika Kahn covered his with a coat of Munxtun Alloy scales. They made him look reptilian and strong while giving him an impenetrable barrier in case the parley turned violent. The coat had two hidden pockets. Into these, he slipped close-range laser pistols. A wide Antacore hide belt was wrapped around his thick waist and held an Ashi dagger with a ring pommel at the small of his back. He didn't relish crossing blades with any of the generals, but he was not above cutting a throat or two, if it meant getting his way.

Satisfied that he looked the part, Sheika Kahn returned to the Bridge of the *Retribution*.

"Shipmaster, what is our status?"

"The command ships are nearly finished linking, Lord Kahn. I expect the assembly will be gathered in an hour."

"Make sure there is rich wine and succulent fare waiting for them," the Kahn said. "What of the fleet?"

"We have lost a third of our strength, Lord. And all the bombers were destroyed. We have only a handful of dreadnoughts left as well."

"How many is a handful?" Ulrech Sheika asked.

"Six, with two more that could be repaired given enough time, Lord."

"What of our eyes and ears across the galaxy? We must know the moment the Arodoni ship is spotted in real space again."

"Aye, Lord, we have vessels in every junction and all the major systems," the Shipmaster explained. "Spies on the minor worlds will inform us of the alien ship's presence should it show up. But the rebellion is growing, Lord. There is fighting on a hundred worlds. The fleet is needed to put down the dissenters."

"The fleet is needed where I say it is needed," Sheika Kahn said. "Do not think to tell me how best to run the Imperium."

"Forgive me, Lord. I meant no offense."

"Yet offense was given," the Kahn snapped. "If it is given again, I will require your head. Do I make myself clear, Shipmaster?"

"Aye, Lord, you have my apologies."

"You are dismissed," Sheika Kahn said.

He turned and looked out the big transparent hull sections that gave him a view of space around the *Retribution*. The other command ships were drawing close. It would have been easier and more efficient to have their parley done via a conference call. But that was not the way of the Ashi. They were a race of warriors. Orders could be given via electronic transmission, but a strategy session required warriors to be face to face, where disputes over strategy, mission goals and leadership could be settled in a violent, physical confrontation.

There was no doubt that the generals were eager to attack Sheika Kahn. They knew him only as a politician, a glorified servant to the true emperor. He would have to make an example and make it quickly once the parley started. They would want answers, and failures had to be made up for with blood. But Sheika Kahn was prepared for the confrontation. He would sacrifice as many of his commanders as necessary, just as he had sacrificed a third of his fleet in pursuit of the Arodoni ship. The foolish generals cared more about grandstanding and battle reports than the real treasure to be had. Command, not just of the fleet, but of the entire galaxy was at stake. And Sheika Kahn would let nothing and no one stand in his way of getting it.

CHAPTER 4

CAPTAIN DARIUS LEAD Commander Lori Lee and Ensign Alex Stanislaus into a small storage compartment on the *Jericho*. The human built ship was built from designs sent to them by GIGI over forty years before contact with the alien artifact was established. The long range fleet ship looked like a long auger used for drilling through ice. The corkscrew shape was useful in mimicking gravity. But little did they know at the time, that the real purpose of the ship was to serve as the *Renegade's* power plant.

Darius was still coming to terms with the reality that everything about their mission had been designed by GIGI, from the building of the *Jericho*, to recovering the Arodoni Power Converter, to taking control of the *Renegade* and fighting the Imperium. The alien device was maneuvering them like pieces on a chessboard. It didn't matter to Darius that what GIGI had manipulated them to do was probably exactly what he would have done anyway. He didn't like being used or spied upon.

The storage compartment on the *Jericho* was just one of many. There was a low shelf in the compartment with a few empty buckets and bottles of deck polish. Otherwise the room was empty. It was barely large enough for three adult humans to squeeze in.

"This is tight," Commander Lee said.

"Sorry," Darius replied. "It was the only place I could think of that GIGI wouldn't be monitoring."

"That we know of," Stanislaus said.

"Correct," Darius agreed. "But there are no human built cameras or microphones in this room."

"Why is that important right now?" Lori Lee said. "There's no doubt GIGI knows we found the firewalls. And like it or not, there's no clue as to what's been hidden."

"It could be completely innocent," Stanislaus pointed. "It's possible that she will give us access if we just ask."

"It's also possible that those files contain information that GIGI doesn't want us to have," Darius said. "Consider the fact that maybe GIGI is using us to fight her battles."

"Again, we don't have any proof of that," Lee said. "The alien device hasn't asked us to do something we don't want to do."

"Agreed," Darius said. "But we're only getting part of the story. We've only been told what she wants us to hear."

"You think there's more?" Stanislaus asked.

"I do," Darius said. "I think once we reach the free worlds, there will be cause for us to do something else instead of returning home. That seems to be the pattern we've fallen into."

"It's not safe to go back home," Lori Lee said. "Isn't that the paradigm we've been operating under."

"It is. It's partly because that's what GIGI told us," Darius explained.

"So, what could she be hiding?" the first officer asked.

"Who made her for starters," Darius said. "Maybe it wasn't the Correll. Maybe there was never a race of beings called the Correll."

"Wait, didn't Nurek say there was a prophecy about Correll?" Lori Lee asked. "Something about our race working with a Guidance Instrument built by the Correll to bring down the Imperium?"

"Oh, yeah, I forgot about that," Darius admitted.

"So far, everything that GIGI has told us was true," Stanislaus said. "I don't think she's hiding secret information."

"Then what?" Darius asked. "Is she hiding what happened to the Arodoni?"

"Maybe," Lee said. "Maybe they all went crazy and killed themselves. Maybe there's something on this ship that isn't good for us."

"That would be information worth hiding," Stanislaus said. "If the goal is to keep us on the *Renegade*, it might not be a good idea for negative information about the builders to come out."

"I want to know what it is," Darius said. "And I want GIGI to be shut out of our computer systems if we think it best. Is that possible, Ensign?"

Alex thought for a moment. "Anything is possible, Captain. But keep in mind that GIGI is smarter and faster than we are. We don't know how she functions. I can't just unplug GIGI to make her go away."

"Jettisoning her into space won't work either," Lori Lee said. "Hard vacuum has no effect and she can control the ship's systems from a distance."

"There has to be a way," Darius said. "We'll blow her up if we have to."

"That might work," Lori Lee said. "The ship's lasers have more than enough power to vaporize GIGI."

"We might not have to go that far," Alex said. "We could overload her systems. She's protected from an EMP but if we feed enough power into her directly, it should shut her down, temporarily, at least."

"How temporarily?" Darius asked. "Long enough to hack into those records?"

"You're assuming we can hack into them," Alex said.

"There's always a way," Darius said. "We shut her down, break through the firewalls and find out what GIGI is hiding."

"That's an audacious plan," Commander Lee said. "We might piss her off and get ourselves killed in the process."

"We have to be prepared for anything," Captain Darius said. "The fact is, with GIGI on board our ship we can't be sure she won't turn on us. We need contingencies in place. Surely, we have protocols for dealing with rogue AI."

"We've always been too reliant on computers to fully integrate truly sentient Artificial Intelligence. A droid is one thing, independent computers is another," Lori Lee said. "That's why AI research and development was shut down centuries ago."

"People were afraid foreign governments or terrorist groups would use them to attack military systems, power and water grids, even banking," Alex added. "All our AI systems have built in checks and balances. If a system goes rogue, it would shut itself down in the process of trying to gain control."

"What do we have to combat against foreign AI?" Darius asked.

"The *Jericho* has a system called Infiltrator," Alex said. "It's a military grade program designed to kick out any foreign presence inside our software systems. But there's a drawback. It will also delete anything that's been added since that presence entered the system. The idea is that if an outside entity gained access, they would almost certainly leave malware on the system. Enough to crash everything, if they were pushed out. So, Infiltrator is designed to stop that."

"Okay, sounds right," Darius said.

"If it does that, Captain," Lee said. "We would lose the navigation system upgrade. We wouldn't be able to calculate a way back home."

"Oh," Darius said, realizing his mistake. "Then we need to copy that system. We need a hard copy of everything from the *Jericho* and from the *Renegade*."

"Which sounds simple enough, but you're talking about Petabytes of information," the ensign pointed out. "We don't have that."

"We can build it," Darius said.

"Not without GIGI knowing," Lori Lee reminded him.

"Of course not," Darius said. "But we don't have to be honest about what we're building it for."

A plan was starting to come together in his mind. One that made sense to him and felt reasonably achievable.

"Stanislaus, get the production plant going on the servers we'll need to make a hard copy of the ships' systems. We'll set it up on board the *Jericho* so it's out of the way. I'll give the order from the Bridge. We'll say we're doing it to share the *Renegade's* advanced technologies, which is true. But if we have to box GIGI out, it's better to be sure we have what we need to carry on without her."

"Aye, Captain," Alex said.

"Better have him ask GIGI about the restricted information, too," Lori Lee said. "It'll be less suspicious coming from him."

"Good idea, Commander. My gut says GIGI will either deny your request or lie about her ability to access those files. Either way, we'll know she's hiding something from us."

"And if she gives us access?" Alex asks.

"Notify me immediately. We're going to call this Operation Odyssey. Never talk about the details of it outside this room."

"Aye, Captain. We know the stakes," Lori Lee said.

They left the tiny compartment and made their way back to the *Renegade*. Once there, they went their separate ways. Darius returned to the Bridge, but he felt like he was being watched. He told himself he was being paranoid, but that was the way of secrets. He couldn't keep a secret without feeling that others were trying to pry it from him. On the Bridge, he settled into his captain's chair, and not for the first time relished how comfortable it was.

"Progress report, Lieutenant Ramos," he said.

"Aye Captain, we are thirty-nine hours from the transition point. All is well on the ship. All systems in the green, sir."

"Very good, any update on the laser repairs, Lieutenant Nash?"

"Actually, Captain, we are proceeding with fabrication of parts," Henry explained. "We can't replace the laser cannon in hyperspace since it is outside the ship, sir, but we'll have all the parts to do it once we're in real space again. All the electronics and power supply issues on the inside are repaired. The maintenance system is calculating eight to ten hours for total replacement of the laser cannon."

"And there's no way to bypass the damaged gun and still utilize the other three?"

"Negative, Captain," Pete Best said. "I've been looking into it. All the laser cannons are on a single power grid. Knock out one and you lose all four. It's a very clean and efficient system, but flawed."

Darius nodded. Flawed was the correct word. The ship seemed perfect in nearly every way, but she had flaws. Given time, human engineers could probably change the power structure and allow the each individual laser to function independently. But time and resources were already stretched thin. They would have to make due with the weapons system as the aliens had devised it.

"I want to meet with the refugees and make a plan for when we reach the free worlds," Darius said. "If we're truly going to disrupt the Imperium, we should share as much of the technology from the *Renegade* as possible. Every world should be able to defend itself. Sharing the tech we have gained should level the playing field. In the meantime, I want us to be ready to defend ourselves once we come out of hyperspace. Lieutenant Best, meet with the Marine platoon and come up with some ideas that would make us ready for battle if it should come to that."

"Aye, Captain," Pete Best said.

"Navigation, can we have a plot set to take us to the next hyperspace portal the moment we come back into real space?"

"This lane isn't on our network, Captain," Vivian Ramos explained. "I have no point of reference for where it might come out. I'll need that to plot our course."

"Get on that slave ship and see what you can learn, Lieutenant," Darius ordered. "Without our laser cannons speed is our greatest asset. I want us ready to run for the next portal the moment we hit real space."

"Aye, Captain. I'll be ready."

Darius leaned back in his seat and drummed his fingers on the armrest. He needed to keep everyone busy. His orders were more than distractions though. As much as he wanted to solve the mystery of what GIGI was hiding, he knew they were facing a very real threat when they dropped from hyperspace. They couldn't take their own safety for granted and Darius was tired of scrambling because of his own mistakes. As far as it was up to him, he wanted a clean run to the free worlds. Maybe then, he thought, they could truly turn their thoughts toward home.

CHAPTER 5

THE COUNCIL WAS ASSEMBLED. Sheika Kahn made the generals wait for him. They stood in a circle, no one speaking. The Kahn watched on a video feed from the Bridge of his ship, noting the physical appearance of the commanders. They were all Ashi warriors, thick chested, with powerful arms and shoulders. Their tusks were long and many had golden rings embedded in the curved teeth that stuck up from their lower jaws.

Sheika Kahn was the opposite of the professional warriors. The skin around his throat sagged, a sign of age and physical deterioration. His arms and shoulders were still large, but so was his stomach. It stretched the front of his armored coat, and hung over the front of his kilt. His hair, what remained of it, was wiry and resisted styling. His whiskers had already turned white from stress more than age. Worse still there were deep lines around his narrow eyes and across his forehead. He was older, weaker and less appealing than the generals. But he had a wealth of experience they did not have. For centuries the Ashi had trained for war that never happened, while Ulrech Sheika was in a constant battle of wits with the leaders of the empire every single day. They had sparred to hone combat skills, he had struggled to survive in a political landscape where one wrong move resulted in shame and ended careers.

He did not fear the generals, although he respected their ferocious nature and their skills in combat. But there was no need to fight them. His greatest weapon was not the knife in his belt or the guns in his hidden pockets, but his mind. He had already considered every possible way in which they would attack him. He had his countermoves ready, not just to parry their attacks, but to crush their vain ambitions.

"I am ready," Sheika Kahn said to the shipmaster.

The career spacer bowed slightly, then led the way to where the other commanders waited. At the door to the chamber the shipmaster stepped aside. Sheika Kahn strode through with confidence. The others watched him without a word and he took his place in the circle, speaking first to assert his control over the proceedings.

"Welcome to the *Retribution*," he said. "As you know, the alien ship has fled the system in disgrace."

"How?" Barked General Creed.

"Through an unmarked portal," Sheika replied calmly. "It was not in the galactic network. I have already sent a scout through the portal to report on where it leads."

"Another failure," General Blean growled.

"That is not true," the Kahn replied. "There is nowhere in the galaxy for the enemy to hide from us. They run away because they cannot succeed in destroying the Ashi fleet."

"You are blinded by your ambition," General Holok said. "Step aside and allow us to take command."

"You propose to lead by committee?" Sheika Kahn asked.

It was the first shot from his arsenal. Nothing was more revolting to the Ashi warrior ethos than decisions made in a committee. The question was immediately followed by several roars of disgust.

"I will lead!" Shouted Blean.

"Never!" Creed swore.

Sheika Kahn didn't move. Five of the assembled generals

moved forward. Their intent was to reach the Kahn and kill him. But they could not confront him while there were other challengers so they turned on each other. They were fast and strong, ripping and tearing one another to pieces. Savage growls echoed off the metal walls and blood splashed onto the deck plates. Three of the challengers were killed quickly, the last two were Creed and Brean. They punched and bit, landing blow after blow. The Ashi were not known for defensive fighting. It was a brawl. Bone shattered, flesh was rended, but neither would submit.

Finally, Creed managed to sink his teeth into the back of Blean's neck. The bite tore flesh, but that wasn't the danger. As Blean tried to shake his opponent off, Creed's powerful jaws tightened. There was a sudden sound, a ~Crack!~ that sounded benign, almost like the breaking of a quill when a writer pressed too hard. It was Blean's neck snapping under the pressure from Creed's bite. Blean dropped to the floor dead, his body limp and covered with blood.

Creed roared in victory and turned toward Sheika Kahn who calmly raised his arm. In his hand, the Kahn had a small pistol. The weapon fired with an electric hum. The laser caused Creed's eye to explode before burning through his brain. The Ashi warrior, Commander of fourteen ships of war, stiffened and toppled like a tree.

There were growls of disapproval from the remaining commanders.

"Why are you surprised?" Sheika Kahn said.

"You have no honor," Holok snarled.

"That's where you are wrong," Kahn said, launching into the speech he had been waiting to give. "Why do we seek the Arodoni ship? It is not to test our prowess, nor for glory in battle. It is for the technology."

He held up the small pistol. "With this little device I slew a giant. I had but to squeeze the firing plunger. It was simple, yet deadly. It took no strength, yet it laid the strongest Ashi warrior low. Understand the lesson at hand or you too will die as Creed has

died. There is no honor in his death. There is no glory in his struggle. And know this, anyone can do this. Even the weakest race
among the galaxy can press this plunger and deal death in an
instant. That is why we alone must capture the Arodoni ship. I
care not about the beings who crew this vessel or what they want.
We must have their technology that can vaporize our ships of war
in a single blast. We must copy their ability to harness energy to
power their mighty ship. We must know what they know and
utilize it.

"As I speak there are over one hundred Imperial planets in
open rebellion. The Ashi fleet is spread thin. Imperial representatives are under threat. Even the Prime Council is attacked. You all
know that Nic'Tal was murdered. These are uncertain times and
we must be ever vigilant to look after the empire."

General Holok shook his massive head. "Fine words. It is no
surprise that you have risen to power, Sheika Kahn. I wonder, did
Emperor Vang fall under your spell?"

"Do not speak ill of the dead," Ulrech warned.

Holok chuckled. "Emperor Vang was a fool. We all knew he
was your puppet, Kahn. His death has played right into your
hands."

"I may not be the emperor yet, but I have been given control of
the Ashi fleet."

"No one would deny it," Holok said, stepping forward from his
place. It was a clear challenge to Sheika Kahn's authority. "But we
are warriors, Kahn, not political appointees. Military command
must be earned, it cannot be given."

"I have earned it with a lifetime of service."

"Your lifetime has been one of manipulation and excess."

Sheika Kahn was growing angry. It may have been traditional
for the battleship commanders to question their leaders, but as the
insults mounted, Ulrech found it harder and harder to maintain his
self-control.

"Look at you," Holok continued. "Fat, weak and slow witted.
You have no discipline and your management of the fleet reveals

your lack of strategic understanding. How many must die for your folly?"

"Enough," Sheika Kahn said quietly.

"Will you shoot me down too, Kahn? You dare not fight me with honor. And yet I stand here challenging you."

"Step back, General. No one else needs to die today."

"I disagree," Holok said.

He leaped forward so fast that Sheika Kahn was caught completely off guard. Holok's first blow was to Ulrech's right forearm. It broke, the bones shattered under the powerful punch. The Kahn dropped the small laser pistol as he reeled backward.

General Holok didn't give the career politician even a moment to recover. As Ulrech staggered back, Holok charged forward. A hard fist landed against Sheika Kahn's stomach. It drove the breath from his lungs and shocked his internal organs. Spots appeared in his vision as he doubled over from the blow. General Holok grabbed the back of Ulrech's head, yanking hard on his thinning hair. He bent low, his hard face close to Ulrech's exposed throat.

"How does it feel to be in a real fight?" Holok taunted.

His arrogance cost him dearly. Sheika Kahn's right arm was broken and useless. But his left arm was strong enough to draw the dagger from the back of his belt. Holok never saw it. He never suspected the Kahn would do anything but die. His taunt gave his opponent just enough time to pull the blade free of its sheath. And as Holok's tusks neared Ulrech's throat, the Kahn drove the blade into the General's side. He brought it in low to make sure it didn't catch on the bones of the chest. The hardened steel plunged in just above the General's hip. It was long enough to puncture through the thick muscles of the warrior's stomach, and reached the vital organs they covered.

General Holok suddenly lost all his strength. He dropped to one knee and Ulrech's blade ripped up through his stomach to his chest. Pain was throbbing from Sheika Kahn's broken arm, but he ignored it and instead pulled the knife free from the General's body. With the other commanders watching, Ulrech slid the blade into Holok's narrow throat. The Ashi anatomy was different from a human's. They had barely any neck at all, but it was there. The knife blade found it and slipped in between the high breast bone and the General's strong chin. Blood gushed from the wound, splashing over Ulrech's hand and onto his battle coat.

"What I lack in physical strength, I make up for in other ways," Sheika Kahn said. "The empire is mine now ... and no one will take it from me, General!"

He shoved the dying warrior aside like a bag of garbage. Holok toppled to the deck. The remaining commanders didn't move to challenge him, which was good. The pain of his broken arm was starting to register in his brain and he felt weak. His body was trembling from rage, fear and pain. But looking around the circle, Sheika Kahn saw a grudging respect from the other commanders.

"Return to your ships," he ordered. "We will track down the Arodoni vessel and take it from them, no matter the cost."

The commanders bowed. He had no doubt they each harbored their own desires to kill him and take control of the empire, but they had seen his resourcefulness. No songs would be written about Sheika Kahn's prowess in battle, but once he was crowned as the emperor, he could adjust the historical record however he desired. And he was proud to think that while he wasn't a physical match for the Generals in close combat, he was more than shrewd enough to make up the difference.

CHAPTER 6

"YOU ARE THE DURA?" Captain Darius asked.

The old woman nodded. She was pale skinned and what was left of her hair was gray. The former slaves were malnourished and infested with lice. Doctor Lanski had ordered their heads shaved, and treated them with red light therapy. They had been washed, given new clothing, their open wounds treated. The Dura looked to be ancient. She only had a few teeth left and her skin was wrinkled everywhere, even on her scalp.

"I am," she said, her voice raspy.

"Thank you for talking with me," Darius said. "I'm captain of this ship. I want you to know you are safe now."

The old woman had an IV in one arm, and wore a medical gown. She seemed both distressed and in wonder at the same time.

"I need to ask you some questions," Darius said. "Is that okay?"

He waited while his words were translated. The old woman seemed to listen intently, then nodded her head.

"Thank you," Darius told her. "What do you know of where your people came from?"

The elderly woman seemed to brighten up. She raised a gnarly hand as she spoke. "It is said, that long ago, we lived in the light."

There was light in the medical bay, but it was limited and dim. To Darius it seemed gloomy, yet he knew that to the humans who had lived their entire lives in the dark, it was very bright.

"We were taken away from our place. No one remembers who took us ... or why. It is said we served in many places. But we were stubborn. We did not serve willingly. So, the masters put us in darkness."

The short explanation seemed to tire the elderly woman out. She lay back on the bed and closed her eyes.

"Are you all right, Dura?" Darius asked.

She gave a shuttering breath. "This place is hard," she said. "I never dreamed I would see so much."

"You never have to go back to the darkness," Darius told her. "You are a human. Where we come from, there is light."

"It is said there is light when we die. Am I dead?"

"No. You're very much alive."

"I have lived too long," she said. "I should have passed the mantle long ago. But I feared the light."

"You have nothing to fear now," Darius said. "You're safe."

He wasn't sure she believed him, but he knew in time she would adapt. The younger members of her group were already adjusting to their new circumstances. Soon, they would be well enough to leave the Medical Bay and move into their own quarters on the ship.

Darius wasn't sure what he hoped to learn from the former slaves. Even if they had known their own history, they had been trapped on the slaver space station so long it probably all seemed like myth and fables to them. But Darius felt a burning desire to understand what was really happening in the galaxy. Perhaps it was because GIGI had orchestrated so much of what they had done since leaving the Sol system. Or maybe, Darius was looking to the former slaves in an attempt to rationalize his own command decisions.

He left the Medical Bay and went to the park. It had become a busy place. There were volunteers and former captive aliens mingling with the humans on the grassy hills.

"It's really something to see," Connor O'Dell said as he approached Captain Darius. "I never would have guessed that we could get along with aliens so well."

"You have so little faith in your fellow man?" Darius asked.

"This is a warship, Captain," Connor replied.

"True, but I think the crew is seeing a cause worth fighting for in our guests. They aren't just aliens; they're prisoners, they're slaves. They've suffered under the Imperial government for a long time and our crew finds purpose in liberating them. I know I do. Nothing in my career has come close to achieving what we just pulled off at that space station, where the humans were kept down in the dark."

"I can't argue with that," Connor said. "I've never seen people looking so terribly mistreated."

Darius had seen the effects of war. He had seen video feed from units on the ground after a naval bombardment from orbit. It was terrible. He sometimes had nightmares about it. It could be incredibly intense at times. In fact, Darius felt almost as good about destroying the Ashi orbital bombing ships as he did about saving the human slaves. But he had to agree with O'Dell. He had never personally seen humans who looked so much like the dead.

"I only wish I knew how they got there in the first place," Darius said.

"Our history is rife with stories of people being abducted by aliens," Connor said. "People have always disappeared without a trace."

"You're saying the rumors are true?" Darius asked. "Should we get our tin foil hats out?"

Connor laughed. "I felt the same way before this trip. Sometimes, I wish I hadn't volunteered."

"You certainly got more than you bargained for," Darius said.

"You can say that again. There's nothing worse than being a civilian on a battleship during a fight."

"I suppose," Darius said, although he couldn't really relate.

"So, what do we do now? Is there a plan?"

"The plan now is to get to the free worlds," the captain said. "That's our purpose and we have even more reason to go there now."

"You mean them," Connor said, nodding toward the refugees in the park.

"I do. Once that's done, I think we have to seriously consider going home. If we can get there without being followed, that is."

Connor took a deep breath, then sighed. "I'm not getting my hopes up."

"I know how you feel, Mr. O'Dell. I'm sorry that I couldn't accommodate you sooner."

"Couldn't or wouldn't?"

"Both," Darius said with a nod. "I won't deny that staying away from the Sol system was my choice. I'll take full responsibility for it when we get back home. But as you have pointed out, we are members of the Space Defense Force. There is a new - very powerful enemy - on our doorstep, and it is our duty to learn as much about them as we can. Just as it is essential that we don't lead them back to our star system."

"You can't control everything," O'Dell pointed out.

"True, and it seems like we've done our part. Hopefully, it will be enough to disrupt the current governmental situation. But either way, we've let the enemy know we're not to be trifled with. It may be enough to keep the Ashi fleet away from our home."

"And if it isn't?"

"At least we'll have the *Renegade* to help us defeat them," Darius said. "It's my aim to share the technology of this ship with the entire galaxy. What they do with it is up to them, but I don't feel like it's ours. We may have found the Arodoni ship, but we didn't build it."

"There are a lot of people back home who will disagree with you."

"I'm sure," Darius said. "And who knows, they'll probably lock me up for the rest of my life because of what we've done. But all I have to do is think of the people we saved from that slaver space station to know I was right."

"I admire your conviction, Captain. I only wish I shared it."

"You don't think saving those people was noble enough to justify what we've done?"

"You're only thinking of one facet of what you've done," Connor said in a grim tone. "You can argue that you didn't start an interstellar war, but it could easily be argued that you did. How many members of your crew died on this cruise, Captain? Were their lives worth those that you saved? And what about the thousands of Ashi that died? If life is the plumb line we're using to justify what you've done, there are many more deaths on the scales than lives saved."

Darius couldn't believe what he was hearing. He told himself that Connor O'Dell was a civilian and didn't really understand war. It was easy to sit on the sidelines and criticize those who put their lives at risk in war. Darius was an officer in the SDF. His duty was to fight all enemies, foreign and domestic. He had done that his entire career. He had served, trained and worked to make the Sol system a safer place. The sacrifices he had made loomed large in his mind when he contemplated the future. The service had been important to him even though it cost him the ability to have a meaningful relationship. He had no family and no friends outside the Fleet. It was a painful reality of what it took to serve in the SDF.

There were scars on his conscience, too. People had died under his command and as a direct result of orders he had given. Not just on their current mission but in the past as well. Some had been accidents. Space was not a safe environment in which to live and work. At times, the unforeseen occurred and usually had permanent consequences. But there were combat deaths, too, and even collateral damage from operations he had been involved in or commanded. At night, those scars often kept him awake. He remembered the people who died under his command. And he didn't take for granted the Ashi that died as a result of his actions on the *Jericho* and the *Renegade*. But he had seen the enemy, too. He had seen them on his ship, killing and trying to sabotage the vessel. He had seen the Ashi protecting the aliens operating the slave trade in the galaxy. They had made the choice to serve in the military, just as Darius had. They knew the risks they were taking and the reasons they were fighting. At times, he felt the weight of responsibility for all the lives he had taken and it threatened to suffocate him. But when he thought of the humans who had lived their entire lives in the dark, subsisting on rats and garbage, with no hope that their lives would ever get any better, he was reminded that all he had done was of value. Zeke Darius fought to free the oppressed. The thousands of Ashi who died because he ordered the *Renegade* to vaporize their ships had fought to keep people, even humans, enslaved.

"I won't argue that we've started a war," Darius said. "Nor do I ever forget that I am directly responsible for thousands of lives who have died fighting us. But I have a noble reason for my actions. I will fight for freedom without hesitation, be it here or at home."

"I hope it isn't at home," Connor said. "I hope we aren't remembered as the people responsible for bringing death from a superior race down on humanity."

Darius thought for a moment, then asked a question. "Do you really think one race of intelligent people is superior to another?"

"I didn't mean inherently superior," the younger man said. "I just meant more advanced."

"They are more advanced than us at this moment, but they won't be once we share the technology from this ship," Darius said. "That's why going wide with what we have here is important. It not only levels the playing field across the galaxy, but it also keeps humanity from becoming a tyrannical race. We can be just as bad as the Ashi. Our history is full of examples of that. But we also have the capacity to do good."

"It'll be all for naught if we don't get home with that technology," Connor said.

"Yes, that's true. We have to complete our mission and get all this home."

He stared out across the park, marveling at the life he saw and the spaciousness of the alien starship.

"This," he said with a wave of his hand, "is our future, Mr. O'Dell. Not the dank, cramped ships we've built in the past ... but this. And the galaxy is open to us now, as well. Space for humanity to spread out, to breathe and to grow. We'll make sure that happens."

"I hope so," Connor said.

And they both knew exactly what he meant. They had a plan, but so did their enemies.

CHAPTER 7

"WON'T BE LONG NOW," Remmy told Laila. "I need to get up to the Bridge, I suppose."

"I haven't decided if I like the fact that you're an officer now," she replied.

"Don't insult me," he said.

"Yes, *sir*," she said with a grin, which she followed with a kiss.

They were in her apartment. The view out on the park was spectacular. Remmy hadn't known that the apartments on the top level also had transparent sections with a view directly out of the ship. It was a billion-dollar property on Earth, something that neither of them could ever afford as long as they were in the Space Marines. But on the *Renegade*, all they needed was the willingness to move in.

Laila had moved out most of the Arodoni furniture. What remained was the large round bed and a set of two backless, padded benches. From the industrial facility a set of reclining vacation chairs had been fabricated. They had no cushions, but using the ship's computers to design a seat for the human body's contours, they had no need of them. Laila had put them on the balcony with a view of the park's incredible avian wildlife. Birds of all shapes and colors flew in looping circles over the park land, in a beautiful display of freedom.

"Whatever," she replied. "All I have to do is bat my lashes and you're putty in my hands."

"In my defense, I've never seen eyes as beautiful as yours," he said. "In fact, I've never seen anyone as beautiful as you."

"Ha! You're hilarious," she replied. "I'm no movie star, Remmy."

"And I'm glad you're not," he said.

"You don't prefer women with skinny little waists and big—"

"No," he interrupted. "I prefer a woman who can shoot straight and look good in camouflage fatigues."

Laila McPherson had an athletic build. She didn't have much body fat, but her thighs were thick with muscle. She had opted not to have her chest enhanced the way most women did.

She laughed and Remmy could tell she was faking it. He was being honest with her, yet she didn't really believe him. If he complimented her martial skills or strategic mind, she lit up with happiness. But if he paid a compliment about the way she looked, it never seemed to land.

"Looking good is subjective," she said.

"In my opinion, you are beautiful," he said. "I love you just the way you are."

"You're not so bad yourself."

They kissed again, but it was shorter and less passionate. Duty was calling. They both had jobs to do and neither was the type to shirk.

"Notify me once you have the Casians set up on the recovery deck," Remmy told her.

"Do you miss it?" She asked.

"Miss what?"

"Being in the middle of everything. Is it hard to hold back and give the orders?"

"Hardest thing I've ever done," Remmy said. "No doubt about that."

"Well, I'll just say this: you're good at it. It's good to know the Marine giving us orders knows his stuff. We all feel pretty good about you being in charge, Remmy."

"Thanks," he said. It was his turn to feel awkward. He had given orders in combat and for years as an NCO on training exercises. Of course, it was different being in command. While he preferred to be leading from the front, he could respect the fact that he was good in an officer's role. He knew every person in the platoon. He knew their strengths and weaknesses. In combat, he could order the Spec Op platoon as well - if not better - than just about anyone alive.

He went to the door of the apartment and looked back. There wasn't much in the opulent domicile, yet it was beginning to feel like home to him.

"I'll wait here a bit, then follow you down," she said.

"Good luck, Staff Sergeant."

"You too, Remmy," she said. "See you soon."

When he reached the Bridge, he discovered all the senior officers were already there. While he didn't really have an active role in commanding the ship, he did enjoy seeing the officers do their jobs. It was better by far than sitting somewhere in the ship with no access to what was happening, just hoping not to die.

"Welcome back to the Bridge, Master Sergeant," Commander Lori Lee said.

"Thank you, ma'am," Remmy said, standing at his post near the door.

Everyone on the Bridge was in emergency suits with helmets on or close to hand. He was in full space armor, which was bulky but not uncomfortable. On his back, his Nelson LTX was connected to the armor plating with electromagnets. He wore the Yagger Hand Cannon strapped to his right thigh. And under his left arm was his own battle helmet. Unlike the crews' emergency suits, his armor was made to endure the rigors of hard vacuum, although he hoped that such measures would not be necessary.

"Alright, we're all here," Captain Darius said. "Time to transition?"

"Five minutes and counting, Captain," Lieutenant Ramos said.

"Commander Lee, please have the ship prepared for combat," Darius ordered. "I want all hands at their battle stations. Let's move all civilians to their designated areas."

"Aye, Captain, preparing the ship for combat."

"Let's talk weapons capabilities," Darius continued. "Master Sergeant, what is the status of your Marines?"

"Staff Sergeant McPherson is on the recovery deck, sir. She has large ordinance from the *Jericho* ready to launch using the ship's gravity beam generator on your command."

"Very good," Darius said.

"Sergeant Dirk Oliver is standing by with Corporal Ricky Thompson in Alpha Hangar, sir; Sergeant Hugo McManus and Corporal Leigh Ann Poh are on Bravo Hanger. Both teams are ready for EVA with shoulder-fired missiles, sir."

"And the Casian volunteers?" Darius inquired.

"They're on the recovery deck, Captain. They can lift and move the heavy munitions faster than we can with cherry pickers and cranes, sir. Corporal Van Winkle is on station in the Medical Bay."

"Let's hope we don't need to use them," Darius said. "What about our drone squadrons?"

It was Lieutenant Best who answered. "We have thirty drones standing by in the primary hangar, Captain. They're armed with ship-to-ship missiles and laser cannons."

"Who is piloting them?" Darius asked.

"Casian volunteers, sir, with GIGI standing by as backup."

"Alright, we're as ready as we can be. Let's have radar ready, Lieutenant Ramos. I want to know if we have company. Lieutenant Nash, I want evasive maneuvering the moment we transition."

"Aye, Captain, standing by for evasive maneuvers," Henry Nash replied.

"Sixty seconds," Vivian Ramos said.

Remmy wondered if she had been to see Lieutenant Micky Colt. They had been lovers on the *Jericho*. Since taking over the *Renegade,* Remmy had been too busy to keep up with who was fraternizing with who, on the ship. That was the way of the military in space, after months of routine with nothing to do but gossip, Remmy found himself so busy he could hardly keep up with all the demands on his time.

"What do we know about this Zutek sector?" Darius asked.

"Nav computer shows it as empty space other than the star cluster. No planets," Vivian Ramos said. "Lots of hyperspace lanes converge there."

"And the route to the Free Worlds?"

"It's not in the Navigation files, sir, but Nurek gave us coordinates to a portal that should take us there."

"Do we trust, Nurek?" Commander Lori Lee asked.

"You tell us," Darius said. "You've worked with him more than anyone."

"He's got a terrific work ethic and seems to really care about the Dudonus."

"But he's a murderer," Vivian said.

"Can't blame him for that," Henry said. "A slave who wouldn't kill their owner would be more suspect in my mind."

"Vang is no loss; I can attest to that personally," Commander Lee said. "The galaxy is better off without him. But to kill a helpless person and a prisoner of war is against all rules of engagement."

"Not to mention the fact that he did it on our ship," Pete Best said.

"Doesn't make him untrustworthy to lead us to the Free Worlds," Henry said. "He's done nothing to hurt us directly; in fact, he helped us during the battle in the Olotimbo system."

"And he's helped with the volunteers and the refugees," Lori Lee said. "Other than the fact that he killed the prisoner, I would say he's been an exemplary member of the crew."

Remmy didn't know exactly how he felt about killing an enemy who was wounded and strapped to a bed. It didn't feel right, but he couldn't put himself in Nurek's shoes. He knew the alien had been a slave longer than Remmy had been alive. He also knew the Dudonus were not fighters. They didn't have the physical strength or martial instincts to fend off attacks, much less initiate a fight against their enemies. They couldn't even hold a standard rifle steady enough to reliably hit a target.

In comparison, the Ashi were a violent species. They fought for pleasure, for acclaim, and for conquest. In comparison to the average Ashi warrior, Nurek was a stick figure, little more than a tall insect that could easily be snapped in half. One punch from the late Emperor Vang would have maimed or even killed Nurek. Perhaps living for so long in that much fear had affected the alien's mind. Or maybe it was just the only opportunity that Nurek would ever have to strike back against his former master.

Remmy thought he might have done the same thing if he were in Nurek's position. And while he understood the loss that resulted from the emperor's death, Remmy didn't think it was too terrible an act to be exonerated in a court of law.

"Ten seconds until transition," Vivian Ramos said.

"All hands stand by for transition," Commander Lori Lee said into her comlink microphone.

"Marines, be ready," Remmy said as he pulled his helmet onto his head.

"Copy that, Master Sergeant," Laila said. "Charlie team is ready."

"Alpha team standing by," Hugo McManus said.

"Bravo team standing by," Dirk Oliver said.

There was nothing left for Remmy to do but wait and see what was about to happen as they dropped out of hyperspace.

The view through the canopy changed. In hyperspace, there were strange streaks of colorful light and long periods of gloomy darkness. All that changed as the *Renegade* dropped back into regular space. Light flooded the Bridge. Ahead of them was a cluster of stars. Remmy's visor darkened, and he could make out the yellow, white, blue, and red stars. They were all different sizes, like a model of a complex molecule.

"Evasive maneuvers!" Darius snapped.

"Aye, evasive maneuvering initiated, Captain," Henry Nash.

"Contact!" Vivian Ramos said. "Captain, they're closing in behind us."

"Who?" Darius demanded. "Friend or foe."

"It's a military ship," Vivian said. "Eighteen thousand kilometers and closing."

"Remmy! Get your people out of the airlocks," Darius said. "Lieutenant Best, launch the drones."

"Aye, Captain, launching drone interceptors."

Remmy was busy giving orders via his helmet comlink to respond immediately.

"Captain," he said after a slight pause. "Alpha and Bravo teams are in position, sir."

Before Darius could give another order, laser fire flashed from behind them. Energy that should have scorched through their hull and devastated their engines was instead deflected by the sonic energy screens.

"Shields held, Captain," Pete Best announced. "But they'll need time to build back to full power, sir."

"Drop them," Darius said. "Master Sergeant, have your teams fire on that ship."

"Yes, sir!" Remmy said. "Alpha and Bravo teams, fire at will."

"Tracking missiles," Vivian said.

"Interceptors are active," Pete Best said. "Screening maneuvers initiated."

"She's turning," Vivian Ramos called out.

"How long until our missiles reach that ship?" Darius asked.

"Those are Vulcan 88 missiles, sir. They will reach eight thousand kilometers per hour, Captain," Remmy explained.

"Distance to target?" Darius asked.

"Just over sixteen thousand kilometers, Captain," Vivian Ramos said.

"That's a time to target of two hours, sir," Commander Lee said. "They'll outmaneuver those rockets."

"We can live with that," Darius said. "Lieutenant Nash, flip us around. Let's bring the gravity beam generator to bear on that ship."

"Contact," Vivian Ramos said. "Looks like an Ashi battleship. It's coming out from around the star cluster."

"There could be more of them out there, too," Henry Nash said.

"Distance and speed," Darius said.

"Two hundred, sixty million kilometers, Captain. Heading is one-niner-seven, traveling at eighty thousand kilometers an hour and climbing, sir."

"Damn, I wish I had our lasers online," Darius said. "What's our position relative to the jump point?"

"One hundred and fourteen million kilometers, sir. We need a little over two hours to reach that portal," Vivian replied. "Laying in a course, now, Captain."

"What the hell?" Pete Best said.

Remmy didn't have to wonder what he was referring to. Without a console to keep track of, he was focused on the view out the Bridge canopy. He had seen the ship turn away from the cluster of stars. After a moment, the enemy ship had come into view. Light from behind them reflected off the rounded nose of the alien vessel. He could see it turning slowly. It wasn't on exactly the same plane as the *Renegade*. And the enemy ship was turning up and away, showing her belly. Suddenly, hundreds of small devices were spewing from the ship like chaff from a fighter.

"Could be defensive measures," Commander Lori Lee said.

"No, they're spreading out too far," Darius said. "Can we track them?"

"They're small, Captain. But I think we've seen them before," Vivian Ramos said.

"Mines," Henry Nash said. "Has to be."

"Are we close to a portal?" Darius asked.

"Just the one we came through," Vivian said. "The others are spread out around the star cluster."

"If there are ships on the far side of the system," Henry said. "They'll know we're here."

"And they might be sending word to their fleet," Ensign Bertoli stated.

"We have to destroy every ship in the system before that happens," Darius said. "If they mark where we make the jump into hyperspace, the fleet will follow us back to the Free Worlds. Lieutenant Best, launch a torpedo toward that ship."

"Aye, Captain, launching torpedo one," Pete replied.

Remmy saw the torpedo go speeding out of the ship. It was moving incredibly fast.

"It worked," Laila McPherson said via Remmy's comlink. "The gravity beam shot the torpedo out of the ship faster than a regular launch."

"Like the bullet from a gun," Pete Best said out loud.

The torpedo was twelve feet long and weighed over four hundred pounds. It was loaded with an Amphion XX warhead, one of the most powerful weapons short of nuclear bombs. It disappeared almost as quickly as it had appeared.

"Radar shows it traveling at over a hundred thousand KPH, Captain," Vivian said.

"And that's without the rocket booster she's equipped with," Pete Best said. "The gravity generator works just like a rail gun."

"Activate the booster," Darius ordered. "Is it locked onto the enemy ship?"

"Aye, Captain, she's got a lock on the Ashi heat register from her exhaust," Pete Best said. "Activating boosters. We can double the speed."

The words were barely out of his mouth when the torpedo exploded. For a moment, the Bridge was silent.

"What happened?" Darius asked softly.

"I don't know," Pete Best said.

"The torpedo reached the mines," Commander Lori Lee said.

"Pull back the drones," Darius ordered. "We can't afford to waste them against the mines."

Remmy felt a pit in the bottom of his stomach. The enemy ship was still launching the mines, seeding the entire section of space. Nothing would be able to move in that area without being in danger of the mines.

"Bring your Marines back inside, Master Sergeant," Darius ordered. "We'll have to find a new way to attack that ship. Lieutenant Nash, get the droids to work on that laser cannon."

"Captain, we could fire more torpedos," Pete Best said.

"Negative, Lieutenant. We have a limited number of ordnance from the *Jericho*. We can't risk wasting it."

"What about the other enemy ship?" Ensign Bertoli asked.

"It's out of range for now," Darius said. "Their lasers are only effective up to five hundred thousand kilometers. What's the ETA on the laser reconstruction?"

"Hard to say for certain, Captain," Nash said. "Eight hours if we're lucky, twelve or more if we're not. And one wrong wire could be catastrophic, sir. The amount of energy involved is staggering."

"We'll have to test it," Darius said. "Looks like we're going to be here a while."

"What if the enemy Fleet shows up before we're ready to fight?" Pete Best asked.

"Then we run," Darius said. "Lieutenant Ramos, please mark all the portals in this system. Designate the most direct route from the Olotimbo system as Whisky One."

"Aye, marking all portals, Captain."

"We don't go near the jump point we plan to use until we've destroyed the Ashi ships," Darius continued. "We can't tip our hand and put who knows how many people at risk."

Remmy thought about it. Who knew what the Free Worlds were and how many people might be there? Still, he had a sense of dread. Eight hours was an eternity in combat. And he could do was hope the ship and her crew were capable of surviving that long.

CHAPTER 8

CAPTAIN ZEKE DARIUS WAS ANGRY, but he couldn't let it show. He was tired of always reacting to what the enemy did. They had surprised him in every engagement. Even though the *Renegade* wasn't in immediate danger, he still felt the sting of being caught off guard.

"These ships must patrol these hyperspace lane exchange systems," Vivian Ramos said. "I don't think every Ashi ship has that many space mines."

There were too many of the tiny explosive devices to count, but the plot showed a cloud of them between the two ships.

"Bring us around on heading two-seven-four by one-eight-eight," Darius said. "That should keep the cloud of mines between us."

"Use their own tactics against them," Commander Lee said with a note of admiration in her voice.

"My guess is that vessel's laser cannons can still get through," Darius said. "Lieutenant Best, raise our shields."

"Aye, Captain, initiating the sonic shields."

"Master Sergeant, are your people all inside?" Darius asked.

"Yes, sir. We are standing by for further orders, sir."

"Very good," Darius said. "Lieutenant, keep tabs on the other Ashi ship's speed."

"Aye, Captain. It's still accelerating. Speed is registering at nearly one hundred thousand kilometers per hour."

"Time to intercept if we remain on this heading?"

"Calculating," Vivian Ramos said.

"Is that the plan?" Commander Lori Lee asked.

"Darius thought for a moment, then shook his head. "If we get another shot at the mining ship, we'll take it. Otherwise, we'll begin to orbit the star cluster."

He knew that speed was their one big advantage at the moment. They were only going a fraction of the *Renegade's* top speed. It would take too long to go all the way around the star cluster and Darius wanted to keep the portal to the Free Worlds on his side of the system. The last thing they could afford to do was to get caught on the far side.

"Captain, the Ashi warship will be in firing range in approximately twenty-seven hours, sir," Ramos said. "That's estimating their top speed to be ten million kilometers per hour."

"How fast did they go in the Olotimbo system?" Pete Best asked.

"Forty million kilometers per hour," Ramos said. "But I don't think they'll want to go that fast here."

"Why not?" Commander Lee asked.

Vivian Ramos turned in her seat to face the Commander. "In the Olotimbo system, they had superior numbers and refueling vessels. My guess is they expend a lot of their fuel to reach that speed. Firing their cannons burns even more fuel. A single warship might not be in a hurry to engage us."

"And if they know our capabilities, they probably know they can't reach firing range before we get our laser cannons back online," Henry Nash said. "If they even realize we can't use them yet."

"We have to assume they know," Darius said. "If they do reach top speed, what does that do to our timeline."

"It drops to just seven hours, sir," Vivian said. "Depending on how long it takes them to reach that speed."

"So it's a race," Henry said.

"We have to stay out of their range long enough to repair the lasers," Pete Best said. "Can we do that?"

"I suppose that depends on factors we haven't identified yet," Darius said just as an idea entered his mind. "Lieutenant, prepare to fire the gravity beam again."

"You want to shoot another torpedo at them, Captain?" Pete Best asked.

"Negative, but let's see what happens if we start pushing the mines toward their ship."

Pete laughed, and everyone leaned forward a little in their seats. Darius wasn't sure the gravity generator could affect the mines. They seemed like a long way off, and he wasn't the only person thinking along those lines.

"Can we reach them with the gravity generator?" Commander Lori Lee said.

"It'll take a boatload of energy," Pete said. "But that's the one thing we've got in spades."

"Do it," Darius said.

"What if they have safety measures built into the mines, Captain?" Henry Nash said.

"Then we'll know when this plan fails," Darius said. "But maybe they won't be expecting it."

"Firing the gravity beam generator now, Captain."

The Bridge fell silent. They could still see the alien ship, but it was just a tiny speck of light in the distance. And there was no way to see the mines. They had no lights and weren't large enough to reflect much starlight. The distance between the mines and the *Renegade* was just too far to make out the tiny objects, so they had no way of knowing if the plan was working or not. But they didn't have to wait long to find out.

It took less than a minute before the Ashi warship reacted to the threat. Even from a distance, Darius could see the flare of the ship's exhaust.

"She's running," Henry said.

"Looks like they're moving to course two-seven-three," Vivian said.

"Master Sergeant, have your Marines prepare another torpedo just in case," Darius said.

"Yes, sir!" Remmy replied.

But a few seconds later, they saw multiple explosions. They were small. Darius guessed they were meant to cause damage, not total destruction. But the little flares were followed by a large explosion.

"That had to be their engines going," Henry said. "Maybe their fuel tanks as well."

"Tango one is in a spin, Captain," Vivian Ramos said. "They've lost all propulsion. It looks like they're drifting free."

"Should we finish them off?" Pete Best asked.

"No," Darius said, relaxing a little in his Captain's chair. "Even if their lasers are still operational, they won't want to waste the fuel shooting at us. Not when the hope of rescue is a long way off."

They remained in the vicinity of the mines for almost an hour before the maintenance drones cut the ruined laser cannon free. Once it was floating away from the *Renegade*, Darius ordered the ship to use the gravity beam to maneuver it several thousand kilometers in front of the ship. Then, the beam was sent sweeping through the minefield, pulling the deadly devices toward them. As the mines got close to the wreckage of the laser cannon, they began to detonate. The shockwaves set off a chain reaction racing through the cloud of mines until the vast majority of them exploded. It was a spectacular display, but all the while, Darius was watching the Ashi battleship as it made its way through space.

"Tango Two is passing twenty million kilometers per hour," Vivian Ramos said.

"Very well," Darius said, knowing his time was running out.

Unfortunately, the course of the enemy ship was directly in

line with the hyperspace portal the *Renegade* needed to use to escape the system and reach the Free Worlds.

"Lieutenant Nash, engage main engines," Darius ordered. "I want to see as much as we possibly can around the star cluster before we engage Tango Two."

"Aye, Captain," Henry Nash said. "Engaging the main drive."

"Speed?"

"We're at sixty thousand kilometers per hour and climbing, Captain," Vivian Ramos said.

"Distance to our pursuer?" Darius asked.

"They are still over two hundred million kilometers, Captain. But it's possible that they are rushing to render aid to their companionship."

"Doubtful," said Pete Best.

"Unlikely, but a possibility," Darius said. "And it's our job to consider all the possibilities. How long is it going to take us to get up to full speed?"

"How fast is full speed?" Henry Nash said. "We've got no specs on that in the ship's computer system. Theoretically, given enough time and space, we should be able to attain any speed as long as the sonic shield holds up and the power core continues to supply the engines with what they need."

"Since we've been on board, we've reached one hundred million kilometers per hour," Vivian said, "when we were on our way to Olo Prime from the hyperspace portal."

"Let's at least get back to that," Darius said. "I don't want to look up and discover that the enemy has gained on us."

"Will that speed affect the repairs?" Commander Lori Lee asked.

"Shouldn't," Henry Nash said. "The automated maintenance system has already expanded gravity in that quadrant of the ship to include the laser cannon they're rebuilding."

"All we need is time," Darius said. "With any luck, we'll be long gone from this system before the Ashi fleet arrives."

The officers took turns leaving the Bridge and getting some

food, as well as stretching their legs. Darius alone remained. He watched the holographic projection of the *Renegade,* which was updated in real-time. It was a marvel to watch the maintenance drones work on the ship. They moved materials and assembled the parts with precision and speed that humans couldn't match. Perhaps it was because they were designed for such work, but Darius thought it came down to the fact that they didn't think about anything else. They didn't marvel at the scope and beauty of the galaxy while they were outside the ship. Nor did they fear getting knocked away from the *Renegade* and drifting endlessly through space. Instead, their entire focus was on the task at hand. And it probably didn't hurt that they were all linked to one artificial brain, so to speak. They were separate units but more like a single entity. There was no wasted effort, no miscommunication and no variation in their skill level. Added to that was the highly technical but precision-crafted design. Each part was exactly the right size, shape and material. The pre-fabrication was perfect so that every hole lined up with every bolt and every groove slipped into place quickly and easily.

Still, despite the high level of efficiency, it took the drones nearly nine hours to complete the rebuild. Darius was hardly able to wait to give the order to activate the weapon.

"Captain, the laser cannon is online and charging, sir," Pete Best said.

"Outstanding," Darius replied. "Helm, bring us around. How far out is that Ashi warship?"

"We've been outpacing it for the last seven and half hours," Vivian Ramos said. "We're slightly over four hundred million kilometers ahead of them."

"Lieutenant Best, begin targeting solutions for both of the Ashi ships," Darius ordered.

"Should we turn for the portal to the Free Worlds now, Captain?"

"Negative," Darius said. "I don't want to tip our hand."

"But if we're going to destroy the enemy ships," Commander Lori Lee said. "What difference does it make?"

"The difference is that we don't know when the enemy fleet might show up or what other resources the Ashi could have in this system," Darius said. "What's the status of our laser cannons?"

"Full power, Captain," Pete Best said. "Ready for testing."

"Target the Ashi battleship first," Darius said. "I want it out of the fight before it knows we have weapons back up and running."

"Aye, Captain, targeting the Ashi warship now."

"Extend the laser cannons and lock them into position," Darius ordered. "Alert the crew. Let's make sure no one is in that area just in case the unthinkable occurs."

"Aye, Captain, alerting the crew now," Lori Lee said.

Darius pressed the transmit button on his seat's comlink. "Ensign Stanislaus, what is the condition of the ship's systems?"

"All green," came the reply. "We're at full strength again, Captain."

"Very good," Darius replied and silently breathed a sigh of relief.

He had let them come too close to total destruction in the battle with the Ashi Fleet. It was a lesson he had learned from. It was also one he hoped to never repeat, but in battle anything was possible.

"Target acquired, Captain," Lieutenant Best said. "Ready to fire on your command."

"Fire," Darius said.

"Fox three!" Pete announced.

There was a flash of light. For a split second they saw the massive laser beam shooting through space, then it was out of sight.

"Time to target?" Darius asked.

"Approximately twenty-two minutes," Vivian Ramos said.

"How did the new cannon perform?"

"It's perfect, Captain," Pete Best said. "Fox three is already recharging."

"No maintenance issues," Henry Nash said. "Everything worked as designed."

"Ensign Stanislaus?" Darius asked via the comlink.

"We're all good, Captain. There was a slight dip in the energy reserves, but that is normal when you fire the laser cannons. No changes in life support or ship systems, sir."

"Excellent," Darius said. "Go ahead and fire on the mining ship as soon as possible. Lieutenant Ramos, please continue to monitor the system. We can't let anyone know where we're making our transition."

"Aye, Captain, continuing our sweep with all detection systems."

"I have the mining ship firing solution ready," Pete Best said.

"Very good. Use the new cannon again, please," Darius said. "If something is going to go wrong, I want to know it now."

But nothing went wrong. The cannon worked properly. The first laser blast reached the Ashi battleship and vaporized the entire thing. It almost seemed like magic. There was no explosion, no ion cloud or drifting particles. The warship simply disappeared. A few minutes later, the mining ship was gone, too. Radar systems showed no other vessels in the system.

"Excellent test," Darius said. "Now, we can make our way toward the portal. But I don't want us pointed right at it. Take us to within a hundred thousand kilometers and then we'll turn and burn for the portal."

"Aye, Captain, setting a new course," Vivian Ramos said.

"Give me two hours, Commander Lee, then I'll relieve you," Darius said.

"Aye, Captain," Lori Lee responded.

It felt good to be on his feet again. Darius walked the upper decks in the Commerce Section of the ship, which was empty. Only the occasional maintenance drone passed him. The droids were built for function, not form. The Arodoni didn't want the robotic serving units to resemble living creatures and Darius thought maybe that came from their abhorrence of slavery. Not that he knew how they felt about the institution, but the deduction seemed rational. At any rate, he was left alone with his thoughts and so he walked half an hour before returning to the Command Section of the ship and getting himself a meal.

There was plenty of food on the ship, but the automated food production was not designed for humans. Fortunately, the crew from the *Jericho* included several culinary specialists. Their job in the regular fleet was to oversee the food supplies on the ship and load ingredients into the automated dispensaries that the crew utilized in the mess hall. Senior officers had things a little better, with a chef who actually cooked two meals a day. But they were limited to SDF food supplies, which means vat-grown protein and dehydrated vegetables, powdered milk and eggs. On the *Renegade*, they not only had fresh vegetables grown in the gardens of the park but also fresh meat from the herd animals that were harvested. The cooks insisted that Captain Darius eat only freshly prepared meals since taking command of the alien vessel. So, he settled into the newly appointed Wardroom and waited while the culinary specialists prepared his food.

"Mind if I join you, Captain?" Remmy asked from the doorway.

"I would be delighted, Master Sergeant. Hungry?"

"Actually, I was just stopping by for a coffee, sir."

"How are the Marines?"

"Fine, sir," Remmy said. "Happy to be off duty for the moment."

"Commander Lee downgraded the alert status?"

"To yellow, sir," Remmy said as he poured hot coffee into a clean mug. "We're standing by."

"You won't be needed," Darius said. "At least, I hope not."

"Me too," Remmy said, settling his bulk into a chair. With the space armor on, he barely fit.

"All systems are back online and there are no other ships in the system."

"I'll be honest, sir. That makes me breathe a little easier," Remmy said. "I don't relish battle in a starship. I never have."

"But you're a Space Marine," Darius said.

"True, but in a space battle, we have very little control of the outcome. I prefer to fight it out on my own two feet with a weapon in my hand."

"Well, then, that's the difference between us. Face to face, I don't know what I'd even do in a fight."

"I hope you never have to find out, sir."

"That's kind of you, Master Sergeant. Have you been to the Medical Bay?"

"Just came back. Corporals Fry and Berry are itching to get back on duty. I'm surprised they're making such a fast recovery."

"As am I," Darius said. "That's surprising. I'm guessing you refused?"

"Didn't have to. The doc turned them down in no uncertain terms. They're not physically ready to be back at work, but it can be difficult to be confined to a bed."

"I'm sure," Darius agreed. "What about Lieutenant Colt?"

"Doc said he's gone quiet. I don't know what that means, but it doesn't seem good," Remmy said. "He was asleep when I looked in. He didn't stir. Gunnery Sergeant Chad Rand is improving. Doc Lanksi has put him to work in the Med Bay looking after the slaves we liberated."

"How does he seem to you?"

"More like his old self," Remmy said. "He'll never be combat-ready again. That part of him is gone."

"How is that possible?"

"I've seen it before, sir. For some people, it's like prizefighting. You can only do it for so long before you lose the ability to take a punch."

"I suppose we all have our limits," Darius said as a crew member brought him a plate of food under a polished dome with an ornate handle.

"Grilled white meat, sir," the culinary specialist said. The animals on the *Renegade* were foreign to humans but much better than the vat-grown protein from the fleet; still, with no better way to identify the meat, it was designated into colors. The white meats were light and mild in flavor, most closely resembling chicken. "Steamed vegetables, freshly baked rolls, butter, and for dessert, lemon sorbet."

"Excellent, thank you, Jean Claude. My compliments to the kitchen team."

"Our pleasure, Captain," the culinary specialist said before backing out of the room.

"Are you sure you won't eat something?" Darius said.

"I've already eaten, sir. The grub here is too good to go hungry."

"That is the truth. In fact, I don't think I've eaten this well in my entire life."

"Perhaps that's what's contributing to the speedy recoveries in the Med Bay," Remmy said. "The former slaves are improving rapidly. They'll be ready to move into their own cabins soon."

Darius cut into his meat and took a bite. It was sublime, juicy and well-seasoned. Then he thought about what the future held. He was a serious person by nature. Being the captain of a ship of war was like playing a constant game of chess but also worrying over the vessel's systems, which often malfunctioned, leaving the commander to limp into battle or crawl back to base. But the *Renegade* was a highly superior ship. Almost nothing went wrong mechanically on the alien vessel. Plus, for the moment, there was no enemy in the system to worry about. Of course, the threat of the Ashi fleet catching up to them was like a weight on his mind, but Darius realized he could relax a little.

"Can you imagine what this ship could be like, Remmy?" Darius asked. "I mean, if she were fully occupied."

"It would be a small city, sir."

"Yes, and what if it was occupied not just by human beings? What if there were people from every planet represented on this ship? Just imagine what variety there would be."

"Hard to picture that," Remmy said. "Just the differences between us, the Dudonus and the Casians are strange enough. We can get along, but we're all so different."

"Yes, that's true, but what if we could learn from each other?

What if we could explore the galaxy together? It would be an honor to command that ship."

"Also, an honor to serve with you, sir."

"When we go home, there's zero chance the Brass will let us take her out again," Darius said.

"They'll probably lock us up in padded cells and throw away the key," Remmy agreed.

"It's not fair to think of never going back, but if I'm being honest, Remmy, I might consider it."

"In comparison, there isn't much to look forward to back home," Remmy Steele said. "Other than the people."

Darius was just finishing his meal when his com-link beeped. "Captain, we have a contact on radar."

When Darius met Remmy's glance, he could see the steady resolve in the Space Marine's eyes. Darius felt a surge of admiration for the Master Sergeant. He was a warrior, of that there was no doubt. How the man could face mortal danger without a trace of fear was awe-inspiring to Darius.

"Can you identify it?" Darius asked.

"No, Captain. It is not a vessel we have encountered before," Commander Lori Lee said. "If I were guessing, I'd say it's a commercial vessel of some type. Maybe a freighter by the size of her."

"Very well, I'm on my way to the Bridge, Commander."

"No rest for the weary," Remmy said. "Let me see to those dishes, Captain."

"My mess," Darius argued.

"You've got bigger fish to fry, as the saying goes, sir. I've got this."

"Thank you, Master Sergeant."

"Happy to help," Remmy said.

Darius left the Wardroom thinking that it really should have been him cleaning up after the Master Sergeant. Remmy was a Medal of Honor recipient, after all. And Darius was feeling more and more like a washed-up ship Captain. Perhaps taking the *Renegade* home was the best thing for everyone, even if it meant the end of Darius' career.

CHAPTER 9

"CAPTAIN ON DECK!" Commander Lori Lee declared as Darius entered the Bridge.

"As you were," he responded before the officers could leap to their feet and salute at full attention. "What have we got, Lieutenant Ramos?"

"Looks like a freight hauler, Captain, about eighteen million kilometers from our present location. She came out of Whiskey fourteen."

There were eighteen hyperspace portals around the cluster of stars that showed on the ship's holographic plot display. They were all marked with orange titles.

"Where are they going?" Darius asked.

"Trajectory shows them headed for Whiskey Three, Captain," Vivian Ramos said. "It's only about four hundred thousand kilometers from their position. They'll pass through it in an hour or so."

"Unless they change course," Commander Lee said.

"Let's get Nurek up here. Maybe he can identify it," Darius said. "It's not in the ship's computer banks or GIGI's?"

"Negative, Captain," Lori Lee said. "I checked both while you were returning to the Bridge, sir. That style of ship is identified as commercial, but the make, model, purpose, and port of origin are unknown."

"Captain, I'm receiving a hail from that ship," Ensign Bertoli said. "It's a video message, sir."

"Put it on the main projector," Darius said, sitting up a little in his seat.

The plot, which showed the *Renegade* and everything in the system that was picked up on the radar systems, disappeared. In its place was the face of a frightening-looking alien. It had long, glistening tendrils instead of hair, and its mouth was long like the muzzle of a wolf. It spoke in growls, huffs, barks, and clicks. The ship's translation function projected the words under the image of the alien.

"Greetings from the Salmantis system," the alien said. "I am Kundis Miz, the quatarp of this galactic transport. We have heard many stories of your kind. We would be honored to confer with the legendary Arodoni if you would be so willing."

"Are we transmitting?" Darius asked.

"Not yet, Captain," Bertoli said.

"Good," Darius said. "Lieutenant Ramos, keep a close watch on the radar."

"Aye, Captain, scanning the system now, sir."

"Captain Darius," Lori Lee said. "Nurek is here."

Darius turned and found Remmy escorting the thin, cone-headed alien.

"What can you tell us about that ship," Darius asked.

"One moment, Captain," Nurek said, looking down at the screen built into his console. "It appears to be a Salmantis ship. They are interstellar merchants. They collect goods in one system and sell them in another."

"Weapons?" Darius asked.

"No, Captain. Weapons are strictly outlawed under Imperium code of law."

"Are they working with the Ashi?"

"They might be willing, Captain, but the Ashi would think it beneath their honor," Nurek said. "They are not from the core worlds, and their ships pay premiums in every system."

"Alright, that's good," Darius said. "We have to be careful."

"Indeed," Nurek agreed.

"Alright, Bertoli, begin the transmission."

"Aye, Captain, initiating communications now, sir," Ensign Bertoli said.

Darius spoke slowly. "My name is Zeke Darius, and I am Captain of the *Renegade*. It is our pleasure to make your acquaintance, Quatarp Miz."

They had to wait nearly two minutes for the response.

"The pleasure is ours, high Captain," Kundis Miz said. "There is news from across the galaxy. The Ashi Imperium is pursuing you. To be honest, I am astounded that no military ships are currently here in this system. We are headed to Nobis, but I would be honored to share the latest news from the U'Nengus system."

"Please do share whatever news you have," Darius replied. "We have met the Imperium Fleet several times. They still pursue us, but we are determined to resist. Our kind is not easily dissuaded. And we have volunteers on board, some Casians, and Dudonus, along with over a hundred refugees freed from slavers."

Commander Lori Lee spoke softly as the message Darius composed was sent to the alien ship.

"They don't trade in slaves, do they?" She asked Nurek.

"No, Commander, they do not. The Salmantis are one of the few races who do not. They are private and prefer only their own race to work on their merchant ships."

"We can't all be perfect," the commander said.

"I guess I nearly stepped in it," Darius said. "No one ever accused me of being diplomatic, I suppose."

"Captain," Ensign Bertoli spoke up, "we're getting a data stream from the alien ship. Not another message. It must be the news information they referred to."

"Thank them for the download, Ensign. GIGI, can you sort

through the data, ensure there are no threats on the download, and give us the highlights please."

"Of course, Captain," the alien artifact replied via the speakers built into Darius' captain's chair.

He didn't know if he could trust the artifact. It was keeping information from the *Renegade's* computer log from them. But there was no better way to sift through the large data stream. As he sat back in his chair, another message from the Salmantis ship came through.

"As you will see in the data, many planets are in active rebellion from the Ashi Imperium. For this, we cannot blame them. Your presence has done much to shake things up in a positive way."

Darius stood up to answer. "War is not our goal. But freedom for all people, regardless of race or where they are from, is a value we hold very dear. Do we have the support of the Salmantis people in the cause of liberty?"

A few minutes later, the reply came through.

"The Salmantis have always been neutral. War is not our way."

It was Nurek who responded, and it was with a huff that was somewhere between laughter and incredulity. "The Salmantis have no issue with profiteering from war, despite their claims of neutrality."

"They wouldn't be the first to pull that trick," Lori Lee said.

GIGI's computerized voice broke in, "Captain, the data pertains to happenings around the Imperium. The most significant is an assassination of Nic'Tal, a representative from Hurz to the Prime Council."

Once again, it was Nurek to respond, this time with a surprised gasp.

"Who is this Nic'Tal?" Darius asked.

"The members of the Prime Council are the highest officials in the Imperium short of the Emperor himself," Nurek said. There was a stiffness in his voice and movements. The news was clearly a shock to the former slave. "There are only five, one from each core world. An attack on a member of the Prime Council is unheard of."

"What's the fallout?" Darius asked.

"Hurz is under attack by terrorist groups," GIGI continued. "The other council members are in fortified locations, but according to the news reports, their worlds are suffering various levels of resistance to the Imperium. The core planets have strong law enforcement organizations, but protests have erupted in the largest cities."

"Seems like we really are shaking things up," Vivian Ramos said.

"Continue your report," Darius said.

"Open rebellion is reported on over a hundred worlds. Many citizens are calling for a response from the Ashi military, but so far, the fleet seems to be focused on finding the *Renegade*."

"Your plan is working, Nurek," Darius said.

"It was not my plan, just my good fortune to realize our opportunity to resist had finally come," Nurek said. "Every planet has revolutionary movements. Some are coordinated; others are completely independent. My task was merely to light the spark and, if the opportunity arose, to stop Emperor Vang's reign of terror."

"You certainly did that," Lori Lee said.

"There is news on that issue as well," GIGI said. "It seems that the Emperor's Kahn, Ulrech Sheika, was denied the opportunity to take up the mantle of Emperor by the Prime Council. The council cited the reports that Emperor Vang still lived."

Darius looked at Nurek, who stared down at the deck between his long feet.

"It seems you were right about the Kahn," Darius said.

"He was leading the fleet in the battle in Olotimbo," Commander Lee said.

"But they didn't crown him emperor yet," Henry Nash said.

"What do you think that means?" Vivian asked.

"Nurek?" Captain Darius prompted.

"It is merely a precaution, but..." Nurek paused, deep in

thought. "It could signal a shift in the Imperium. It is possible that the council might try to replace him."

"Replace Sheika Kahn with someone else?" Darius asked.

"Remove the emperor all together," Nurek said. "It has been tried before, but the Ashi Fleet put down the revolution of the Prime Council. If the fleet is weakened or destroyed, I have no doubt that they will try to regain power."

"Will they be able to hold the Imperium together?" Darius asked.

"The core worlds will via for supremacy but they will remain loyal. Some of the more wealthy worlds will, too, but the others will break away unless the Council finds a way to coerce them into staying."

"There's only one way to do that," Commander Lee said.

"What are the odds the core worlds are building a secret army?" Pete Best said.

"High," Darius said. "If the Ashi fleet falls, the galaxy could descend into war."

"Better a fight for a chance to live free than peace that leads to enslavement," Henry Nash said.

"Not everyone would agree," Ramos said.

"You don't?" Nash asked her.

"Yes, I agree with you. I would fight, but what about worlds like Olo Prime or the Dudonus people? How will they defend themselves?"

"Ultimately, that will be up to them," Darius said. "But we have the technology they need. The only question that remains is how we disseminate it."

"Not with the Salmantis," Nurek said. "They would certainly charge top dollar for the technological secrets."

"Agree," Darius said. "We'll decide after we deliver the refugees to the Free Worlds."

An hour later, the Salmantis ship transitioned into hyperspace. The *Renegade* was once more alone in the system. It took several more hours to reach their own portal but no other traffic entered the system. As they approached the jumping-off point, Captain Darius gave the order and the *Renegade* once more leaped into hyperspace.

"How long until we reach the Free Worlds?" Darius asked.

"My calculations show that we have just over twenty-four hours to reach the transition point," Vivian Ramos said.

"Engineering report?"

Henry Nash cleared his throat. "All good, Captain. Engines are in optimal condition. We have plenty of power."

"It is strange to not have to stop for refitting," Commander Lee said.

"Indeed," Darius said. "But you won't hear me complaining." He hit the transmit button on his comlink. "Ensign Stanislaus, any problems?"

"Negative, Captain. We're green across the board."

"Alright, we'll use this time to get some rest," Darius said. "I know the Free Worlds are supposed to be unknown by the Imperium, but we can't count on that. I want the crew back at battle stations when we drop out of hyperspace."

"Agreed," Commander Lee said. "We'll be ready, Captain."

Captain Darius felt a sense of relief. The ship was whole and the weapons systems were repaired and tested. With any luck, they were proceeding to a system where the Ashi fleet couldn't find them. Darius knew they all needed some rest and the chance to consider their options. He didn't feel like there was any reason why they shouldn't return home, if they could reasonably do it without drawing the Ashi fleet back to the Sol system, too. Of course, there were no guarantees. Only time would tell what the Ashi were truly capable of but he was determined to be ready. And not just the *Renegade* or the human race, but if it were up to him, the entire galaxy would be prepared. He thought that if he had to disappear into obscurity, he could live with that legacy. He had used the alien ship to bring liberty and hope to hundreds of worlds. It would be up to them how they held onto it. But, at least, he would make sure they had the means. In addition, he would get his crew, the ones that still wanted to go, back home where they belonged.

CHAPTER 10

REMMY WALKED Nurek back to the cabin he was being held in. The alien had no restraints, and there was no guard at his door. Most of the crew were completely unaware that Nurek had murdered Emperor Vang. And the alien wasn't mistreated. The berth he was assigned to had furniture and even a computer terminal.

"Was it worth it?" Remmy asked him.

"It was," Nurek said softly.

"Even if the Captain kicks you off the ship and hands you over to the authorities?"

"I doubt any authority on the Free Worlds would condemn me for killing Emperor Vang. But even if you took me to Galactic Core and turned me over to the Prime Council, it would still be worth it."

Remmy opened the door to the cabin and then stood leaning against the door frame after Nurek had entered.

"He was not a good person," Nurek said. "Would you care to sit down, Master Sergeant?"

"No, I'm good," Remmy said. "Thank you."

"Your courtesy is almost shocking to me after over a hundred-star cycles in slavery to the Imperial family. Not once in all that time were they ever courteous to me. I was a non-person with no rights. I was unnoticed until I failed to do something exactly as my masters expected. Then, I was berated or beaten. I have suffered broken bones on numerous occasions by the emperor and was forced to work despite my injuries. In all that time, I was never asked for my opinion, was never given any consideration whatso-ever, and always treated as a disposable commodity that could be replaced at any time. Can a warrior such as yourself even compre-hend what it is like to live in fear that at any moment you could be killed?"

"I've been in combat situations," Remmy said, "that was dire. I think I can get some idea of how you must have felt, although I'll admit I don't think I would be much good to anyone living with a constant sense of terror."

Nurek nodded. He was standing by a cabinet where a tall decanter was filled with green liquid. He lifted it and began to pour the pale fluid into two tumblers.

"I knew that if I displeased the emperor, he would most likely beat me to death," Nurek said. "Fear can be a powerful motivator."

"True, but it corrupts," Remmy said. "On our planet, we have a saying: you catch more flies with honey than vinegar."

"Interesting," Nurek said, holding out a glass of the pale green drink to Remmy. "This is Vanar. It's a traditional Dudonus bever-age. I would be honored if you tried it, Master Sergeant Steel."

"Call me Remmy," he said as he took the tumbler. "What's it made from?"

"The juice of several fruits and a base of water mixed with a variety of minerals," Nurek said. "It is a testament to the wealth of this ship that fruits from different worlds can all grow together here."

Remmy gave the drink a sniff. It smelled pleasant, almost tropi-cal. Nurek took a drink from his glass, and Remmy did the same. The beverage was room temperature and tasted tangy. It was refreshing and light. There were no harsh flavors like a hard cider would have.

"It's good," Remmy said.

Nurek smiled, but there was a sadness in his eyes. "I have never been so honored as I am on this vessel. That you would drink Vanar with me is the highest honor, Master Sergeant."

"I'm honored that you would share it with me," Remmy said. "And please, call me Remmy."

"I'm not sure I can do that," Nurek said. "Ludus has told me of your bravery on Casasil. You fought the Ashi. You faced hundreds of them all alone."

"That's not exactly true," Remmy said. "I was part of a team."

"I can't imagine fighting just one," Nurek said. "Does that make me a coward in your eyes?"

"No," Remmy told him. "That makes you smart."

Nurek chuckled. "And what if I told you that I trembled like a leaf in a strong wind as I murdered Emperor Vang? Or that my sleep is plagued since I did it?"

"I would say this," Remmy told him, "killing is never easy. Taking a life is difficult to do and harder to live with. We are different, you and I, but we are the same too. I never knew a human who killed another person and wasn't plagued by it afterward."

"I knew I had to do it," Nurek said. "It was wrong by your standards and wrong to do what I did without informing your Captain Darius beforehand, but I knew he would forbid me from doing it. I... I could not let the opportunity to strike a blow against the Imperium—not just for myself, but for all my people."

Remmy thought he could understand what Nurek was telling him. Most people couldn't fathom the need to fight. Billions of humans lived in civilized societies with no real violence. He was glad of that but also knew there were times when a person had to act. Perhaps Nurek didn't need to kill Emperor Vang for the purpose of liberating the galaxy, but he might have needed to act for his own sanity. He may have needed to strike a blow to prove that he wasn't helpless against the Ashi despite having been forced into slavery for over a century."

"What do you think Captain Darius will do to me?" Nurek asked.

"Under normal conditions, you would be turned over to the SDF authorities to stand trial for your actions."

"What does it mean to stand trial? Is that torture or some type of death penalty?"

"No," Remmy said. "A trial is a chance for you to defend your actions. We believe in allowing anyone accused of a crime to defend themselves and to be judged by an independent authority."

Nurek thought for a moment. "But these aren't normal conditions?"

"No," Remmy said. "My guess is he'll send you down with the refugees who are going to be left on whatever planet we find at the end of this run."

"Libertine," Nurek said. "That is the destination that I shared with your Lieutenant Ramos. I will regret having to leave this fine ship. It is a wonderful vessel and it is crewed by a most unique race."

"Well, that's just my opinion," Remmy said. "Don't count on that. The Captain may have other ideas for you."

Remmy finished his drink and found that he felt good. There was no buzz like he might get from alcohol, but he certainly felt refreshed, as if he had just stepped out of the shower after a good night's sleep.

"I will not soon forget our conversation," Nurek said. "Would you give the other Dudonus volunteers a message from me?"

"Sure," Remmy said.

"Thank you, Master Sergeant. You honor me and I am delighted by your kindness. Tell them I am well and being looked after. You can tell them I have helped Captain Darius in some small way. Be sure to tell them that I shared a glass of Vanar with you. That will let them know that you are telling the truth."

"Is there something in your beverage that keeps me from lying?" Remmy said with a chuckle.

"No," Nurek said with a slight bow. "But Vanar is a beverage the Dudonus only share with those we have the utmost respect for, and hopefully, a bond of friendship."

Remmy nodded, "I get it. I'm happy to be your friend, Nurek."

"The honor is all mine," he said again with a deep bow.

Remmy left the prisoner in his quarters. Nurek was still, officially, a prisoner. He had committed murder, but Remmy couldn't help but think that if Nurek was guilty of a crime, that Remmy himself was much more guilty. Nurek had killed one Ashi, but Remmy had killed hundreds. And by that logic, Captain Darius was responsible for killing thousands in space combat. Obviously, Emperor Vang was not a threat while he was strapped down to a table in the Med Bay, but he had been let loose during the battle in the Casa system. And Remmy knew that Vang was responsible for killing several crew members. He might have killed Commander Lori Lee if Specialist Elgersma hadn't sacrificed himself to save her. In Remmy's mind, Nurek had simply carried out justice.

Then he had to admit there was a difference in the way a person of high rank and authority was treated. Emperor Vang was just a murderer. In fact, it could be argued that as a prisoner on an enemy ship during a time of war, that his acts were justified. But Remmy didn't agree. He hadn't known the crew members killed by Vang, but he knew they were human beings. The Ashi had invaded the *Renegade* with the aim to disable her and kill or capture the entire crew. In his mind, Vang got exactly what he deserved.

Of course, there were the political implications to be considered. Having the emperor as a prisoner would have given the crew leverage with the Ashi. But politics were above his pay grade, even if he was acting as an officer for the Marine platoon. What he didn't do was blame Nurek. Remmy didn't know him and didn't know if he or any of the Dudonus could really be trusted, but Remmy understood why Nurek had killed Emperor Vang. Additionally, he thought if he were in a similar situation he would have done the same thing himself. So, it was hard for Remmy to find guilt with Nurek.

After drifting down the gravity ring, he stepped out on the main deck. Everything on the Arodoni ship glistened, from the polished deck to the diamond accents that graced the bulkheads. People were moving through the concourse. Some were having conversations by the big statue near the ramps that led to the upper levels of the commerce section of the ship. Others were moving toward or away from the Admin Center, which was directly across the wide concourse from the Med Bay. Above the wide walkway, the area was open all the way to the upper hull. People on the upper decks could look down to the concourse with all its hustle and bustle. There were humans mingling with a dozen different species. He still thought of them as aliens simply because they weren't human. Most of the aliens were refugees and yet they all seemed to get along. There was no fighting, no arguments or misunderstandings. Perhaps, given time, that would change. Remmy knew that most of the beings on board the *Renegade* were simply happy to be alive. His platoon had rescued the Dudonus from a slave ship. They had fought the Ashi on Casasil, which would have been overrun otherwise. And the other aliens had been rescued from holding cells on a slave space station. Compared to forced slavery, minor misunderstandings could be easily overlooked, he supposed.

Remmy made his way to the Dudonus social club. He didn't know what they were calling the place, but that was what the human crew had named the room. It was big, larger than most stores or bars on Earth. Almost every facility on the space station was larger than what humans normally built. He stepped inside and looked around. It was a colorful place. There were bright paintings on the walls, ornate furnishings, rugs with intricate designs, and even tall, narrow, cylinder-shaped cups made from strange materials. In the hands of the Dudonus, which were thin and delicate but much longer than human hands, the cups seemed natural.

"Master Sergeant Steel," one of the Dudonus said in a soft voice. "Welcome."

It was a female. At least Remmy thought she was female. Her name was Mura, and while she looked not different from the other Dudonus, she spoke in a more feminine tone of voice.

"Thank you," Remmy said. "I have a message from Nurek."

Several more of the aliens were moving closer to hear what he was saying.

"Go on, then," Mura encouraged him.

"He says to tell you that he is well and being looked after. Also, that he has helped Captain Darius."

The Dudonus had big eyes. Their heads were tall and conical, with small mouths and tiny noses. Remmy couldn't read much of their body language, yet he noticed the big eyes narrowing in suspicion. It was an almost human gesture.

"He shared with me a glass of Vanar," Remmy said. "It was very good."

"You have taken the cup of friendship?" Mura asked.

Remmy nodded. "I did."

"Thank you, Master Sergeant. Your news is welcome."

There were nods. The murmuring among the onlookers wasn't picked up and translated by his language app, so Remmy had no idea what the others were saying, but he thought they seemed relieved.

"Some have feared that Nurek's actions would reflect poorly on our race," Mura continued. "It is hard to believe that a race as courageous and strong as yours would be able to understand what we have endured."

"Maybe not," Remmy said. "But I don't think anyone on this ship blames Nurek for what he did."

"I hope that is true," Mura said. "While we do not condemn his actions, we still fear the consequences."

"If there are consequences to be meted out, they will not pass onto you or the Dudonus. Nurek's actions were his alone."

"Do you know what will happen to him?" Mura asked.

Remmy could only shake his head. "That's up to Captain Darius."

"Can you intercede for him?"

Remmy thought for a moment. He wasn't used to being part of the decision-making group on a starship. Normally, that was reserved for senior officers only, but his position on the *Renegade* was different. As was his friendship with Captain Darius. Remmy didn't think he could offer much hope, but he could at least try.

"I will try," Remmy said. "And we will keep you updated if any decisions about Nurek are made. In the meantime, he is being well-treated and is proving himself useful to the command crew. I have been witness to that."

The Dudonus bowed in respect. Remmy copied the gesture and left to go find his Marines.

CHAPTER 11

THE *RETRIBUTION* WASN'T the first ship to drop out of hyperspace in the Zutek system. Sheika Kahn was no fool. If the Arodoni ship was waiting for them, he didn't want to be the first vessel they targeted.

"Lord, the enemy has fled the system," the shipmaster declared.

"Not surprising," Vang said. "There is nothing here."

"Commander Ollug requests to deliver news of the alien ship personally."

"Connect him," the Kahn ordered.

A holograph appeared before him. The Ashi was older than most commanders. One tusk was broken off and capped with silver. There were soft portions of fleshy skin under his narrow eyes.

"Lord Kahn," the hologram declared with a deep bow. "It is a great honor to serve you."

"Indeed," Ulrech Sheika said. "What service do you have to offer?"

"News, my Lord. The Arodoni ship was here."

"And where are the other ships I ordered to his location?" the Kahn demanded.

He had sent a mining ship, a spy vessel and a battleship to all of the hyperspace lane exchange systems. It was one of the first orders he had given upon seizing control of the Ashi fleet.

"Destroyed, Lord Kahn, by the alien ship no less."

"They have repaired the damage to their laser cannons?"

"Aye, Lord Kahn. We recorded their time in system. Some ten hours were spent on the repairs. We were too far out to get good visuals, but the ship fired on the *Berserker* and destroyed it in a single blast. Likewise, what remained of the mining ship was vaporized by the alien's powerful laser weapons."

"What do you mean, what was left?"

"That was why I begged the favor of a personal audience with your Greatness," Ollug said, bowing again. "When the alien ship came out of hyperspace, it was attacked by the mining ship *Loathing*. She was deploying mines across the portal which the alien ship came out of. It's not on any of our navigation charts, Lord. We have checked multiple times."

"That is not unexpected," Sheika Kahn growled. His patience was growing thin.

"Well, sire, what I wanted to tell you was that the alien ship used its gravity beam to manipulate the mines. They pushed them straight into the *Loathing*.

"That's... not possible," Sheika Kahn said.

Artificial gravity was a little-understood technology. It could be generated and even harnessed. The Ashi fleet had several interdictor vessels that could produce large gravitational fields. But even though researchers had spent lifetimes trying to find a way to reverse gravity, none had ever been successful. Eventually, the Prime Council declared an end to the research after deciding that a reverse gravitational wave could not be produced.

"But that's what happened, Lord Kahn. I am uploading the data to your flagship now."

"They used gravity to push the mines back onto the mining vessel? You're certain?"

"Aye, Lord. That's the only plausible explanation."

Only, it wasn't plausible, Sheika Kahn thought. The technology to generate artificial gravity was possible, but not to manipulate and reverse gravity. If the Arodoni ship contained such a secret, he absolutely had to seize the alien vessel and steal their advanced technology.

It was a shift in Sheika Kahn's strategy. He had planned to requisition the alien ship if possible, but all he really cared about was attaining the throne. If the alien ship was destroyed, and more importantly, Emperor Vang was destroyed in the process, then so be it. She had incredibly powerful laser weapons. And no one knew what fueled the ship or where it managed to get more energy, but Sheika Kahn didn't really care about that sort of technology. Who needed ultra powerful weapons when he had an entire military fleet at his disposal? And who cared about energy production, when he had entire worlds whose entire purpose was the creation of energy for his needs.

But a gravity weapon? That was another matter entirely. A gravity weapon was useful. It would not only cement his rule as the new emperor, but it would be the crowning achievement of his rule. He would be known as the emperor who developed the gravity weapon that would define the Ashi military might for the next millennium. That was a goal worth pursuing. The first step was to find the alien ship again.

"Commander Ollug, where did the alien ship go?"

"It disappeared, Lord. Vanished into thin air, like a ghost."

"Don't be a fool!" Sheika Kahn snapped. "They passed into hyperspace. Where?"

"Lord, we checked the navigation charts three times. There is no portal in that section of the system."

"That - we - know - of," the Kahn growled. He wondered how Ollug had ever risen to the rank of commander, even on a surveillance vessel. The man was an utter fool. "But the alien ship came out of a portal we knew nothing about. It stands to reason he would know of others. It is, in fact, why the alien ship was in this system in the first place. Where!"

Ollug had to have someone pass him the information. It was

directed immediately to the scout ships which went to find the unlisted portal. In the Olotimbo system, the alien vessel had taken another unmarked portal. Sheika Kahn had sent a scout ship through the portal. It returned in less than a day reporting that the portal led to an unknown system which had been occupied by unauthorized slavers. That much of the report was not a surprise. Outlaws had long been known to slip out of systems by means that no one could explain. The best theory was that they had knowledge of hyperspace lanes that were not on the Imperium's navigational systems.

What was a surprise was the condition of the system. Among a myriad of derilict spacecraft was a massive space station. Sheika Kahn could only surmise what types of illicit dealings went on in the station. Even more surprising was the fact that the station was catastrophically damaged. The scouts reported gas and smoke venting from the station and one section that was blown apart. It had exploded from the inside out.

It seemed the alien ship knew of the secret hyperspace lanes. Sheika Kahn wondered if perhaps that was why the alien vessel had remained hidden for so long. It took his scouts less than an hour to discover the portal. And Sheika Kahn made a bold decision.

"Send the fleet to the unmarked portal," he ordered. "All ships, save for Ollug's spy vessel. Have the fool relieved of command."

"Yes, Lord," the shipmaster responded. "It will take some time to get that far out and reassemble. Maybe two days."

"So be it," Sheika Kahn said. "We'll send the scout ships through. I have a feeling the alien vessel will soon be in our hands."

He was close. He could feel it. In many ways, it was like the warriors of old. His destiny lay before him. All he had to do was take it. The cost didn't matter. He would throw the entire fleet at the alien ship. If they all died, he would rebuild it. Nothing else mattered but Sheika Kahn's future and he was determined to do everything in his power to ensure the secrets on the alien ship were his alone.

CHAPTER 12

THE *RENEGADE* CAME out of the portal and into the Libertine system. At first glance it seemed like a very hospitable place. There were four gas giants in the system and four planets closer in to the system's bright, yellow star.

"No other ships on radar," Vivian Ramos announced. "Continuing to scan."

"Lots of places a ship could hide," Pete Best said.

"The entire Ashi fleet could be behind one of those gas giants," Commander Lori Lee said.

"Let's stay focused," Captain Darius told them. "We'll do our due diligence. Lieutenant Ramos, start plotting a course back out of the system just in case we need to run."

But they didn't. After lingering by the hyperspace portal for several hours they launched drones toward the gas giants. Darius was in no hurry to get caught unaware again. After over fifteen hours in the system, he felt fairly certain that they were alone. The plot showed the entire system. There were no other ships except for two old cruise liners in orbit around the third planet.

The *Renegade* was making for the planet. More drones with

orbital instruments were being launched from the ship. More information was coming in minute by minute.

"First readings are in from the planet," Vivian Ramos said. "It looks hot."

"A dust ball," Pete Best said. "Wonderful."

"Surface readings are very hot," Commander Lee said. "In fact, there's no vegetation below the 66th degree parallel in the northern hemisphere. The same is true in the south it appears."

"It's a pretty barren place," Henry Nash said.

"Probably was completely barren before people showed up," Darius said.

"Why pick such an inhospitable world?" Pete Best asked. "There has to be other options."

"Not outside the Imperium," Nurek said.

He had been summoned from his quarters once it appeared that the system was safe. The alien was seated at the same console he had used to help during the battle of Olotimbo.

"I don't suppose they're here to have a cushy lifestyle," Henry Nash said. "When you're running from tyranny, you do what you have to do."

"They don't even have satellite intel," Pete Best said. "I'm getting very little electromagnetic signatures from the planet itself."

"What do you know about this place?" Darius asked Nurek.

"It's one of five worlds that are hidden from the Imperium," Nurek said. "Libertine is the most inhabited."

"How was it discovered?" Commander Lee asked.

"No one knows for certain," Nurek said. "As you might imagine, it cannot be discussed openly. The entire subject is outlawed by the Imperium. It was labeled as disinformation long ago. We hear of it only in whispers. I know of it through the network of rebels across the galaxy. I am but a single link in that chain. I know several others due to the emperor's extensive travels, but we cannot openly meet or talk about it."

"Someone, somewhere knew about this place and how to get here," Darius said. "They probably gathered some resources. We need to speak to the leaders. Ensign Bertoli, start hailing the planet. We need to let them know we have people to land."

"Aye, Captain, hailing the planet now," Jacee Bertoli said.

"What about those ships?" Darius said.

"They're empty," Commander Lori Lee said. "I've already scanned them. No power. They're just frozen hulks lingering in orbit."

"Look at this, Captain," Henry Nash said. "I think I just found a drilling platform and refinery."

"Where?" Darius asked.

"Well south of the sixty-sixth parallel, sir. See that."

It was just a spot on the chief engineer's console screen, but it was registering heat and movement.

"Why would they be drilling?" Pete Best asked.

"Fossil fuels," Henry Nash said, as if that explained everything.

Darius saw the confused look on his weapons officer's face. "They're burning fossil fuels to release CO_2 into the atmosphere. By thickening the atmo, they're hoping to regulate the surface temps and usher in a more hospitable environment."

"Can they do that?" Pete asked.

"Sure, given enough time," Commander Lori Lee said.

"But won't the CO_2 make the air unbreathable?"

"It will to humans but not to flora," Darius explained. "More carbon dioxide will make it possible for more vegetation, which in turn will produce oxygen. It's a delicate balance, but if they can strike it, they'll open up much more of the planet's surface to people."

"Some people think that happened on Earth," Lori Lee said. "They've found the remains of what looks like a tropical forest deep under the ice at the south pole."

"That's a result of planetary shifting," Vivian Ramos said.

"Maybe," Lori Lee said.

"Seems like someone here had the same idea," Darius pointed out.

An hour later, no contact had been made. The *Renegade* was

settled into orbit, and the refugees were gathering in the main hangar. Darius was there too, along with the Marines.

"You're ready to go?" Darius asked.

"Yes, sir!" Remmy said. "We'll escort both ships."

Darius looked around. There were nearly twenty Casians with big machine guns on their backs. The six legged pachyderm aliens were also pulling large crates, currently located aboard a third shuttle.

"We'll be back to a skeleton crew soon," Darius said.

"And then what, sir?" Remmy asked. "Have you made a decision?"

"Not yet," Darius replied. "It's hard to understand why the people here haven't developed planetary defenses."

"Maybe they don't have the resources," Remmy said. "I know how to use guns, but don't ask me to build one from scratch."

Darius nodded. It made sense to him, even though he wasn't sure he agreed. How could people from other planets in the galaxy, travel through space and colonize a new world without being technologically astute? And who was bringing them? It didn't seem possible that the program had been going on for long, otherwise the small land masses at either pole of the planet would be overrun.

"I want a full report, Master Sergeant. Get these people settled and find out as much as you can. Then get back up here."

"What if there's no one on the planet, sir? What if something has happened to them all?

"Then bring everyone back. We'll move on to the next planet. But Nurek assures me that Libertine is the main world. I can't say why they aren't answering our hails, but you'll know soon enough. Once you find out, Master Sergeant, don't linger around any longer than you have to."

"Are you worried the Ashi might find us?"

"I have to be," Darius said. "We can't get caught off guard again."

"Roger that," Remmy said. "It's good to know we're in good hands, Captain."

"That's very kind of you, Master Sergeant. Good luck."

"Yes, sir. Thank you, sir."

Darius waited and watched. He felt a bit out of place. The Dudonus volunteers had taken the lead. They were organizing everything. Most of the volunteers were leaving the ship along with the refugees. Only a handful remained, mostly Casians. Darius had insisted that Nurek stay on board the *Renegade*. It might not have been what the alien wanted, but after murdering Emperor Vang, he had forfeited his rights. In addition, Darius thought it only fitting that Nurek serve to help the ship carry out it's mission. He was, in fact, very helpful.

"Looks like they're ready to lift off, Captain," Staff Sergeant McPherson said. "It might be better if we step off the deck, sir."

"Yes, of course," Darius replied.

They returned to the gravity lift. It carried them both up to the park. Staff Sergeant McPherson was in charge of the human Marines while Remmy was away. It made sense that only the Casian volunteers should go down, since they would be staying on the planet with the others to help defend them in case of an invasion.

"Sir, may I ask what we're going to do now?" Laila said.

Darius couldn't blame her for asking. He didn't normally spend much time with enlisted personnel, and even less time with enlisted Marines. But being in the park seemed to lower the boundaries that normally separated Officers from the crew. It was such a peaceful, beautiful space that they seemed more like friends than Captain and crew member.

"I wish I knew for sure, Staff Sergeant," he admitted. "I'm trying to decide that now."

The walk up to the Bridge helped. There were things he liked about the *Renegade* and things he didn't. Her size was an issue at times, but the longer he commanded the Arodoni ship, the more he appreciated that size. It gave him time to think. A standard fleet ship was small, cramped, and uncomfortable. At times it felt like people were literally crawling all over one another. The *Renegade* on the other hand was spacious. If he wanted time alone he could find it. If he needed to retreat to his cabin, there was still room to move around. He could even pace in his quarters, a luxury no human space captain had ever enjoyed.

As he walked, his blood pumped harder and he felt like he could focus more intently. As he saw it, he now had two options. They could stay in the greater galaxy or go back to the Sol system. Staying meant fighting and he wasn't opposed to that. It was what they trained to do. Every member of the crew had known that warfare was possible before they agreed to join the Space Defense Force. But, as great as the *Renegade* was in a fight, they were still just one ship. If he made a mistake or if the enemy got lucky, they could all die. More important, if they died, Earth and humanity would be robbed of the technology from the ship and from the alien artifact who called herself GIGI.

Going back home wasn't a perfect choice either. It was possible that he could lead the enemy right to their gates. No one wanted that. Additionally, for the crew it would mean weeks of debriefings, maybe even charges. No one had authorized the *Jericho* to leave the system. That had been GIGI's efforts. The alien artifact had blocked all communication signals, forcing Darius to make command decisions. That was protocol. Unable to communicate with the SDF brass, Darius was the senior officer. He had command control and the full decision making capabilities for the ship. Of course, that was just SOP, it didn't mean he wouldn't suffer grave consequences for his actions. He could have just as easily turned the ship back into the system and turned everything over to his superiors. The truth was, GIGI had manipulated him, but only because he wanted an excuse not to return. He was a decorated officer at the end of his career. Administrative duties didn't interest him and Darius hadn't invested the time and energy into politicking his way into a command post. Retirement or a new career were all he could reasonably hope for and those options simply held no interest for him. He was a leader, a starship captain, what else could he possibly do that would measure up to that? So, he had left the Sol system, but he felt deep down that despite his selfish desires, it had been the right thing to do.

Before he knew it, he found himself back on the Bridge. Commander Lori Lee was there, but the other stations were manned by enlisted crew members.

"The shuttles are on their way down," Lori Lee said.

"Any issues?"

"None," Lori Lee said. "Sometimes I get the impression that we aren't really needed to fly this ship."

"I suppose we aren't," Darius said. "The *Renegade* got along pretty well without a crew before we came along."

"Except for their power supply issues," Lori Lee said. "Makes me wonder what happened to the Arodoni."

"You don't buy into the idea that they committed ritual suicide?"

Lori Lee shook her head. "I'm more apt to believe their species grew old and died out," she explained. "This ship was built for thousands. We don't have anything like it. And I don't believe that thousands of intelligent beings all decided to kill themselves."

"Maybe that was part of their culture. In the past, some human communities saw value in suicide."

"Only after a great failure," Lori Lee said.

"True, but maybe the Ashi defeated the Arodoni, and that was their great failure?"

"Is that what you believe?"

"No," I said. "To be honest with you, I keep thinking about what GIGI did to the outlaws on the slave ship when they tried to abscond with it."

"Not to mention that we did something similar to the Ashi who boarded the ship and tried to sabotage the engines," Lee pointed out. "When they were dead, the ship's drones carried the bodies away and cleaned up the mess."

"Who's to say the same thing didn't happen to the Arodoni?" Darius said.

He was keenly aware that GIGI was listening to every word he said. There was no way to keep his thoughts private and share them with anyone on board. The artifact had eyes and ears everywhere.

"Why?" Commander Lee asked.

"I have a theory," Darius said. "What if they weren't resolute enough in stopping the Ashi?"

They both fell silent as Lori Lee pondered the idea. "They had the means, just not the will to see it through?"

"Maybe they didn't think it was important," Darius said. "If the Ashi weren't really a threat to them, the Arodoni might have had other priorities."

"But their allies wanted them to fight."

"And when they wouldn't..."

He let the idea hang in the air. He didn't have to spell it all out for Lori Lee. He knew her to be a shrewd officer and very intelligent.

"They found someone else who would," she said in a very soft voice.

Darius nodded, then looked ahead. Outside the transparent canopy over the Bridge, he could see part of Libertine. It was a dull, gray-colored planet. In the distance were the two cruise liners. They were old, but he wondered what it would take to get them, or at least one of them, running again.

"Let's send over a surveillance drone to get a closer look at those cruise liners," Darius said.

"Aye, Captain," Lori Lee said.

He respected the fact that he didn't need to explain himself to his executive officer. It was enough for her that he gave the order. Darius just hoped that his decisions were good enough to be worthy of her trust.

CHAPTER 13

REMMY MADE the trip down to the surface of Libertine without incident. He wore space armor and carried weapons, but he kept his rifle strapped to his back and his hand cannon in a thigh holster. It wasn't his intention to intimidate anyone ... and he certainly wasn't there to fight. His task was to meet with the officials on Libertine and ensure the refugees would be well taken care of.

Stepping out of the ship was a bit like stepping back in time. He found himself on a dusty planet just outside a village. It wasn't big and certainly wasn't impressive. In fact, he thought it looked like a wild west town. The buildings were made of unpainted mud bricks. Everything seemed old and worn out. People were coming out of the buildings. They looked almost exactly like the refugees he was escorting down from the *Renegade*. There were several different races, most in little clusters. They wore what appeared to be homespun clothing that was made from some type of grassy fiber. Just like the unpainted buildings, they were dull grey in color, with no adornment and not even much in the way of contour.

"We're down," Remmy said, letting his comlink carry his words up into orbit. "It's pretty sad down here."

"We read you, Master Sergeant," Captain Darius said. "We have visuals, too."

Remmy walked toward the aliens who lived on Libertine. The planet had oxygen in the air and the climate was hot but within normal human conditions. Unfortunately, to keep his helmet camera functioning, he had to keep it on, which meant the locals couldn't see his face.

"Hello," he said, pausing while the language app translated his message. "My name is Remmy Steel."

There was bowing and whispered murmurs from the crowd of aliens. One, a thin biped with thick fingers and a massive hooked nose, stepped toward him. The alien's back was bowed with age; his eyes were bloodshot and had a yellow cast to them. When he spoke, it was with a raspy voice.

"Are you a robot?"

"No," Remmy assured him. "This is armor. I am a soldier."

"You are an Imperial warlord?"

"No. I am part of a group that is fighting the Imperium," Remmy said. "We have rescued hostages from a slave station. We have trained Casians to help defend your planet."

The alien looked confused. "Defend us from who? We are isolated. We have nothing of value."

"You are an example of people living free," Remmy said.

The alien made a strange noise. It was part laughter, part cough. It was Remmy's turn to be confused.

"If we are the example, it is no wonder that no one wants freedom," the alien managed to say.

"Is there a place where we can settle these refugees?" Remmy asked.

"They can settle wherever they like," the alien said. "Space is plentiful, but resources are few."

Remmy followed the elderly alien into the village. It was shocking to see a water well in the center of the town. Most of the locals returned to their chores. Some carried water; others were harvesting some type of vegetables from a wide garden on the far side of the single-street community. Young aliens played in the street in front of the hovels they called home.

"I came here fifty cycles ago as part of the terraforming team," the old alien said. "As you can see, our efforts fell well short of the mark."

Remmy bent down and ran his fingers through the soil. It was dull grey, with no moisture that he could detect.

"You have liquid water?"

"It's mostly underground," the alien explained. "We do what we can to repurpose and recycle, but you are the first visitor we have seen in more than twenty cycles. What we have is old, worn out, and broken. The last domesticated animals died long ago. Most races cannot survive here for long. There are more people in the ground than above it."

"You need help," Remmy said.

"We do, and yet, we have no way to request it."

"No communications outside the system?" Remmy asked.

"Not even to the other colonies in the south," the old alien said. "The cruisers that brought us here were salvaged. But we have no way to repair technology. This world offers so very little by way of natural resources. The airships broke down. Crossing the planet without them is impossible."

"So, you were left here? Abandoned? Aren't there other villages to the north?"

"None any better off than we were," the elder alien said.

At the far end of the dusty street was the frame of a spaceship. It was old, the metal bent. The hull plates, wiring, circuitry, and flight components had long been removed.

Remmy switched his helmet to mute so that the locals wouldn't hear him as he activated his comlink. "Captain, things here are pretty desperate."

"We saw that," Darius said. "I've already ordered all available resources to be shipped down to the planet, including some of our livestock."

"That will be a major upgrade for these people," Remmy said. "Do we have communication equipment?"

"Affirmative," Darius said. "I've already ordered Sergeant McManus to take down fifty percent of all the resources we can spare to your position. Sergeant Oliver will do the same to the colonies in the south. In the meantime, I intend to see if we can get the cruise liners operational."

"That is very generous of you, sir."

Remmy relayed the good news to the locals, who, despite their enormous needs, seemed uncertain. Perhaps, Remmy thought to himself, he just didn't know the aliens well enough to read their body language, but they seemed crushed by the isolation on Libertine, as well as the lack of hope.

There weren't very many individuals from any one race in the village. It appeared to be a family of one kind, a few members of another race, but not enough for any species to procreate. What had probably begun as a very hopeful colony soon became a world of desolation. It was hard to be hopeful, knowing that one's children could never fall in love and have children of their own. In time, they would simply die alone.

"We need to get word to the other settlements," Remmy told the elder alien and the small group of locals who cared enough to want to help. "We can take the shuttles and ensure that the supplies from the *Renegade* are equally distributed."

Soon, the ships were in the air. It didn't take long to reach the next village. GIGI flew the shuttle around the settlement. It seemed even poorer than the first. After alerting the townsfolk, they moved on. The landscape changed as they flew north. There was grass growing and even a few narrow streams. At the third village, Remmy found sod houses. The people supplemented small crustaceans found in the little stream that ran through their community to the diet of meager vegetables. Unfortunately, the aliens in the village seemed no better off than those from the first two settlements.

When they returned to the original colony, two new shuttles from the *Renegade* had arrived. Remmy's transport was full of representatives from each of the small settlements. They were nervous and quiet. Remmy met Hugo as he led the way off the ship.

"I've got your supplies, Master Sergeant," Hugo said.

"Outstanding. What'd you bring?"

"One shuttle is full of building supplies. It's mostly prefab buildings, but it's wired for solar power and has hook-ups for water."

"I doubt these people have the means of running water to their domiciles, but maybe I'm underestimating them," Remmy said. "What else."

"The second shuttle has communication equipment, tools, and basic tech supplies."

"Let's get it offloaded and send them back for more."

"Roger that, Master Sergeant."

Remmy found the elderly alien he had first dealt with. The creature had a name that Remmy couldn't pronounce. Instead, he called the alien Elder.

"Our first priority is to set up the communication equipment," Remmy said, glancing up at the sky. "Probably better to do it indoors."

"That building is empty," Elder said, pointing a thick finger at a crumbling edifice. Most of the building had been scavenged, but there was a corner still intact, with a sloping roof above it.

"That will do," Remmy said.

He and Hugo put the Casians to work. A few moved the main communications console into the empty building. Hugo directed the offloading of the rest of the equipment. Some stayed in the village; some were put into the other shuttles to be transported to different settlements. Meanwhile, Remmy got a big receiving dish mounted to the roof of the crumbling building. The structure would need to be repaired soon. He called up for some metal support beams.

It didn't take long to get the communication unit running. There were old satellites still in orbit. The comms gear synced up and soon Remmy was chatting with Sergeant Dirk Oliver.

"I'm with Leigh Ann Poh," he said. "We're in the primary settlement. It ain't much, Master Sergeant."

"Same here," Remmy said. "But there's hope. Perhaps we can turn things around for these people."

"Is it our responsibility, though?" Dirk asked. "This isn't a human settlement."

"No, but it is a free world. And we have the means to make a difference here, wouldn't you agree?"

"Yes, Master Sergeant, there's no doubt about that."

"Then we should. A little work on our part can make a huge difference in the lives of the locals."

Remmy turned the communication gear over to Elder, who made contact with members of his original team that he hadn't spoken to in years. For the first time, the stooped alien seemed hopeful.

Using the comlink in his battle helmet and the signal amplifier in the shuttle, Remmy could stay in touch with the *Renegade*.

"Master Sergeant, you have livestock in transit," Ensign Bertoli alerted him.

"Roger that," Remmy said.

"There are insulated crates with frozen victuals, too. Each would have the capacity to stay cold for two weeks unless it's opened."

"Copy," Remmy said. "The locals will certainly appreciate that. Food is scarce down here."

An hour later, a herd of short, wooly animals was being led out of a shuttle and into a makeshift pen. There wasn't enough grass at the primary settlement to raise them, and Elder set about assigning the animals to villages farther north.

"They will grow fat on the sod there," Elder said.

"You won't have trouble keeping them alive for breeding?"

"Not from lack of food," Elder said. "But there is a predatory animal that is native to this planet. We call them sand vipers."

"They're around here?" Remmy asked.

Elder shook his head. "They come up from the sand sea about thirty kilometers from here. They are nocturnal and mostly subterranean."

"But they don't attack your people?"

"No, we mostly stay indoors at night. But there is no way to protect livestock. We are not warriors. We have no weapons."

"You do now," Remmy said. "There are ten Casian soldiers here and ten at the South Pole. They have weapons that should be able to deal with any threat. How big are the vipers?"

"Usually two meters in girth. They range from three to six meters in length."

"That's manageable. Do they come in groups or alone?"

"They are solitary creatures."

"Then we're in business. You'll be able to build defensive systems as the herds grow. What about trees? I didn't see any."

"None were planted," Elder said. "When we began our colony, the atmosphere wasn't rich in carbon dioxide. We could not sustain anything more than grass and some vegetables."

"And now? Could you grow more if you had them?"

Elder shrugged, his slumped shoulders rising and falling like pistons in an ancient machine. "We no longer have the capacity to measure the gases in our air."

Remmy cycled through the apps in his battle helmet, eventually finding an atmospheric register app. He activated it and got a readout of the gases in the air.

"Looks like CO_2 is at eight hundred parts per million," Remmy said.

"That is ideal," Elder said. "Given enough water, we could grow most anything now."

"Good. We've got crates with a variety of seeds being shipped down. You'll have everything you need to thrive."

"We cannot thank you enough," Elder said.

Remmy looked around. The aliens had changed since he first arrived. They seemed hopeful. He heard what sounded like laughter. That was all the thanks Remmy needed. The crew of the *Renegade* was making a difference. And that was all he cared about.

CHAPTER 14

"THAT'S THE LAST SHUTTLE, CAPTAIN," Commander Lee said.

"What's the status on our stores?" Darius asked.

Nurek was on the Bridge again and helping keep track of the supplies being offloaded onto Libertine.

"Captain, we've sent all the prefabricated building supplies, along with an entire load of various sizes of steel beams. That leaves our natural resources down to half of the normal supply, but the refining plant is producing more from the slave ship you ordered, cut down, and processed. Rare minerals are at sixty-seven percent. Iron and processed steel are down to one-third but rising. Copper is down to forty-one percent."

"What about the biological surplus?"

"We focused on the plants currently growing in the agricultural park," Lori Lee said. "That way, we can resupply, if needed. We sent a thousand seeds of every species of tree and bush and then a thousand of the leafy green plants that the Casians favor for food, along with other fruits and vegetables that the computer designated as being optimal for Libertine's atmosphere, soil, and climate."

"That's hardly enough for an entire planet," Vivian Ramos said.

"Especially when you consider it will be spread across two separate continents."

"Time and nature will have to do the rest," Darius said before turning to his chief engineer. "Henry, are we ready to board those space cruisers?"

"Staff Sergeant McPherson has a team of engineers outfitted in space suits now, Captain. They are boarding a shuttle as we speak."

"Very good. I want a status report on the systems that are left on those ships," Darius said. "The locals need reliable transportation."

It was true. The *Renegade* could supply shuttles to ferry the citizens of Libertine up into orbit, but they needed a ship to bring supplies. And if what Darius had seen on Master Sergeant Steel's vid feed from the surface, they needed more people. The human ship captain found it a bit strange to think of the aliens as people. They looked completely different from anything he had ever seen before. And yet, despite their differences in anatomy, background, and culture, they were just people. He found that he couldn't think of them in any other way. They had hopes and dreams, triumphs and tragedies. They were skilled at certain things, but not the same things as humans. It was shocking to Darius that so many highly intelligent races had no concept of weapons or even ways to defend themselves. Fighting, it seemed, while not exclusive to the human race, was incredibly rare in the wider galaxy.

In the short time they had been in the Libertine system, Darius had realized that the Free Worlds needed more than just technological information. They needed resources, supplies, manufacturing capabilities, a link to the greater galaxy, and most importantly, someone to defend them. The volunteers from the crew, about ninety percent of the Casians and half of the Dudonus, were going to stay on the planet. That included the twenty or so Casians that had been trained by the Space Marines and supplied with guns that mounted onto their backs for combat. But that wasn't enough to protect even one settlement against an invading force, much less the entire planet. If they could produce drones and orbital defense platforms the Casians who had learned to fly drones on the *Renegade* could put those skills to use defending the planet. But would even that be enough against a fleet from the Imperium military? Darius didn't think so.

He also didn't think it was fair to ask his crew to protect the alien world. It wasn't their home. In fact, they didn't even have a human presence on the planet. So, he had to send them home, but perhaps it wasn't necessary to take them. Maybe, he considered, he could stay. The ship needed a crew, but many of the jobs could be carried out by the ship's automated systems. He and whoever else wanted to could remain on the *Renegade* if they could get both of the space cruisers working. One could be reserved for the inhabitants of the planet and one could ferry the humans back to the Sol system, along with GIGI and all the alien technology.

It was desertion on a certain level, yet Darius found himself rationalizing the idea. He would be staying to fight. The Imperium fleet, upon finding the *Renegade,* would have no idea that the human crew had gone back to their system, which would keep the aliens from looking for Earth, thus carrying out Darius' highest priority to protect the human race. It would also establish a link to the Free Worlds for humanity, which could prove useful at some point in the future.

So he had sent a crew to the space cruisers in hopes that they could get the old ships up and running. He had also ordered the manufacturing plant on the *Renegade* to replicate the Arodoni Power Core. The alien device was still a mystery to the human crew. Henry Nash had studied the plans for the device but couldn't explain the science behind it. What they could do, however, was have the *Renegade* produce more so that the copious amounts of energy that the power core could convert from dark matter could be used by the space cruisers in lieu of traditional fuels.

If the rest of the ship was intact, meaning the electronics, the engines and life support systems, they could utilize the ships however they wanted. With near-unlimited power, they could even be converted into warships, if necessary. But Darius hoped it wouldn't be necessary. He hoped the Imperium fleet would never find them.

"Engineering team is en route," Vivian Ramos said.

Darius looked at the holographic plot. It showed the *Renegade*, the planet, and both of the cruise liners in low orbit around the dust-colored world. It also showed a little shuttle moving steadily from the large Arodoni ship toward the derelict vessels.

"Very good," Darius said. "What about the rest of the system."

"We have three quarters mapped," Vivian said.

"Are there other portals?"

"Aye, Captain," the navigation officer said. "There are three. Two lead to other worlds, Subterra and Typhana, respectively."

"Are there routes from those worlds to the wider galaxy?" Darius asked, as he wondered about how best to secure the Libertine system.

"Not according to our records, Captain," Vivian said.

"Pete, how's the beacon near the portal working?"

Weapons officer Pete Best looked up from his console. "It's one hundred percent, Captain. I get a ping every sixty seconds. So far, we're the only ship that's come through."

Darius breathed a small sigh of relief. It was exactly what he wanted to hear. Not that he feared combat. In fact, with just one way in or out of the system, he was already thinking of ways to secure the area. It wouldn't take much to build a series of powerful laser weapons that could cover the portal. A ship coming through that couldn't identify itself would be fired upon, either with disabling precision lasers or larger blasts intended to destroy entire space vessels. In fact, he found it surprising that there weren't defensive batteries around most portals. But with the Imperium having the only ships of war, they had little to fear.

"Sir, we're getting good scans of the cruise liners," Henry Nash spoke up. "Looks like the hulls are in good shape."

"Excellent. Have they found a way in?"

"Looks like it, Captain. They're extending a docking tube now."

"Zoom in on them, please," Darius said.

The holographic projection grew larger until they could see the shuttle clearly. A white tube was extending toward the larger of the two space cruisers. It would connect with powerful electro-magnets but wouldn't be strong enough to seal out the hard vacuum of space. Instead, the engineers would pass through in their space suits.

"Shogun, this is Onna-Bugeisha actual. I am passing through and opening the derelict cruiser's airlock. Standby."

"Standing by, Onna-Bugeisha," Darius said.

"I have the video feed from her helmet camera," Ensign Jacee Bertoli said.

Another holographic projector activated, and Darius could see what was being recorded from Staff Sergeant McPherson's battle helmet. She was halfway through the white tunnel. The only light was from her helmet, but they could see the emergency airlock clearly. There was writing on the alien ship in a strange, wavy script.

"Can we get a translation of that signage?" Darius asked. "GIGI?"

"It is simply the ship's call sign, Captain, and her system of origin," the computer voice replied. "It is Mangalise. The name of the ship in your language is *Independence*."

"How apropos," Darius said. "Thank you, GIGI."

"It is my pleasure to serve, Captain."

Darius glanced over at executive officer Lori Lee, who was looking back at him. They both shared the same feeling that GIGI was manipulating, not serving the human crew, but they would have to worry about that another time.

Laila McPherson pulled the emergency hatch lever and then twisted it. The airlock made a noise they couldn't hear in the hard vacuum of space. There was a grinding vibration of metal on metal as the airlock cycled, then the hatch popped open.

"We're in," Laila said. "Engineering team, standby. I'll make sure it's clear inside then; call for you to cross over one at a time and join me."

The airlock was small. Laila McPherson, in her bulky space armor with weapons attached, barely fit inside. She managed to get everything in the small airlock and run the cycle. This time, everyone heard the old metal grinding.

"Is that normal?" Darius asked.

"Old metal can become attached, especially if there's rust or some other substance involved. Most likely, it just needs to be oiled, Captain. Nothing to worry about at this stage of the game."

"Thank you, Henry," Darius said.

Laila stepped through the airlock on the other side and found herself in a well-appointed passenger cabin. There were rows of small seats. They had thick cushions on the seat and narrow back-rests with safety straps. The ceiling was low for human standards, but the interior seemed intact.

"Looks clear," Laila said as she moved down the aisle. "Plenty of room in here. Vince, start sending your people over."

"Copy that, Staff Sergeant," a male voice replied.

"The passenger cabin won't tell us much," Henry said.

"Moving into the cockpit," Laila announced.

She stepped into a wide area with four large pilot chairs. It was all foreign, but nothing looked as though it had been ripped out of place.

"Hey, we may get lucky," Henry said.

"It all looks intact," Darius agreed.

"Doesn't mean it's connected to anything," Pete Best pointed out.

"But if the hardware is there, we should be able to reconnect to it," Henry said. "Staff Sergeant McPherson, can you look under those consoles?"

"Sure," she replied. "What am I looking for?"

"Loose wires, missing panels," Henry said. "Any indication that things have been removed."

"Copy that."

She spent the next ten minutes inspecting the cockpit. There was no sign of any tampering that she could make out. Darius felt a slight thrill. It really might be possible that he could send his crew home. It would mean never going back for him, but he didn't mind. The *Renegade* felt more like a home to him than any place on Earth. And he could keep doing what he loved most, commanding a starship. That alone was worth any sacrifice he could make. It was almost within his grasp.

CHAPTER 15

IT WAS ALMOST dark when Remmy set the last sentry radar device into the soft turf. They were designed to detect enemy movement in combat situations, which was why he had them in a crate of supplies that included weapons and ammunition. He had set up a line of them about forty kilometers apart in the hopes that if the livestock they had brought down from the *Renegade* would draw the sand vipers north, the radar would pick them up.

"That's the last one, Master Sergeant," Hugo said.

"You check coms?" Remmy asked as he got on board the shuttle.

"All settlements are squawking. If the predators come this way, we'll know it, and there should be plenty of time to prepare the Casians."

"Let's see how they hold up," Remmy said. "This will be a good test for them."

There were three Casian Marines in each of the settlements where livestock had been sent. From what Remmy was told, the animals were enjoying the tough grass that grew on Libertine. If the Casians could keep them alive, there was no reason to think they wouldn't thrive.

"Never thought I would ever see anything like this place," Hugo said from the cockpit of the shuttle as the automated transport lifted off.

They didn't bother flying the ship. GIGI controlled it from orbit, freeing the Marines to do other things. In this case, it was to gaze out at the verdant world while they waited for their combat radar to pick up movement from the south.

"It's beautiful," Remmy said.

There were no clouds in the sky, which had turned a dark pink as the sun set. Stars were just starting to glimmer. Below them, the rolling landscape was covered with dark grass, but there were no trees and very little signs of liquid water. Further south, the grass ended in an arid strip of rocky soil that stood between the livable territory to the north and the sea of sand that covered most of the planet to the south.

"It's like being on a young planet," Hugo said. "There's nothing but potential here."

"You don't mind the ruggedness?" Remmy asked. "There's no modern conveniences on Libertine."

"But there's room," Hugo said. "A man could own a thousand acres and raise whatever he wanted without seeing another person for months at a time."

"Sounds kind of lonely."

"Not to me," Hugo insisted. "Horses would thrive here. Can you imagine a herd of horses out there roaming free?"

"It would be a beautiful sight," Remmy agreed.

"You think we'll get the chance to come back here one day? I mean, when the fight is over and done."

Remmy shrugged. "I don't see why not. It might not be cheap to get transport this far out, but it won't be difficult."

"Unless the government forbids it," Hugo said. "That wouldn't surprise me. We finally have the ability to roam free through the galaxy and the bureaucrats will find a way to ruin it."

"I prefer to think of settling on a world that is a little more habitable," Remmy said. "Casasil was a nice place."

"It was," Hugo said. "It's the kind of place that everyone would want to go. That's why I would choose this world. No one will want to live here for a century at least. The civvie was telling me about it."

"Connor O'Dell?"

"Yeah," Hugo said. "That's him. He said, eventually the planet's atmosphere will thicken enough that everything will change."

"To make more of the land more habitable?"

Hugo nodded. "But I'll be dead and gone before that happens."

"Wouldn't you rather find someone to settle down with? Raise a few baby Hugos?"

"No," he said matter-of-factly. "I... the Marines saved me, Master Sergeant. Everyone said I was a lost cause, even my drill instructor. They thought I would run headlong into the enemy on my first combat op."

"Didn't you?"

"Sure did," he said with a chuckle. "I was ready to end it all and that seemed like a good way to do it."

"Why?"

"My old man beat us. He killed my mother and would have killed me, too, but the government stepped in. I was put into the system at age five, which was no improvement over my home life, believe you me. I had to fight to survive, to get enough food, to get anything at all. I don't think I ever got enough to eat until I enlisted."

"You don't look like you've missed many meals," Remmy told him.

Hugo wasn't fat. In fact, he had very little body fat, but his big frame was thick with muscles that would have made a bodybuilder jealous.

"I've worked at it the last ten years," Hugo said. "The gym is one place I can do something productive on my own. Just put on some headphones and lift something heavy. When everyone else was putting in an hour, I was putting in four."

"What happened during that first combat op?"

"The enemy saw me coming. It must have freaked them out. They broke and ran. Suddenly, people are saying what a great Marine I was when all I wanted was a way out."

"Suicide by combat?"

"Something like that," Hugo said. "I was a dumb kid. Pain didn't frighten me, relationships did. Girls? I just never understood the nuance of it. I tried a few times, but it only reinforced to me that I wasn't built for normal."

"I think you're too hard on yourself," Remmy told him. "I'd share a foxhole with you."

"Thanks, Master Sergeant. But I've learned a lot about myself over the years. Trauma affects the brain. I don't have to tell you that."

Remmy shook his head. He understood the toll trauma could take. Gunny Sergeant Chad Rand was a perfect example.

"My trauma came early in life and left major scars," Hugo went on. "I prefer my own company. And I'm not looking to pass on these genes. The McManus line can end with me and I think it's for the better."

"You're a damn fine Marine," Remmy pointed out.

"I don't mind hard work and I don't fear dying," Hugo said. "What more could anyone want from a professional soldier?"

"You're selling yourself short."

"I don't think so. I don't have the qualities that make a good leader. I can't relate to other people the way you and McPherson do. I'm not good at motivating others. That's a burden to me. Trying to understand another person's feelings? No, I'm better off alone."

Remmy wanted to argue with him, but he decided it wasn't wise. Remmy had no idea what Hugo McManus had endured in his life. He couldn't explain away the trauma that plagued the big man or help him relate to people better. If Hugo preferred solitude, who was Remmy to try and convince him otherwise?

"Wherever you end up," Remmy finally said. "You'll be an asset."

"Thank you, Master Sergeant. I hope that's true."

They fell silent for a few minutes. Remmy didn't mind the quiet. It gave him time to think. Libertine wasn't the type of world he wanted to spend the rest of his life on. It was a big step up from Mars but nothing close to the pristine beauty of a world like Casasil. Hugo's musing on the future made Remmy think about what he could look forward to as well. What he wanted was a life with Laila, somewhere peaceful, where they had the space to live their lives. Earth was crowded, expensive, and dirty. Since leaving the Sol system, Remmy understood that there were other places where they could find what they needed to thrive, where their love could flourish and they could build a family.

It was odd that having met Laila had shifted Remmy's perspective on so many things. He had lived his adult life focused entirely on his career. In fact, if it hadn't been for the unusually long cruise on the *Jericho,* Remmy would never have admitted his feelings for Laila. And without a doubt, the moment the cruise ended, they would have both been shipped off to other assignments. The chances for a love affair would have been almost zero.

But that long cruise had been more than his iron will could stand. Seeing her day in and day out—his admiration for her growing with every training exercise and combat simulation. Eventually, despite the taboo against fraternizing within their own platoon, Remmy simply couldn't deny his feelings for her any longer. He sometimes wondered how he would have survived if she hadn't felt the same way. But she did, and they were more than two Marines fraternizing. They were in love and Remmy was thinking about a future beyond the Space Marines for the first time in his life.

He had always assumed there would come a time when he would meet someone, fall in love, get married and start a family, but it also seemed distant. It was always something he would do down the road. He hadn't expected to meet the woman of his dreams on a cruise that ended up taking them both to star systems millions of light years from Earth.

His musing about the future was suddenly interrupted by a chime from the radar.

"Got something," Hugo said. "Unit nine has a biologic entity moving north at twenty klicks per hour."

"Size?" Remmy asked.

"Seven meters in length. It's moving toward Havershed."

"GIGI, take us to the settlement called Havershed," Remmy ordered. "As fast as possible."

"Confirmed, Master Sergeant," the computerized voice replied.

He could have just thought the order, but he preferred to do things out loud when he could. It seemed to make the people around him feel a bit more comfortable.

"ETA?" Remmy asked.

"Six minutes, Master Sergeant," GIGI responded.

"How long will it take the sand viper?"

"It's about sixty kilometers from that thing's position to the settlement," Hugo replied. "Three hours at its current speed."

"We'll have to form a reception party," Remmy said. "Alert the town. Have the Marines meet us a full kilometer from the stock pens."

Hugo went to work alerting the locals and Remmy turned his thoughts to matters of combat. Not that the predator would fight back. It should be a straightforward kill by the Casians, but in Remmy's experience, nothing was ever that easy. He had to be ready for the unexpected, which was sure to come. It always did.

CHAPTER 16

"CAPTAIN, I HAVE CONTACTS!" Vivian Ramos announced.

Darius had been watching the video feeds from the engineering team on the *Independence*. It was fascinating to watch them working. GIGI was offering help as well, but the human engineers had identified most of the space cruiser's engine components. The most surprising thing was how much was still intact. It was a fuel-burning engine with an electrical booster that would get them moving fast enough to jump into hyperspace. The team of engineers were already brimming with ideas of how to convert the ship's engines to fully electric and get the old vessel running again.

"What?" Darius said, his head turning back to the holographic plot.

"Three ships," Vivian said. "Looks like they're turning around."

"Can you identify them?"

"Ashi, I believe," she said.

"Those are scouts," Nurek said. "The smallest ships in the Ashi fleet."

"How the hell did they find us?" Darius said. "Lieutenant Best, prepare the laser cannons."

"Aye, Captain, preparing the laser cannons for battle."

"Distance?" Darius asked.

"They just came through the portal," Vivian said. "From what I can tell, they're going back through."

"They won't stay," Nurek said. "Their job is to ensure the portal is safe to pass through. And in this instance to identify where the portal leads to."

"They won't have this system in their charts," Vivan said. "It isn't on the main navigation system."

"Somehow, they knew about it," Darius said. "Can we stop them?"

"Negative, Captain," Pete Best said. "I don't have a firing solution, and we're over nine million kilometers from the portal. They'll be gone by the time we fire at them."

"With our exact location," Darius said with a sigh. "It took us twenty-four hours to make the jump. Can we assume it will be the same with them?"

"Affirmative, Captain. It should be exactly the same travel time between systems," Vivian Ramos said.

"Then we have two days to prepare. Just two. A fight is coming to this system. Let's get our ducks in a row. Someone alert our people on the ground."

"Can the locals help?" Henry Nash asked.

"I don't see how," Darius replied. "But they should be ready for whatever the Ashi Fleet brings to the system. There's no guarantee that we can stop an entire fleet."

An hour later, everyone knew. The *Renegade* was prepping for battle. They had limited resources, but what they had could be put to good use. Darius had already made up his mind. All that remained was for the crew to return to the ship, and then he would tell them, starting with his senior officers.

"Report is in from the *Holiday*, Captain," Henry Nash said.

"Very good," Darius replied, looking up from his data tablet. "What's the story?"

"The *Holiday* isn't as whole as the *Independence*, Captain. I can't say what the cruiser had been carrying, but there was obviously some sort of humidity in that vessel that wasn't in the other."

"Rust?"

"Aye, Captain, and a lot of it. The hull needs work, and the engines are locked up. We could probably get it running in time, but not in two days."

"That's fine," Darius said. "I want your team to focus on the *Indy*. I want that ship up and running as soon as possible."

"Is that the best use of our resources, Captain?" Vivian Ramos asked.

"I believe it is," Darius said.

"We could probably mount some guns on her," Pete Best said. "The power core should be ready. If we can task some of the *Renegade's* drones to attach lasers to the hull, we could probably be ready when the fleet arrives."

Darius shook his head. He had other plans for the space cruiser.

"Captain, the shuttles have returned," Ensign Bertoli said. "Master Sergeant Steel is on his way to the Bridge."

"Have him meet us in the Wardroom, Ensign. We'll be there for the next hour. Until then, I trust that you can handle things here on the Bridge?"

"Me, sir?" Jacee Bertoli asked.

"That's right," Darius said. "You have the con, Ensign."

"Aye, Captain!" She said in a loud voice. "I have the con."

"Senior officers with me," Darius said.

Vivian Ramos, Pete Best, Henry Nash, and Commander Lee rose from the consoles. Darius had already summoned crew members to take each officer's place. Outside the Bridge, he turned to the others.

"Let's take five, then meet in the Wardroom," he said.

They all agreed. Most of them had been at their stations for hours. Everyone was tired but that was life on an SDF battleship. It was one of the reasons most patrols only lasted a few weeks before returning to port and giving the crew some much-needed rest.

By the time they returned, Darius was in his chair at the head of the conference table, which doubled as a dining table. He had a mug full of black coffee in one hand. There was a pot on a tray in the middle of the table. Several of the officers took cups from the tray and filled them with hot coffee, fresh cream and real sugar. Darius didn't blame them. He preferred his coffee black, but real ingredients were so rare in space that it was tempting to add them anyway.

They were just settling in when Remmy Steel appeared in the doorway. Darius stood and filled a mug with coffee for him.

"Here, Master Sergeant, I'm sure you're tired."

"Thank you, Captain. I'm fine, sir."

"But a little caffeine won't hurt," Darius said. "Alright, people, we have some decisions to make. The Ashi Fleet will most likely arrive in system in just forty-six hours. There's a lot to be done in that time."

"For all they know, that portal is the only way out of the Free World systems," Vivian Ramos said. "If they were smart, they would just seal it off with mines and hope we never come out."

"Wouldn't that be nice," Pete Best said.

"We can't count on that," Darius said. "We have to assume they expect us to flee another way. The Free Worlds are known about in the Imperium, according to Nurek, but no one knew how to get to them outside of a handful of people. We have to prepare for the reality that the fleet will come through and attack as soon as possible."

"And we can't run?" Henry Nash asked.

"That's a good question. What happens when ships pass through a portal at the same time?"

"Don't ask me," Vivian said. "I only have the maps. How they work is still a mystery."

"Let's ask GIGI," Darius said. "Master Sergeant, can you do the honors?"

Remmy nodded, waiting a moment, then replied, "It's possible.

The ships are equipped with avoidance controls that would move us out of their path and vice versa."

"So, we can run," Darius said. "Or, we can stay and fight."

"Great options," Henry said. "If we run, they'll just pursue us."

"Which is why I'm offering a different alternative," Darius said. "Since we left the Sol system, the goal has been to return. Events have made that difficult, if not impossible. We have advanced alien technology, but taking it back to our home system while the Ashi are pursuing us is too dangerous."

"Which means we have to stay and fight," Pete Best said.

"I will," Darius said. "But you don't have to."

For a moment, there was silence in the Wardroom. Everyone stared at him, their coffee forgotten.

"I don't understand," Lori Lee said.

Darius nodded. "I've been considering this for a while. Operation Odyssey has been successful. And now the *Indy* is close to being ready to fly again. I'm going to allow anyone from the crew who wants to go home to take this opportunity. Commander Lee will be in charge of the *Indy*. She will see that the rescued slaves and a handful of Dudonus, along with GIGI and all of the Arodoni technology, return safely to the Sol system. Any crew member that so desires can go with her and any that wish to stay can do that, too. It will be up to every individual to make the decision for themselves."

"Wait, you're sending us away?" Lori Lee asked.

"I'm sending you, Commander."

"Have I done something to offend you, sir?"

"No," Darius said with a soft smile. "Just the opposite. You are the finest executive officer I've ever served with, Commander Lee. And I would give you the choice, but SDF protocols require that command of the *Independence* be given to the most senior officer available. That's you, so you'll be in charge of that ship. As soon as the logistics are finished, you'll take her out of the system. I want you gone before the Ashi arrive."

"Won't they just follow us back to the Sol system?" Vivian asked.

"I don't think so," Darius said. "They want this ship. Or at least, to destroy it. The *Renegade* is their enemy. My guess is they won't even notice the *Indy* is gone."

"What if we don't want to leave," Lori Lee asked.

Darius looked around the room. He could see the desire in the eyes of his crew. He knew them well enough to guess who would stay and who would go.

"They do, Commander. I'm sorry to foist this responsibility on you, but we all know how invaluable the technology we possess is. The Imperium has sent their entire military fleet to possess it. The only thing stopping us from taking it home was fear that we would be followed. I'm staying behind to ensure that doesn't happen."

"By yourself?" Remmy asked softly.

"We all know this ship practically flies itself," Darius said. "I can run it from the Bridge with just a few hands. We have enough volunteers left to keep us in tip-top shape."

"Unless you get damaged in battle again," Henry said.

"I'm confident that this is the right plan of action," Darius said. "We will have technical superiority in battle. We know exactly where the enemy is coming. I'll have the Renegade sitting exactly six hundred thousand kilometers from the portal. That's well within our range but out of theirs. We can fire rapidly at mid-range power and create havoc around the portal."

"That won't defeat an entire fleet," Lee pointed out.

"No, but it will even the odds a little," Darius pointed out. "The *Renegade* is more than a match for most of their vessels. And once they break through the choke point, we'll slip through to the next system and do it all over again."

"If you're able," Vivian Ramos said.

"We will be. The question now is, what will you do? I'll make the announcement to the rest of the crew as soon as the *Indy* is ready. Until then, if you want to share the news with people in your department, please do so."

"I have a question, Captain," Remmy asked.

"Go ahead, Staff Sergeant."

"I'm assuming you will be sending Lieutenant Colt back?"

"That's not a given. I'll be speaking to the doctor before making that decision."

"Fair enough," Remmy said.

"Alright then, unless there are any more questions, I'll let you have some time to yourselves."

Darius stood up. He felt their eyes on him, like little stinging insects, as he moved toward the door. The die was cast. All that remained was to see who would stay and who would go. But for the first time since leaving the Sol system, Darius felt relieved. He would be a starship captain for the foreseeable future and that was just fine with him.

CHAPTER 17

"IT'S DEAD," Hugo said, his voice slightly muffled by the distance from the planet's surface into orbit.

Remmy was in the Admin Center with Nurek and Connor O'Dell. In front of them was the holographic video feed from Sergeant Hugo McManus' battle helmet. It showed the sand viper. The creature was big, half again as tall as Hugo and just as wide as it was tall. It had short tentacles around the cone-shaped head. It's mouth was set low, and there were no nostrils or eyes that Remmy could see. Bullets had torn into the tough skin and smashed bone, brain, and flesh into a gruesome pulp.

"We can see that," Remmy replied.

"Was it hard to kill?" Connor asked.

"Negative, sir. The Casians made quick work of it. The sand viper never saw it coming."

"I don't think they can see," Nurek said. "There are no optical organs that I can make out."

"If it lives underground, it may not have any," Remmy said.

"The hide is pretty tough, but it didn't stop standard .223s," Hugo said. "We were expecting more of a fight. The recruits hit this thing head-on and stopped it pretty quickly."

"What are .223s?" Nurek asked.

"Ammunition," Remmy said. "The number refers to the size."

"I see," Nurek said.

"Was that the work of all three Marines?" Remmy asked.

"Negative, just the primary," Hugo said. "We let them decide how to form up against this thing. They had a primary shooter and two backups to either side of the primary. But there was no need. The initial volley was thirty rounds, fifteen from each mounted gun. That stopped the creature. They waited for movement, but there was none."

"Outstanding work," Remmy said.

"There are three more on radar moving toward different targets. I'll hop between them and give a little encouragement, but the volunteers should have no trouble dealing with the predators."

"And who said you weren't leader material?" Remmy teased.

"Sergeant," Connor O'Dell spoke up. "Do get full scans before you leave."

"Roger that, sir," Hugo said, even though O'Dell was just a civilian.

"Captain Darius wants everyone back on board the *Renegade* shortly after sunup," Remmy said. "We'll see you soon. Good work, Hugo."

"Thank you, Master Sergeant. McManus out."

The hologram remained. It was slowly rotating.

"It's fascinating," Connor said.

"You are a student of biology?" Nurek asked.

"Not really," Connor said. "But I have interests across the spectrum."

"You are fortunate to have the ability to pursue your interests," Nurek said.

"Pretty soon, you will too," Remmy told the alien.

"I believe I will be too busy paying for my crime," the Dudonus said. "But I knew that before I acted and have no one to blame ... but myself."

"We all have obligations," Connor said. "Yet, we make time for the things we find most important."

Remmy agreed and so he took his leave of the two. He would have preferred to stay on Libertine to help the Casians work through the process of preparing for and eliminating the predators on their new world. Stopping the sand vipers would be paramount for the people who would depend on the newly arrived livestock. If they could keep the predators at bay, there was enough room and resources for all of the people to flourish.

But, Captain Darius had been right to recall him. With Lieutenant Colt out of action, it was up to Darius to inform the Space Marines of the choice they faced. Stay or go; it was not as easy a decision as he thought it would be. Remmy had feelings about the decision. Home always sounded right, but surprisingly enough, the thought of leaving the *Renegade* didn't seem like going home. And he hated the thought of leaving Captain Darius in the lurch. Not that Remmy was much help in a space battle, but still, it didn't seem right to leave a ship without any Marines.

Ultimately, he wanted Laila's opinion. Their choices would have a big impact on one another. So, he made his way to the primary hangar and waited for her shuttle to arrive. It didn't take long. The engineers on the *Independence* were making fast progress, but they needed more materials and tools. She was escorting two of them back to gather the needed supplies.

She saw him waiting for her when she stepped off the shuttle. What she hadn't expected was the surge of emotion at finding him there. He was in fatigues and leaned casually against a nearby bulkhead.

"You lost, Master Sergeant?"

"No, just waiting for you," he replied.

"A lady can't have too many handsome gentlemen waiting on them, now can she?"

"I don't know about that," Remmy said. "I like to think I'm all the man you need."

"She already had her helmet off, but the bulky space armor

made it difficult to get close to one another. Still, he managed to lean in, and they kissed.

"You're all the man I want," she said softly.

"That's good to know," he replied. "There's news."

"Good or bad?"

"I'll let you decide. How much time do you have?"

"Maybe half an hour. It depends on how quick they load up the supplies needed for the cruise ship."

"Then we should talk now," Remmy said.

There was no shortage of space on the *Renegade*. And there were plenty of empty rooms and workspaces just outside the hangar. While the engineers loaded their supplies, Remmy took Laila into an empty room to talk.

"There were Imperium scouts in the system," Remmy said. "Captain Darius thinks we've got just over forty-two hours before they lead the Ashi fleet into the system."

"No rest for the weary," Laila said.

"No kidding," Remmy said. "They're relentless. Captain Darius plans to hit them hard the moment they come through the portal. He's got a decent game plan, but we're still just one ship against who knows how many."

"True, the Ashi could be reinforced already," Laila said. "It might be better if we weren't here at all when they arrive."

"That could be, but the Captain has an ulterior motive for the attack. He's offering to send us home in the *Independence*."

"You and me?"

"Anyone who wants to go back to the Sol system. The slaves we rescued, the crew, Marines, anyone."

"But he's staying here?"

Remmy nodded. "That's the plan. Part of the reason is so the Ashi don't know we've gone."

"They're after the *Renegade*," she said. "They won't even be looking for the old space cruiser."

"Exactly," Remmy said. "He'll make an announcement to the crew as soon as the *Indy* is space-worthy."

"That won't be long. Ten, maybe twelve hours, but the engineers are pretty confident they can get it flying. And the ship is in decent shape."

"My guess is we have maybe twenty-four hours in this system before the *Independence* leaves for home. So the only question is, will we be on it?"

"We? As in, you and me?"

"That's right," Remmy said with a nod. "What do you want to do?"

She thought for a moment. Her face took on a serious expression. Not quite what he had seen in combat, but it was close. Remmy thought she looked especially beautiful.

"I know I want to be with you," she said.

"I agree," he said. "I want us to make this decision together."

"Do you mind if I think about it?" She asked.

"Not at all," he said. "We can chat on a private channel when you're ready to talk."

"What about the others? Are you going to tell them?"

Remmy nodded. "The Captain left that up to us, and I'm planning to gather the platoon when everyone gets back from the planet. Do you want me to wait for you?"

"No, just leave an open comlink when you break the news," she said. "I want to hear reactions."

"I'll set my helmet up, and you can have eyes and ears," he said. "I'm bringing Gunny Rand down from Med. Tex and Izzy are already out."

"You know they're together, right?"

"I figured, but haven't pressed the subject."

"Looks like we aren't the only ones who found something special on this cruise."

They kissed again, but Laila was called back to the shuttle. Remmy walked her into the hangar. The engineers were waiting.

"Looks like my ride is waiting on me," Laila said.

"Those engineers work fast," Remmy said.

"Thank you," she told him.

"For what?"

"For telling me."

"Of course."

"No, it's not a small thing, Remmy. It's our future. At every turn, I keep expecting to find something that isn't right about us. But you always come through."

"I'm far from perfect, Laila, but I really do love you. All I want is to make you happy."

"And you do," she said. "So keep it up, mister."

He watched her walk up the ramp and into the shuttle. It immediately began preparations for lift-off. Remmy had to back away. There were things to do, and even though his heart was on the shuttle with Laila, his responsibilities were to the Marines, who would soon be returning to the *Renegade*. He couldn't help but wonder what they would decide to do.

CHAPTER 18

THERE WAS no place on the entire ship where Zeke Darius felt he could be alone. He took his old leather-bound journal and an old-fashioned ink pen into the bathroom of his quarters. If the Arodoni had anything close to the same ideas of privacy that humans had, there shouldn't be video access inside the bathroom. He closed the lid to the toilet, which had been manufactured to human physiology, and replaced the larger alien facility. It was an odd place to write, but even the practice of writing in a physical book was an old-fashioned discipline. Zeke's mother had given him the journal after being accepted to the SDF Fleet Academy. He had kept it all through his career, although he rarely wrote in it.

He turned to a blank page and began to write his last official report to the Space Defense Force. It was not up to the standards of the modern military, but it was the only way he could communicate freely without GIGI becoming aware of his suspicions. He made quick work of summarizing his command decisions from the time they made contact with GIGI. That led him to the purpose of the report.

It is without question that the alien artifact is hiding things from us. My hope is to discover those secrets once the Indy *has left the* Libertine *system. And supposing that I survive the battles with the Ashi fleet, I will find a way to communicate whatever has been hidden by the device. But it is not my intention to return, personally. This is my official resignation from the SDF. I intend to remain on board the* Renegade, *in one capacity or another, for the rest of my days. It is my great hope that those of you reading this report will approve of the decisions I've made, but ultimately, I have done what I think is best. As long as I and the* Renegade *survive, we will continue the fight for freedom wherever that takes us in the galaxy.*

He signed the bottom of the page, then tore it from the journal and folded it up. Going back into his quarters, he sat down at his desk where another memento was kept. It was an ornate candle stick, thick and covered with wax. He held it over the fold of paper and lit a match. The heat quickly melted the wax, which dripped onto the paper. When a puddle had formed, he took off the class ring he had purchased upon graduating from the SDF academy. It had his number from the class of graduating cadets and the date of the graduation. He hoped that would be enough to ensure the note was given credence as his own. He pressed the top of the ring into the wax, holding it there long enough to make an impression as the wax dried. When he pulled it away, he felt like the seal was effective.

His task done, the last thing he needed to do was give the report to Commander Lee, and while he doubted he could pull it off without GIGI noticing it, he still hoped he could do it in a manner that would not reveal the importance of what he was doing. Lori Lee was not in her quarters or on the Bridge. It took nearly an hour to track her down. She was walking barefoot in the park. Darius left his boots on but joined her.

"I'm sorry to disturb you," he said.

"Are you here to apologize?" She asked.

"For what?"

"For sending me away."

"No, I hadn't realized that I needed to."

"You don't think I would prefer to stay here and fight alongside you, Captain?"

"I assumed you would set aside your desires in respect to your duty," he said. "Am I wrong?"

"Why would you assume that I would do something you aren't willing to do yourself."

"What?"

"Duty," she said. "Your duty is to get the artifact back home along with as much of the alien technology as possible. Yet here you are, leaving it all behind, so that you can remain in command of the *Renegade*."

He knew she wasn't wrong.

"I'm sorry," he said.

"Thank you. I accept your apology. Just know that I would have chosen to stay if I had been given that choice."

Darius fell silent. He thought about how he would feel if he had been forced to leave. It wasn't pleasant. In fact, part of the reason he was staying was because he didn't want someone telling him he had to step down or step aside. Being a ship Captain was all he ever wanted to do and that didn't go away just because he was a certain age.

"What's the latest on the *Indy*?" Lori Lee asked.

"It should be flight-ready in a few hours. You can take command of her, make a few laps around the planet, then take on passengers."

"This isn't how I thought my time on this ship would end."

"It is a magnificent vessel," Darius said.

"Yes, maybe too good," she said. "Have you considered that deciding to put your life at risk just to stay on board the *Renegade* isn't the best idea?"

"Staying on this ship is just part of the reason I'm staying. You know what I'm looking at back in the Sol system. Even if I weren't at the end of my career, I'd never be given command again."

"You don't know that."

"I do know that. I've seen officers lose their commands for much less. But it doesn't matter. They were benching me no matter what. I thought I had come to terms with it, but the *Renegade* has given me a second chance and I'm going to take it. Besides, it's the only way I can think of to get people home safely."

"Which is the only reason I'm not fighting you about it," she said. "I think you're wrong about the SDF. I think you would be hailed a hero at home, but I suppose it doesn't matter now."

"I hope you're right," Darius said. "I hope you are welcomed with open arms and given a promotion. You deserve it. You'll be a phenomenal Captain."

"Thank you," she said. "That means a lot coming from you, sir."

"It's the truth. And we both know it, so I hope the Brass can see it too."

He reached out, offering to shake her hand. She frowned, clearly realizing he was up to something. She took his hand and felt the paper note. For a moment, their eyes locked. She realized he was being secretive on purpose.

"For the Brass," he said, releasing her hand and the note.

She discretely tucked it into the pocket of her uniform and left her hands in the pocket so that it wasn't obvious she had put something there.

"I'll leave you to your own devices," he told her. "If I can do anything for you, Commander Lee, all you need to do is ask."

"Thank you, Captain. It has been an honor to serve with you."

"The honor's all mine, Lori. Good luck."

"You too, Zeke. And God bless."

He turned away and headed back through the park. It was mostly empty of people and aliens. The refugees and most of the crew had left the big ship to start new lives on Libertine. Darius looked up at the grand apartments with their spectacular views of the park. It seemed wrong for the ship to be so empty again. Not that it was ever full or even close to it. Even with the refugees and volunteers, they only ever made up a fraction of what the *Renegade* was built for. It was a flying city, but in many ways, it looked more like a ghost town.

Darius felt a shiver run down his spine at the thought of the ship being full of ghosts. He tried to shake it off but the feeling persisted. And it felt like he would soon be one of them.

CHAPTER 19

"THEY SAID WHAT?" Leigh Ann Poh asked.

Remmy had the Marine platoon gathered in the armory. Everyone except for Laila was present. Even Gunnery Sergeant Rand looked as though he had lost a lot of weight since his mental breakdown.

Tyler "Tex" Fry was there, along with Izzy Berry. They both had bandages showing from the recent surgical procedures, but they both looked well considering the short amount of time that had passed since they were wounded.

Corporal Al "Rip" Van Winkle was back to active duty. Corporal Ricky Thompson had gone down to the southern polar region of Libertine with Sergeant Dirk Oliver and Corporal Leigh Ann Poh.

"You can go home if you so choose," Remmy said again. "Captain's orders. Staff Sergeant McPherson is overseeing the repairs on the transport cruiser now."

"You really think that old ship will be capable of taking us through hyperspace?" Tex asked.

"Captain Darius does," Remmy replied. "I have no reason to

doubt it. The engineers are fixing it up now. Staff Sergeant McPherson reported the transport to be in very good shape."

"So, we're going home?" Izzy said.

"If that is what you want. Captain Darius is keeping the *Renegade* in the system to fight the Ashi fleet when it arrives."

"It's kinda crazy, ain't it," Rip said. "One ship against an entire fleet."

"There isn't much we can do to help, is there?" Leigh Ann Poh asked.

Remmy shrugged. "I don't think so. Each of you needs to decide what you want to do. The Captain will be making the announcement to the rest of the ship soon. And they'll be heading out in less than twenty-four hours. We want the *Indy* gone from the system before the Ashi arrive."

"We? Does that mean you're staying, Master Sergeant?" Hugo asked.

"No, I haven't made a decision yet," Remmy said.

"Seems like a no-brainer to me," Dirk Oliver said. "I'm going home."

"Me too," Leigh Ann Poh said.

"Is the offer for everyone?" Gunny Rand asked.

"No, Gunny," Remmy said. "Captain says you have to go back."

Chad Rand looked relieved.

"How's the Captain going to fight the enemy without a crew?" Izzy asked.

"From what I understand, he can control everything from the Bridge," Remmy explained. "And he'll have the remaining volunteers to help."

"If something goes wrong, he'll be in a world of hurt," Tex pointed out.

"Especially if the ship takes damage," Hugo agreed. "I think I'll stay, Master Sergeant. Who knows, maybe I'll get my spot down on Libertine when all is said and done."

"Maybe you will, Hugo. I'll make sure the Captain knows that's what you want."

"Only once everyone is safe," he said.

"Sure," Remmy said. "The rest of you take your time making the call, but let me know once you do. I'll have my comlink on."

Remmy left the platoon in the armory. Some followed him out. Tex and Izzy labored to catch up but managed it.

"What are you and Laila going to do?" Izzy asked when it was just the three of them.

They had gone up to the main level and were lingering in a pavilion in the park. In the distance, Remmy could see a small herd of animals. They were grazing peacefully. Butterflies, or creatures that reminded him of them, flittered among a row of shrubs. He could smell the soil and hear the trickle of water as it gurgled over the stones of a creek nearby. It was like being on a peaceful, beautiful world, but still in a starship.

"I haven't decided," Remmy said. "I have no idea what Staff Sergeant McPherson's plans are."

"We know, Master Sergeant," Tex said. "I mean, we all sort of knew it, but Laila told us that you were together."

"She told us when we told her that we're together," Izzy said, taking Tex by the hand. "We don't care who knows."

Remmy knew he should have been bothered that Laila had shared their secret. But he wasn't. If she needed to tell someone, then he was glad she did. And he was glad that it was their fellow Marines.

"Good for you," Remmy said. "I'm happy for you both. But Laila and I haven't made our decision yet."

"You know they won't let you stay together if you go back," Izzy said.

"There's a lot I don't know," Remmy said. "Maybe they'll hold us; maybe they'll ship us off in different directions. Hell, I might even retire. We can make a life together wherever we end up."

"Or you could stay here," Tex said.

"That's right. All I can say is, whatever we do, it'll be together. I'll update the Platoon list with your decisions to stay if you're sure."

"We are," Izzy said.

"No doubt," Tex added.

"Then you should get some rest," Remmy told them. "Once the others are gone, you might be needed, whether you're physically able or not."

"Roger that," Tex said. "We'll be ready when they call."

Remmy watched them leave together. It was obvious they were still in pain, but their eyes had been clear and he respected their decision. Soon, it would be time for him to make his own and he knew what he wanted to do. He hoped that Laila felt the same way.

Pulling his data tablet from the cargo pocket he kept it in; he brought up the platoon list. There were lines through the names of the Marines who had died during the mission. Remmy regretted their loss. He also thought they would have volunteered for the mission anyway. Death was part of the job. They all knew it when they signed on and were reminded of it every day during boot camp. Every mission carried risk, some more than others. Remmy didn't know of any Marines who hadn't lost a friend in combat or due to an accident in space. It still took a heavy toll.

Beside Hugo, Tex, and Izzy's names on the list, he typed the word *stay*. They had made up their minds. Beside Gunny Rand, Sergeant Oliver, and Corporal Leigh Ann Poh, he wrote *leave*. He didn't think it would take long for the others to decide. Soon, he would be able to turn in the list of Marines who would stay and fight alongside Captain Darius. All Remmy could hope for was that his name was one of them.

CHAPTER 20

IT ONLY TOOK the engineers six and a half hours to get the *Independence* fully operational. Commander Lori Lee took charge of the vessel. Chief engineer Henry Nash joined her in the cockpit, and together, they learned the basic controls of the spacecraft.

"No issues, Captain," Lori Lee radioed to the *Renegade*. "All systems are green for go. We have emptied the water tanks and sealed off the fuel compartments."

"How's your air, Commander?" Darius asked.

"We have full O2 tanks, Captain. The cabins are pressurized with breathable air. We are ready for passengers."

"Outstanding. Bring her up alongside the *Renegade*. I'm going to make the announcement to the crew now."

Remmy and Laila were in her apartment overlooking the park. She had wanted a shower upon her return. It was SOP after hours spent inside a space suit. Remmy had waited on the balcony, his mind turning his idea of how to decide their future over and over in his mind.

The problem wasn't coming to a consensus. He would do whatever she wanted to do. The problem, as he saw it, was that he feared she would choose what she thought he wanted. So, the best way to proceed was for them both to say what they really wanted to do at the same time, which was why she found him on the balcony with his data tablet open on his lap.

"Work?" She asked.

"No, not yet," he said. "It's time for us to make our decision."

"I heard the captain's announcement. Do you think anyone didn't know about it at this point?"

"No," Remmy said. "You?"

She shook her head. "The engineers were talking about it on the *Indy*. I was glad I heard it from you first, though."

"Me too. I've been thinking about things."

"I suppose we all have," she said. "Why don't you just decide what to do? I'm fine with that either way."

"We know each other pretty well," Remmy said. "I'm betting we're already on the same page. But I don't want you to resent me … and I don't want you to choose based on what you think I want."

"What's the solution?"

"We both write down what we really want," Remmy said. "Without the other seeing it. Then we can reveal at the same time."

"What if the answers don't match?"

"Then we have a harder conversation. But at least we'll both know how the other really feels, and we can find a way to agree."

"I'm really fine either way," she said.

"But if you aren't honest now, I'll never really know for certain that you don't resent the choice."

She chuckled. "You've put a lot of thought into this."

"You have people back on Earth, right?"

Laila nodded. "My parents, aunts, uncles, cousins, we're sort of a tribe."

"That's a lot to give up if we stay."

"If we go back, we have a lot to figure out," she said. "I've got three years on my term of enlistment left. We have to find out how to make things work long distances. And when we're out of the Marines, then what?"

"Are you wishing we had just stayed on Casasil?"

"Every single day," she said with a sigh.

"So, let's be honest and let's make sure we don't leave any consideration out of our decision."

She agreed and sat down opposite him. She held her own data tablet in her lap but didn't immediately write down her answer. Remmy jotted his on the smooth surface. His handwriting wasn't very neat, but it was readable. Then he thought about the list. Everyone else had made up their minds. Ricky Thompson was going home. Rip Van Winkle had decided to stay. That was four staying and three going back, not counting Gunny Rand or Lieutenant Colt, who didn't have a say in the matter.

"I'm ready," Laila said.

"You're sure?"

"Absolutely."

"And you didn't just write down what you think I want to do?"

"No, did you?"

"No," he admitted. "I was honest about this."

"I hope we can always be honest with each other."

"Me too," he said.

They turned their tablets over and Remmy felt a wave of relief that they said *stay*.

"What about your family?" Remmy asked.

"I want to start a new family," she said. "With you. I love my people, but they all have their own lives. I've been in space for over ten years. When I go home to visit, I'm just in the way. We have the chance for something different, something better."

"I feel the same way," Remmy said. "Besides, I didn't want to leave the Captain in the lurch."

"I knew that the moment you told me we were being given a decision. It would have killed you to leave."

"But I would have for you," Remmy said.

They both stood up and he gathered her in his arms. When they kissed, they held nothing back.

On the Bridge, a memo came through on Captain Darius' tablet. He glanced at the screen, saw that it was from Remmy Steel, and opened the Master Sergeant's message. It was a list of the Marines staying and going. Remmy's name was at the top of the stay list. Darius felt a little tension leave his body. He couldn't say why having the Master Sergeant on board made him feel any better. In the fight to come, Remmy wouldn't play a major role, but they were friends. And as the Captain of an SDF warship, Darius knew friendship could be rare. He didn't know what the future held, but he felt better facing it with Master Sergeant Steel by his side.

"Sir, the *Indy* is in position," Vivian Ramos said. "We can start moving supplies and personnel when you're ready."

"Copy that, Lieutenant. I suppose that means you'll be leaving soon."

"I'm all packed, Captain," Vivian Ramos said. "But I'm happy to stay as long as you need me, sir."

Darius stood up. Vivian joined him. "It's been a pleasure, Lieutenant," he said. "You are dismissed."

"Aye, Captain, the pleasure was mine. Thank you, sir."

They shook hands. Darius felt a slight tremble in hers. Vivian Ramos didn't come across as the type who was easily shaken. But something made her nervous.

"Are you okay, Lieutenant?"

"Yes, Captain, thank you. It's just hard not to worry about you, sir. I feel guilty leaving you."

"Don't," Darius said. "I made my decision knowing full well I might be the only human who decided to stay."

"But you aren't," she said.

"No, I'm not. You go ahead. You've got a bright future in the SDF, Vivian. Maybe we'll meet again someday."

"I hope so, Captain. Good luck."

She left the Bridge. Nash was already on the *Indy*. Ensign Bertoli would join them, as would most of the crew. He had about twenty enlisted members who volunteered to stay and six Marines. Lieutenant Pete Best would remain as the weapons specialist. His decision had been based on the opportunity for combat and Darius couldn't blame the young man. In the Sol system, a ship's weapons were rarely used, and when they were, it was to fire on ships with humans on board. In the *Renegade,* he would have the chance to make a difference doing what he was trained for, and in the process, he would be defending humanity, not killing them.

Ensign Stanislaus has volunteered to stay as well. He would be promoted to Lieutenant and would take Henry Nash's place. The *Renegade* was operated by a computer system. It was powerful but not sentient like GIGI. That made Alex Stanislaus the ideal engineer to have on board. The young officer knew more about computers than the rest of the crew combined.

And there were the alien volunteers, twelve Casians, and twenty-one Dudonus. It wasn't a full crew by any stretch of the imagination, but it was enough. The *Renegade* was almost completely automated, which meant the crew were backup. He had enough to get through the next combat engagement. After that, he would begin looking for more recruits, maybe on two of the other free worlds, Subterra and Typhana.

Behind him, Darius heard quiet footsteps. He was already turning when Nurek said, "You asked to see me, Captain Darius?"

"I did. I've been trying to decide what to do with you."

"I see," Nurek said quietly.

"Where I'm from, my superiors will have a lot of questions for you," Darius told the alien. "You were the closest to the Imperial family with the best knowledge of how the Imperium works. You would be treated well; I will vouch for that personally. We are not a cruel race. I would, however, have to inform them that you murdered Emperor Vang, who was helpless at the time. How they might deal with that, I cannot say."

"I understand," Nurek said.

"But I've decided to give you the choice that I've given everyone else. If you stay, I plan to put you to work here. You have a working understanding of the navigation system and knowledge of hidden portals as well."

"I have already input all I know into the navigation system, Captain," Nurek said.

"You could still be useful if you choose to stay. You'll be an acting officer on this ship, in charge of the volunteers, as well as helping with navigation. It won't be simple. This ship will probably be under duress for a long time. But at least you know what you'll be getting yourself into."

"You would allow me to have contact with the other Dudonus?" Nurek asked.

"I would. You would have free range of the ship, just like any other officer. Although you would be required to have your primary quarters here in the Command section like the other officers."

"I accept, Captain. And gladly. You have no idea what your offer means to me."

"You've proven your worth, Nurek. I don't approve of what you did to Vang, but I can't say I understand what you've been through at his hands. Nor can I say that I wouldn't have done the same thing if I were in your shoes. So, we'll let bygones be bygones."

"That is an interesting turn of phrase," Nurek said. "Thank you again, Captain. I am in your debt."

"No, Nurek, we are equals. I have command of the ship, but no one on board is more important than any other."

Darius extended a hand, and Nurek shook it. The alien hand was long and delicate. It felt slightly cold, but Darius felt the fingers tighten around his own. The two beings understood one another and the Captain of the *Renegade* had a new comrade in arms.

CHAPTER 21

"THE SCOUT SHIPS HAVE RETURNED, Lord Kahn," the shipmaster stated.

"The way is clear?"

"It is. The Arodoni ship is there."

"Do we know what system?"

"Negative, Lord. It did not register on our charts of the known galaxy. It could be one of the hidden systems that the rebels call the Free Worlds."

"Very good," Sheika Kahn said. "We will capture the alien vessel and seize new territory at the same time! The Prime Council will be very pleased."

Sheika Kahn needed positive news. Everything coming in from across the galaxy was negative. Over three hundred worlds were in open rebellion. Some had even slaughtered the Imperial representatives and burned Imperium properties. The Prime Council was in hiding after the assassination of Nic'Tal. They were all useless cowards but Sheika needed them to bestow power to him. After that, he would sweep them off the board. Better to have administrators who answered directly to him rather than elected officials running the galaxy. He would implement a streamlined, aggressive government. And with the technology gained from the Arodoni ship, he would ensure his dynasty for a hundred generations.

Unfortunately, securing the Arodoni ship had not been as simple as he hoped. Simply overwhelming the alien ship hadn't worked. It was too powerful and too fast. Plus, the crew knew of hidden portals that weren't in the Imperium's hyperspace network. Still, he wasn't going to give up. He either had to capture the ship, destroy it, or chase it out of the galaxy. Each of those options came with their own rewards, but soon, he would need to turn his attention back to the rebellious worlds. Those openly defying the Imperium would answer for their treason in blood.

"All battleships are refueled and prepared for battle, Lord Kahn," the shipmaster said. "What are your orders?"

"We must move through the portal in battle formation," Ulrech Sheika said. "The Arodoni ship will be waiting."

"Or it will have fled again," the shipmaster said.

"We must prepare for what it could do, not what we think it will do," Sheika Kahn replied calmly. "We will be weakest upon arrival in the new system. Have our vessels form up battle lines."

"Aye, Lord."

"I want the Dreadnoughts around the *Retribution*. And the refueling ships to the rear. Send in Holok and Creed's ships first. Then Brean's battlegroup. Let them try to regain the honor their commanders lost when they turned against me."

Sheika Kahn saw the look on the shipmaster's face. He obviously didn't agree with his commander, but he didn't argue either.

"It will be done, Lord Kahn."

"I want them to spread out immediately upon entering the system," Kahn said. "Evasive maneuvers in case they are fired upon. Have them form a screen to allow the rest of the fleet through."

"Even if that puts them in danger, Lord?"

"Their commanders put them in danger. I will not tolerate insubordination. They have only their own misplaced allegiance to blame if they die. Let it be a lesson to the rest of the fleet."

The shipmaster bowed, then hurried away. Kahn knew he was being cruel, but someone had to take the lead. Why should it be a loyal commander when there were several battlegroups without leadership in the wake of the parley? It would be dangerous to go through the portal first, but it would also be an excellent chance for the new leaders to earn glory through battle. That was the way of the Ashi. The strong prevailed, the weak fell away, and the entire race was better for it.

Through the transparent hull section immediately in front of Ulrech, he could see the ships moving. The invisible hyperspace portal was over ten thousand kilometers away. The ships needed enough space to get up to speed. He saw the fleet moving into position. They would proceed in staggered groups. Holok's group was moving to the front of the line. It was twelve ships in all, ten battle frigates and a pair of fast-moving corvettes. The odds against the Arodoni ship were not in their favor, but that was their concern, not Ulrech's. He would command from the rear, where it was safe, where his intellect could be utilized to the fullest extent. They had wounded the alien ship in their last encounter. Soon, they would disable it.

He imagined returning to the galactic core with the alien ship in tow. He would parade the vanquished Arodoni before the Prime Council, which would have no choice but to name him emperor. Then, he would strip every technological secret from the alien ship and use it. Vang may have been stronger and faster, his generals more lethal in battle, but none of them could match his intellect. Only he could make the best use of the alien knowledge. Vang would have squandered it. Worse still, he would have allowed others to steal it from the Ashi. Not Sheika Kahn; he knew exactly how to utilize the Arodoni secrets. This would make the Ashi more powerful than they had ever been.

CHAPTER 22

"YOU SURE THIS is what you want?" Remmy asked.

"One hundred percent, Master Sergeant," Dirk Oliver said.

"Then I wish you luck. All of you."

Remmy shook Dirk's hand. Gunny Rand was there too, but wouldn't look Remmy in the eye. The man had been a skilled commando, but his experiences outside the Sol system had broken him. Remmy put a hand on his shoulder.

"Take care of yourself, Chad."

"Yeah, you too," Gunny Rand said.

They were joined by Leigh Ann Poh and Ricky Thompson. They both looked a little sheepish. Remmy couldn't blame them for making the choice to return home. There was no guarantee that those who stayed behind would ever return to the Sol system. And for those who held dear to the idea of home, staying behind simply wasn't an option. Not that Remmy would ever blame anyone for walking away from combat. It was the people like himself who ran toward it that were crazy.

"It's only right that the *Indy* has Marines on board," Remmy said. "Look after one another. It was an honor serving with you."

"The honor was ours, Master Sergeant," Leigh Ann Poh said.

"Makes me wish I could be in two places at the same time," Ricky Thompson added.

"You've all done your duty and more," Remmy said. "Don't think of the *Indy* as a retreat. You are fulfilling the mission we were sent to do. It's important that our people get this tech and you three are making that happen. No matter what happens to the rest of us, you getting back home is a victory for all mankind."

They picked up their rucksacks and weapons cases. The Marines were leaving in full space armor. It wasn't necessary, but it was the easiest way to move their gear. The *Independence* wasn't as big as the *Jericho* and nowhere near the massive size of the *Renegade*. Room on the cruise liner was precious, so the Marines would take up as little as possible.

Remmy watched them board the shuttle, then headed over to where Captain Darius was waiting. Together, they walked toward GIGI. The alien artifact hovered off the deck near another shuttle that would take it to the *Indy*. Remmy still had some reservations about sending the device away ... and not just because it had been so valuable in controlling the drones from the *Renegade* in combat, or that it was instrumental in helping the humans decipher the alien languages and customs outside the Sol system. His biggest hesitation was the bond he shared with the device. Since encountering it, GIGI had linked to his mind. He didn't understand the how or even the why, but GIGI had saved his life and helped the crew of the *Renegade* more than once. He had no way of knowing what the separation would do to him. Maybe nothing at all, but maybe it would wreck his mind. He wasn't anxious to find out.

In all the time that GIGI had been in his thoughts, she never judged him or criticized his decisions. It wasn't as though she intruded into his consciousness unbidden. If he had to have someone in his head, GIGI would have been the best choice. That's not to say that Remmy would miss having the alien artifact inserted into his consciousness. The truth was, he never really felt GIGI's presence. It was more like he had a new, almost supernatural ability. When she left, he would be giving that up.

Captain Darius was the first to speak. "We have been honored by your presence and constant help on this mission," Darius said.

"The mission is not finished, Captain. I would be more help to you here than in returning to the Sol system."

"That may be true," Darius said. "But our mission parameters are clear. You were to be taken back as soon as possible. Besides, we have the *Renegade* now and the Dudonus. I believe we're in good hands."

"There is still much to be done," GIGI said.

"I understand your position and I think you understand ours," Darius insisted. "Join the *Independence* and help them home. That's your mission, now."

"He's right," Remmy said. "Humanity needs you."

"Appealing to my vanity will not change my mind, Master Sergeant. You, of all people, should understand that."

"I do," Remmy said. "But that doesn't make what I said any less true. We need you, not just here but back home, where you can help our entire race move forward. It wouldn't be right for us to keep you on the front lines where the risk is the greatest."

"I cannot refute your logic," GIGI said. "Although my purpose is to guide you."

"So, guide the human race," Darius said. "You've given us the tools we need here on the *Renegade*. We'll be fine."

It wasn't true. They would be in a fight for their very lives. There was an alien fleet seeking to destroy them, but everyone on board the *Renegade* understood that risk. And they had to ensure that GIGI wasn't endangered before she could be a boon to humanity.

They watched as the alien artifact glided up the ramp and into one of the shuttles. Soon afterward, a group of medical technicians brought Lieutenant Colt into the hangar. He was unconscious and strapped to a gurney. Doctor Lanski followed behind them.

"How is he, Doc?" Remmy asked.

"Certifiably insane," Lanski replied. "There is no doubt about that now. The parasite must be interfering with his mental faculties, but we won't know how without an autopsy."

"You mean?" Darius asked.

"I believe his condition will worsen until he dies, I'm afraid," Lanski said. "I don't believe anything can stop that now."

"How long?" Remmy asked.

"That I cannot say," Lanski said. "Lieutenant Colt is a strong, healthy young man. Under the right conditions he could survive a long time. But I'm not sure that's in his best interests."

"Thank you for looking after him," Darius said.

"Thank you for finding a way to get us back home," Doctor Lanski said. "I only wish I was leaving some of my staff to help you."

"Everyone had the right to decide what they wanted," Darius said. "Besides, we've got the tech. You're leaving us in good hands, Doctor."

Lanski knew that wasn't true but he still wanted to leave. He nodded in appreciation, then boarded the shuttle.

"I think that's everyone we needed to see off," Darius said. "Will you stay and let me know when the shuttles have departed."

"Yes, sir," Remmy said. "The refugees are already on board?"

"We sent them over first. Commander Lee got them settled before the crew members crossed over."

That was a relief to Remmy. He had risked a lot to rescue them. Their presence on the *Indy* was proof that they had done the right thing in leaving the Sol system and fighting the Imperium forces. The Brass might not see it that way, and people back home would always have their opinions, but in Remmy's mind, they were doing the highest work they could aspire to.

It was another twenty minutes before the last shuttle left the *Renegade's* hangar. Remmy used his comlink to alert Captain Darius, then started for the armory. With the crew members that were going back to the Sol system getting settled on the *Indy*, those that remained with the *Renegade* needed to start preparing for the onslaught ahead.

"Everyone's away," Remmy said as he walked into the Armory, which seemed too large for just the five Marines that were left.

"What's the plan, Master Sergeant?" Rip Van Winkle asked.

"A long night in space armor," Laila McPherson said.

"Oh, the joy," Izzy Berry complained.

"Better to have it and not need it," Tex said slowly, "than to need it and not have it."

"We'll be moving ordnance to the fore deck," Remmy said. "Priority one is to have everything we can deploy in a fight ready for when the Ashi arrive in system."

"If they arrive in system," Izzy said. "I still got fifty that says they don't show."

"I'll take that action," Laila said.

"Me too," Rip interjected. "How are we going to move the torpedoes into place without the Casians?"

"The old-fashioned way," Remmy told him. "Cherry pickers and dollies."

"I won't be much help," Izzy announced. She had been shot in the shoulder from above. The surgical droids had repaired the damage, but she was still healing. Her arm was immobilized in a sling."

"We don't have any weapons specialists left in the crew," Remmy said. "Your job, Corporal Berry, will be to keep tabs on what is available in the *Jericho*. You'll have a direct line to Staff Sergeant McPherson and to the officers on the Bridge."

"Not bad," Tex said. "You're moving up in the world."

"Lieutenant Berry has a nice ring to it. Does the job come with a promotion?" Izzy asked.

"Negative, Corporal," Remmy said. "But you'll have a squad of maintenance drones to help move ordnance to the capture deck as needed."

"Roger that," Izzy said.

"What's the point?" Rip asked. "Is it really possible that we could take out an entire fleet?"

"Maybe not in one fell swoop," Laila said. "But we'll chip away at it."

"We can hit 'em and run," Remmy said. "We've got the distance on them. Plus, it's doubtful that they know where the hyperspace portals are in this system."

"Which gives us a big advantage," Laila added.

"Won't they just follow us again?" Rip said.

"That's the point," Remmy said. "We want them focused on the *Renegade* and oblivious to the *Indy*."

"It's not our job to wipe them out," Laila said. "Worlds all across the galaxy are rising up against the Imperium."

"But we're the tip of the spear," Rip said. "And I want payback."

"We'll get it," Remmy said. "But this isn't the time for a decisive battle. Let's go make sure that Captain Darius has everything he needs to put the hurt on the Ashi fleet."

CHAPTER 23

DARIUS WAS ON THE BRIDGE. He knew he would be living there for the time being and it was a shame that he already felt worn down. There was no one left to send on errands like warming his coffee, so he sipped the tepid liquid and watched as the *Independence* headed out into space.

Pete Best was at the Weapons console. Ensign Alex Stanislaus had taken Henry Nash's place at the Engineering station. Nurek was going over the navigation controls and getting familiar with the system. Alex had already converted that computer station's readout to the native Dudonus language, making it so that Nurek could do what Vivian Ramos had done in the past. Darius didn't know if the alien had the same mathematical expertise that Vivian had, but the ship's computer would do the work. If they lost the navigation computer, that would be a different story, but Nurek had memorized the exact locations of the hidden portals to the free worlds. It seemed only natural that he should take up the navigation officer's duties.

Everyone on board the ship, the skeleton crew, was assuming new duties and ensuring that everything was functioning as it should. The shuttles were being controlled by the last dozen

Casian volunteers. Most of them had already returned and were safely docked in the *Renegade's* primary hangar. It was a job usually performed by GIGI, but the alien device was on its way out of the system.

"Time until they make their jump?" Darius asked.

"Four hours, thirty-eight minutes," Pete Best replied.

"Alright then, let's get into position," Darius ordered as he checked his watch. "We should still have a full twenty-four hours before the enemy can arrive."

"Aye, Captain," Alex Stanislaus said. "Moving us into attack position."

The ship was ready. Her huge laser cannons were fully operational and they could also utilize the gravity beam generator to fling torpedoes and ship-to-ship missiles at their foes. The advantage would be all theirs when the enemy fleet began to arrive in the Libertine system, but it wouldn't take long for their overwhelming numbers to force the *Renegade* into retreat. It was a strategy used throughout mankind's long history of warfare. Although the captain had wracked his brain for a way to end the conflict in a decisive fashion, they simply didn't have the resources to do it with just a single ship.

Perhaps in time, after they had chipped away at the Ashi fleet, they could take them all out. But the Imperium had the advantage. They could pull back, reinforce their numbers and come at the *Renegade* over and over until Darius made a fatal mistake. It was the plain and simple reality of the situation. For all Darius knew, the Imperium had ten thousand warships. It was also possible that they could build ships faster than Darius could destroy them. The plan only really worked as long as enough planets were in rebellion to tie up the rest of the fleet. Maybe it would all work out. More likely, they would eventually be overwhelmed and destroyed. Yet, Darius liked his odds. He might not win the war, but he had already won several battles. The Ashi fleet had lost entire squadrons against the *Renegade*. In the Olotimbo system, Darius had managed to destroy all the fleet's orbital bombing vessels. It was a small victory, but hopefully, one that saved the people on Olo Prime.

What Darius still didn't know, and what plagued him with doubts, was how the Ashi Fleet always seemed to know where they were. It wasn't clear if they had some advanced tracking technology or if they were keeping tabs on the *Renegade* via more traditional means, but no matter where they went, the Fleet always seemed to show up. That fact alone made Darius extremely nervous.

They would come after him and that's exactly what he wanted. But could they also go after the *Indy*? The cruise liner had no weapons. The SDF fleet would be hard-pressed to defend them if the Ashi arrived in the Sol system. There were no promises in combat. Darius couldn't protect them. Commander Lori Lee would have to do that on her own. His job was to engage the enemy, which he planned to do in such a way that it left them reeling. On the other hand, if they managed to somehow chase down the *Independence,* then humanity would have to fight.

Darius had insisted they take a second Arodoni Power Core. The device would be instrumental in providing the SDF with enough power to do whatever was necessary to defend themselves. Hopefully, they would listen to Commander Lee and take Darius' handwritten message to heart. He had urged them to begin building long-range laser platforms. There were already dozens of remote-controlled weapons around Earth but they had a much shorter range than the Ashi battleships. It would be child's play to knock out Earth's defenses. A ground war would be much more costly, but the Ashi's superior ships could defeat the SDF fleet and simply bomb Earth into submission. Darius was under no illusions that he had taken out all of the Ashi bombers. They could have a thousand more spread across hundreds of star systems. No one really knew what kind of resources the Ashi fleet had, not even Nurek. He had not been privy to such information and, while he could have obtained it in secret, he had not thought to do so before escaping his captivity.

What Darius did know was that the Ashi were a militant race.

They were able to focus solely on the military industry because they were made rich off the taxes and tariffs placed on other worlds in the Imperium. To the victor go the spoils, it was said, and the Ashi had complete control of the Imperium's vast horde of wealth.

The hours ticked by slowly. There was nothing left to do but wait. Darius watched with satisfaction as the *Indy* made the jump into hyperspace. He was relieved but left with a feeling of being all alone.

"Permission to come onto the Bridge," Master Sergeant Steel asked.

"Granted," Darius said. "And, like it or not, you are now a senior officer on this ship. Keep your rank if you want to, but you don't need permission to enter the Bridge. I'd like you to take Commander Lee's console. You'll be in charge of the crew when combat comes. You'll make the ship-wide announcements and give specific groups orders if necessary, as well as overseeing the Marines."

"Yes, sir," Remmy said, settling into the seat slightly behind and to the right of Darius' own chair.

"That may not sound like much on a ship like this where everything is automated, but it can be a chore," Darius continued. "Most of all, I want your input on strategy."

"I don't know how good ground operations experience will be in a space battle," Remmy pointed out. "But I'll do everything I can, sir."

"That's all I ask," Darius said.

An hour later coffee was delivered to the Bridge via a robot. Darius was surprised but not unhappy with the new development.

"What's this?" he asked. "Who ordered coffee?"

"That would be me, Captain," Alex Stanislaus said. "With almost all the crew gone, I took the liberty of reprogramming the *Renegade's* automated culinary system. The Casians have their own food set up, but Nurek and I input hundreds of recipes into the system. We won't have to worry about meals, sir. And everything can be delivered to any part of the ship. The Arodoni already had the bots designed for that purpose."

"I like the initiative," Darius said, taking a mug of hot coffee from the small robot with a retractable dome where the food could be carried and kept warm until the recipient was ready for it.

"The results ain't bad either," Remmy said as he leaned over and took a mug of steaming coffee.

"What's our estimated timeline?" Darius asked.

"Two hours until anticipated arrival," Nurek replied.

"The final countdown," Pete Best said.

Darius understood the sentiment, and while he hoped for a major victory over the Ashi, he feared it might be their final fight. He silently wondered if Remmy got scared before a battle. Darius did. He wasn't afraid of dying - although he didn't like dwelling on the subject - but what really frightened him were the lives of his crew, who depended on him to make the right choices in combat. If he failed, they all suffered ... and that was something he feared more than death itself.

CHAPTER 24

THE *INDEPENDENCE* WAS IN HYPERSPACE. Commander Lori Lee felt both excitement and regret. The small cruise ship wasn't small at all, but it was in comparison to the *Renegade*. She had gotten used to the bigger ship's dimensions and amenities.

"I'm going to take a walk back through the ship," she said. "Lieutenant Nash, you have the con."

"Aye, Commander, I have the con," Nash said.

He already had control of the ship, which was built to be flown by civilian pilots, not naval officers. GIGI was in sync with the *Indy's* computer and had translated the readouts and controls so that Nash could operate the vessel. Commander Lee had actually been in the co-pilot's seat. Vivian Ramos was behind them in the navigator's chair, and opposite her was Ensign Bertoli in what Lori Lee considered the Radio Operator's station.

Just like on an SDF Fleet ship, everything was close together. Lori carefully climbed out of the co-pilot's seat and made her way out of the cockpit. The space just behind the ship's control center was a tiny lounge for the crew. It was mostly storage, with a pair of small seats against the bulkhead separating the cockpit from the lounge. There were cabinets both high and low. Some were floor-to-ceiling. They had all been emptied when the ship was left in orbit around Libertine. The SDF crew had used the space to pack supplies for their return journey home.

What they didn't have were cabins. The cruise ship was built for speed. Beyond the crew lounge was what Lori Lee considered the attendant's station. It was more storage, yet also work space for the cruise liner's stewards to mix drinks and prepare meals. She passed through the attendant's station and stepped into the first-class cabin. Just like a human vessel, the designers of the cruise liner had built a series of sections into the ship.

"Commander," Lutus the Dudonus exclaimed from his seat on the very front row. "How are we proceeding?"

"Fine," Lori Lee answered.

"How long will we be in transit?"

"Thirty-one hours in hyperspace," Lori Lee said. "We'll need another forty-eight hours to reach our destination."

"I see," the alien said, not looking pleased.

Lori Lee understood the trepidation. Being locked in a cruise liner for days with nothing to do was a daunting challenge to face. But it was better than real suffering or even days of hard labor. All the passengers needed to do was wait. They all had small items to help them pass the time, as well as conversations with their fellow travelers.

The Dudonus volunteers were given special placement in the ship's first-class compartment. They had more space between their seats and the ability to recline if they desired. The rest of the ship was less accommodating. As she made her way back, she found crew members in seats and others who had created pallets on the floor. It wasn't as packed as it could have been and some of the people were up moving around. They would adjust. The rest of First Class had been used by the sick and wounded, along with the medical staff who oversaw them.

In the back of the ship, the engineers were busy taking readings and making sure nothing went wrong with the ship's propulsion. They had bins full of tools and replacement parts that had been fabricated on the *Renegade*. Everything in the engineering space was cramped but neat.

On her way back through the ship, Lori Lee was stopped by one of the Marines. Sergeant Dirk Oliver seemed nervous.

"Can I ask you a question, Commander?"

"Sure," Lori Lee said. "Fire away."

"Are we really going back home?"

"Why would you doubt that?"

Dirk shrugged. "I guess it sounds too good to be true."

"I assure you we will be in the Sol system very soon. Captain Darius gave us clear orders to return home and share everything we've discovered with our people."

Dirk nodded and sat back down. The seats were small with very narrow backrests. It was a little like sitting on a bucket and leaning back against a fence post, she thought. Not that many people had ever experienced such a thing. Only one out of every fifty humans ever saw wide open spaces. Earth was filled with sprawling megacities that were constructed of towering high-rise apartment buildings and offices. Nature preserves and farmland was strictly controlled by the government. Not that most people wanted to leave the cities where every conceivable luxury was within reach if one could just afford it. There were wide sections of low-income housing in every city—ghettos where over half of Earth's population lived and worked. Lori Lee had grown up in a cramped little apartment in a slum where the utilities only worked about half the time. She had never experienced a hot shower until she joined the Fleet. The cramped conditions on the *Indy* were very familiar to her.

Lori Lee hoped that things got better in the Sol system, but she knew it could get worse. The Brass would undoubtedly be unhappy that the *Jericho* had left the Sol system to begin with. It wouldn't matter that they had done so for good reasons. The SDF was commanded by a board of officers who oversaw every facet of the fleet and they had sent the *Jericho* out to bring the alien artifact known as GIGI back to them. It didn't matter that they would actually arrive faster in the *Indy* than they would have if the *Jericho* had immediately turned for home after retrieving the artifact. Lori was amazed by that fact. They had traveled across the solar system, fought battles, visited alien worlds and collected a few alien species willing to share their knowledge with humanity ... in less time than it would have taken the *S.D.F. Jericho* to make the return voyage from Saturn to the inner system.

She made her way back to the cockpit satisfied that everything was under control. All that remained was to wait while the ship made the passage from Libertine to the Sol system. When they were back in their home space things would get busy fast. It would take the *Indy* just over two days to reach the inner system from the hyperspace portal, but the fastest ship in the fleet couldn't do that. Most ships couldn't even reach the hyperspace portal. They didn't have the fuel efficiency to travel that far into the outer system. But the *Independence* would be in radio range, which would mean a lot of reports and debriefs.

"How we looking, Commander?" Nash said as Lori Lee entered the cockpit.

"We're good," she said, staying on her feet and leaning back against the door. "In fact, we need to start taking shifts to get some rest."

"Might as well," Henry said. "Ain't nothing else to do."

"Is there any place to rest?" Vivian Ramos asked.

"I think it's best if we stay in the crew lounge," Lori Lee said. "There's no beds, but we can make do."

It would be a hardship, especially after the luxurious amount of space and accommodations on the *Renegade*, but they were military officers. Personal comfort wasn't part of the job. It would be an arduous three days and then, well, she didn't know what would happen. They might be lauded as heroes or thrown in the brig for disobeying orders; she really didn't know. But they were better off, at least from the perspective of what was safe and what was dangerous, than the crew who volunteered to stay on the *Renegade*. Lori Lee glanced at her wristwatch and thought that the Ashi fleet was probably jumping into the Libertine system at that very moment.

CHAPTER 25

THE CREW of the *Renegade* was ready when the first Ashi ships dropped out of hyperspace. They were close enough to make quick shots, which didn't give the enemy time to outmaneuver them. But in space, a ship could move in any direction and the tight formation that dropped out of hyperspace first did exactly that.

"Contact!" Nurek said.

"Fire!" Darius ordered.

"Aye, weapons hot!" Pete Best shouted.

Remmy felt the adrenaline pumping through his veins even though he was actually just an observer in the battle. Pete Best was the weapons officer and he had all four of the *Renegade's* massive laser cannons dialed in on the hyperspace portal. Using manual controls, he fired at the enemy battleships using just a quarter of each laser's cannon's power capabilities. It was still enough strength to do damage even from over six hundred thousand kilometers away.

The four laser cannons were mounted on either side of the big, fish-shaped vessel. They extended out from the hull on massive hydraulic arms into their firing positions. The lasers blasted out in a quick staccato. Remmy saw the flashes of light racing through space. It was a bit like firing artillery. The cannons went boom but the shooters had to wait several seconds to see if their aim was true.

The laser blasts from the *Renegade* took two seconds to reach their targets. Eight ships were hit as Pete Best sprayed his laser fire across the group in a static line. It was hard to see how many ships there were in total, especially as those hit began to break apart.

"That's it," Captain Darius said. "I count four more vessels."

"Recharging the cannons," Pete Best said.

"Nurek," Darius said as he jumped from his seat and moved toward the holographic plot. He was pointing at the undamaged ships. "Track these on your radar."

To everyone's surprise, when Darius reached out and pointed to the ships on the plot, his finger passed through one, and it suddenly lit up in a bright red outline.

"Captain," Pete Best said. "Fox One is tracking that ship on its own."

Darius reached out and touched the holographic image of another battleship. It lit up in red.

"Fox two is tracking," Pete Best said.

Remmy saw the excitement on Captain Darius' face. He reached out and tapped the last two ships. They were wisely reversing course and moving behind the debris field left by the other ships.

"Can we hit them through the wreckage?" Darius asked.

"It's doubtful," Pete said. "Lasers are at fifty percent. Captain, I've got a notice. Looks like the computer wants permission to fire the cannons."

"Interesting," Darius replied. "Do it. Let's see how it works."

"Setting the power levels at twenty-five percent," Pete said. "Activating automatic combat."

Almost instantly, two of the cannons fired. Everyone was watching. The lasers lit up as they passed through the dust from the initial barrage. It was like shining a flashlight on a foggy night. And then the lasers ripped through two of the ships. One was a battleship. It took the shot, which burned a massive hole in the side of the hull and sent gas spraying out, but it kept moving. The other ship was smaller—a fast-moving vessel but with less armor and fire-power. The smaller ship exploded from the impact of the laser beam.

"Wow," Alex Stanislaus said.

"Fox two is no longer on the board," Nurek said.

"Impressive," Pete said. "It found a seam in the debris and timed the shot perfectly. I couldn't have done that."

As he was speaking, another laser blast lit the bridge through the transparent canopy like a bolt of lightning. A second later the fourth cannon fired as well. Both were hits.

"Alex, how are we looking?"

"Great," Ensign Stanislaus said. "All systems are green. Power is recharging the cannons."

"Seventy-five percent, Captain," Pete Best said.

"Outstanding," Darius remarked. "Retake command of the firing controls, Lieutenant. I want to be ready for the next squad that appears. You can do the heavy lifting and let the computer mop up."

"Aye, Captain, I have firing controls," Pete Best said.

"Ensign, get us moving," Darius said. "We need clear fields of fire for the next squad coming through the portal."

The master sergeant recognized the tactic. He wondered if the lead ships were even manned. They weren't there to fight but to create cover for the real fighters who could come afterward.

"Aye, Captain, engaging thrusters at full power," Alex declared.

"We're going to be moving from this point forward, Lieutenant. Take that into account as you make your targets."

"Aye, Captain," Pete Best said.

They didn't have to wait long. Nine more ships suddenly appeared in real space.

"Contact," Nurek said. "Nine ships just came through the portal."

"We're not clear of the debris field," Pete Best said.

It was true. The ship was moving upward but had to travel a

long distance to move around the debris field. Fortunately, they didn't have to right away. Remmy didn't know for certain, but he guessed that blowing the ships up was part of Captain Darius's strategy. There were massive sections of the ships still intact and lots of smaller debris. All of it was dangerously close to the portal, which meant the nine ships just coming through had to immediately take evasive action.

"Hang on," Darius said.

Remmy thought the stoic captain was transformed in battle. He seemed as excited as a child on Christmas morning. His face was lit up and he had a broad smile across his face.

"Let's see what they do," he added.

Five of the nine ships crashed. Three couldn't avoid the debris. They weren't destroyed or even disabled, but they were knocked off course and damaged. Another of the ships, trying to avoid the debris, accidentally collided with another. Both ships were severely damaged in the crash.

"Okay, have at them, Lieutenant," Darius said.

"Aye, Captain, weapons hot."

Pete Best's first barrage had been a devastating spray of laser fire. His second volley was neater, more contained. It reminded Remmy of Marines picking off select enemies with carefully aimed shots. Their rifles might have the capacity for fully automatic fire, but they could also be used in a more surgically precise fashion. And that's exactly what Pete Best did.

Lasers flashed from the *Renegade's* cannons. Some found gaps in the debris field; others hit objects that blew apart and sent smaller fragments sailing toward the alien ships. Remmy almost felt like it wasn't a fair fight. Two of the ships fired back at the Jericho, but their laser beams faded away before reaching them.

"So far, so good," Darius said.

"More will be coming," Nurek said. "Many more."

"Lieutenant, can we use the gravity beam from here?" Darius asked.

"Negative, Captain. We're too far away," Pete Best said.

"Let's launch torpedoes," Darius said. "I don't want to be wasteful, but let's put some high-yield explosives near the portal."

"Copy that," Pete Best said. "Master Sergeant, do the Marines have torpedos ready?"

"One on the deck, one standing by, Lieutenant Best," Remmy reported.

"Activating gravity propulsion," Pete Best announced. "Gulf one, weapon hot."

Remmy watched the torpedo shoot from the front of the ship like a bullet. It altered course slightly, angling down then streaking straight toward the debris near the hyperspace portal.

From his comlink Remmy got word the next torpedo was in place.

"Second torpedo is in place," Remmy said. "All personnel is in the safe zone for firing."

"Make it happen," Darius said with a smile.

"Gulf two, weapon hot," Lieutenant Best said.

The second torpedo went streaking from the ship, propelled by a directed gravity beam that sent it flying into space like a bullet from a gun. At the same time, a third group of alien ships appeared. Radar picked them up but they were well positioned behind a screen of destruction. Only one of the ships from the first two waves was still intact, although it had a massive hole in one side and was drifting out of control.

"Contact!" Nurek said. "Eight more Ashi Battleships in system."

"I see them, but we can't reach them through the debris," Pete lamented.

"Increase laser power to full," Darius said. "We'll fire a little slower. Try to take down the ships moving the fastest."

On the plot, Remmy could see the wreckage floating in space, along with several new ships. They came out of hyperspace and immediately began evasive maneuvers. Only one was unlucky enough to get hit by the debris.

"Targets locked in, Captain," the weapons officer announced.

"Fire," Darius said.

"Fox one," Pete Best said.

The flash from the laser was much brighter than before. Remmy watched, silently counting in his mind. It reminded him of a child who sees the flash of lightning and then counts the seconds until the roll of thunder is heard. It took the blast traveling at the speed of light two full seconds to reach the debris field and the ships behind it. Another flash, far in the distance, signaled the hit, but Remmy was watching the holographic plot. A hole suddenly appeared in the debris field, and one of the alien ships disappeared from the plot.

"Keep it up," Darius said. "I want you to continue firing at a steady rate. Ensign Stanislaus, begin evasive maneuvers. We can't be predictable."

"Do you think they can target us this far out?" Alex asked.

"We can't take the chance that something coming through that portal won't be able to shoot this far or that they aren't utilizing weapons we haven't seen yet."

"New contact," Nurek said. "Twelve Ashi battleships."

There were still three from the third wave. The new ships immediately gained speed and flew away from one another.

"Keep firing, Lieutenant," Darius said.

"We can't keep pace with the numbers arriving," Alex Stanislaus said.

"That's true, but we've still got the advantage. We need to take out as many of their ships as we can. Nurek set the course out of the system."

"Confirming that you want to exit the system via the portal to Subterra, Captain."

"Affirmative," Darius said. "Be ready. Ensign Stanislaus, do you have the main engines ready?"

"Aye, Captain, primed and ready to go."

The alien ships were moving away from the portal, but none were headed toward the *Renegade*. Their purpose wasn't to fight, but to distract.

"Contact," Nurek said. "Eight more ships. Four light cruisers, four battleships."

There were still a dozen ships from the previous arrivals. The debris field was starting to look like a chunk of Swiss cheese. The diameter of the laser blasts from the *Renegade* was large enough for the smaller ships to fly through. Remmy could see that the situation was quickly becoming untenable. If it were a Marine op, he would begin ordering the retreat.

But Captain Darius wasn't finished yet. He still had the upper hand.

"How is the power core holding up?" Darius asked.

"It's good," Ensign Stanislaus said. "We're using a lot of power, but the system is fully functional. The risk is to the connections. They may get overloaded and meltdown."

"Laser cannons are getting hot," Pete said. "Another few minutes and we'll need to take a break."

"Keep cycling your shots. I don't want to harm the ship, but we've got to keep hammering as long as we can," Darius said. "Ensign, get the maintenance system on standby. If something breaks down, we have to fix it ASAP."

"Aye, Captain, setting the maintenance system to high alert."

"Master Sergeant, I want all personnel ready to assist if the power system goes down."

"Yes, sir," Remmy said. "We have gear laid out already. The crew is ready for anything."

Remmy knew that wasn't exactly true. Even before most of the crew left for the Sol system, they didn't have enough humans to stand by every junction and every component that might need attention during combat operations. The maintenance droids would do the work, but they wouldn't have the same sense of urgency as a human or a Dudonus would. They were machines. They had no concept of anything outside their programming. They couldn't conceive of danger or war.

Add to that the fact that the *Renegade* was a massive ship. She was seven kilometers stem to stern and four kilometers wide and deep. All together, that was over a hundred square kilometers. Most of the dome cities on Mars weren't that big. Which meant getting to the source of a problem took time. They needed two hundred skilled engineers to fully man the ship for combat, not to mention the other areas of the ship that would require specialists. Ten thousand people on the *Renegade* wouldn't have been too many, and yet there were less than fifty humans, Dudonus, and Casian volunteers.

"Contact," Nurek said. "More than before. I can't keep count."

"It's the bulk of their fleet," Pete Best said.

"Target the newcomers," Darius said. "We might damage two or three vessels with every shot."

There were fifty-seven ships in the last wave. They came out and immediately formed a shield of ships that guarded the portal. Darius was right. The laser blasts vaporized a ship and continued on, damaging two or three more, but they only managed to get seven laser blasts at the enemy before the weapons lost power.

"Weapons are down," Pete Best said.

"Looks like the junction in section L just overloaded," Alex said. "Maintenance system is activated."

"What level?" Remmy asked.

"Beta level," Alex replied. "That's the main power supply to Fox Four."

As Remmy ordered his volunteers to that section of the ship, which was all the way out past the mid-way point, Captain Darius gave the order to retreat.

"Do we still have power to the thrusters?"

"Aye, Captain, ship's engines are good to go."

"Get us moving toward the jump point," Darius ordered. "Nurek, how many ships do they have in the system now."

"Sixty-two and counting, Captain," Nurek said. "We destroyed or disabled thirty-three."

"Not bad," Darius said. "That was some damn fine shooting, Lieutenant Best."

"Yes, Captain. Thank you, sir," Pete said.

"Contact," Nurek said. "dreadnoughts, Captain. They've just entered the system."

"They're in protective positions around that ship," Darius said, tapping it with his finger. The ship in the hologram lit with a red glow. "What do you think that is?"

"The Emperor's flagship," Nurek said. "The *Retribution*. It was Vang's father's before he died. Sheika Kahn must have taken it unless he, too, was toppled."

"Any chance we can hit it when the lasers are back online?" Remmy asked.

"Doubtful," Pete Best said. "Those dreadnoughts are lining up between that ship and us. Even at full power, we couldn't reach it."

"Keep a count on that fleet," Darius said. "We need to know if they have reinforcements. Ensign Stanislaus, how long until the lasers are back online?"

"Hard to say," Alex replied. "Maintenance droids haven't even reached the problem area yet."

"We're too far out for conventional weapons," Darius said. "The torpedos we launched won't reach the portal for another five hours. The entire fleet could have moved by then. How long will it take us to reach the Subterra portal?"

"Thirteen hours, maybe less if we increase speed beyond what is needed to make the jump," Nurek said. "I'm not well versed in exactly what the ship is capable of."

"I don't think any of us are," Darius said.

"What's keeping their dreadnoughts from firing at us?" Remmy asked. "They have the range, don't they?"

"They do," Darius said. "But they're staying behind the debris field. Looks like they're more interested in protecting than attacking."

It took an hour to get the lasers back online. By that time, the *Renegade* was nearly two million kilometers from the enemy fleet, which had formed up, but it didn't pursue.

"What do you suppose they're planning?" Pete Best asked.

"Hard to say," Darius replied.

He was back in his Captain's chair but leaning forward, studying the plot. The hologram had expanded out to give them a greater view of the system. A yellow dotted line showed their trajectory and the portal that led to the Subterra system. It also showed Libertine and the portal from the Zutek star cluster. The Ashi fleet was huddled around it.

"They're on the defensive," Remmy said. "They want to control that portal out of the system."

"Probably because the others aren't in their navigation program. They think their portal is the only way in or out of the Libertine system," Darius said. "They assume they have us on the run."

"But they haven't even fired a shot that could reach us," Pete Best said.

"Doesn't matter," Darius said. "We're the ones in retreat."

"The Ashi place great value on overwhelming force," Nurek said. "Most species flee from their very presence."

"We have our guns back," Pete Best said. "Why don't we just pick them off from here?"

"Start calculating your targeting solutions," Darius said. "Those dreadnoughts are the top priority. But don't fire until I give you the command."

He turned and faced Remmy. "What do you think they're doing?"

Remmy shrugged. He was no expert on naval warfare. But a battlefield was a battlefield, and what he saw led him to two possible conclusions.

"You're probably right," Remmy said. "They probably think they have us where they want us. They don't know the *Renegade's* capabilities."

"You said probably," Darius remarked. "What's the other possibility?"

"That we aren't the target," Remmy said. "It's possible that we're doing what they want already."

"Running away," Darius said.

"Moving away," Remmy corrected him. "If there's another target, they'll want us as far away from it as possible before they attack. By the time we get turned around and can engage the enemy, they'll have accomplished what they set out to do."

"There's only one other possible target in the system," Darius said. "But the settlements on Libertine aren't worth their time."

"They might not know that," Nurek said. "There are many rumors about the free worlds."

"They might think there's whole armies down there," Pete suggested.

"I guess time will tell," Darius said. "Until they do something, we'll make them pay. Charge the laser cannons. Continue evasive maneuvering. Lieutenant, when you have the shot … take it."

"Aye, Captain!" Pete Best said. "Preparing to engage."

Remmy was glad the *Renegade* could still land shots, even from long range, but he feared they were missing something. The key to any battle was anticipating what your enemy would do. And at the moment, Remmy had no idea what the Ashi fleet was preparing for. It left him feeling cold and nervous. He gripped the arms of the chair he occupied and waited to see what would happen.

CHAPTER 26

"WE HAVE SUSTAINED HEAVY LOSSES," the shipmaster said.

It was a redundant statement. Sheika Kahn could see the debris of dozens of ships drifting around them. Some were reduced to space dust that glittered in the light of the system star.

So this is the Free World, he thought. It was unimpressive. In fact, it looked more like an undiscovered world. There was a planet with only the slightest activity. His ship's scans revealed only the barest traces of electromagnetic energy. There were supposedly other Free Worlds, but if the planet in the system Sheika Kahn found himself in was any indication, they were not the type of places he would want to live. The rumors of beings escaping the Imperium to live free were greatly exaggerated. Given the choice, Sheika Kahn thought most beings would choose the Imperium.

The Arodoni ship was still in the system but had, for the moment, stopped firing on the Ashi fleet. Perhaps it was due to the fact that their numbers were so overwhelming, but Sheika Kahn was keenly aware that he had already lost more than half of the massive fleet he started with. By all indications, the battles in the Olotimbo system and the uncharted system they were currently in had been devastating losses for the Ashi. But Sheika Kahn had thousands of ships and billions of warriors. What was the loss of a couple hundred ships and crew in the pursuit of advanced alien technology that would propel the Galactic Imperium into the next ten thousand years?

"Lord, I have the data from the scouting drones," the shipmaster announced.

"At last, some information that may prove useful. Tell me," Sheika Kahn ordered.

"It appears the Arodonis landed on the planet with supplies," the shipmaster said. "Our drones had no way of knowing what they were offloading, but several flights were... interesting."

"What is so interesting that it interrupts your report, shipmaster? Or do you forget to whom you are speaking!"

"No, Lord, forgive me. It's just that several ships went to the planet, but one went to a space cruiser. There were two abandoned vessels in orbit when the scout ships arrived and deployed the surveillance drones."

"But there is only one now," Sheika Kahn said.

"Yes, master, only one remains in the system. The Arodoni ship completed delivery of the supplies to the surface, then it appears that supplies and possibly crew transferred over to the space liner, Lord. The *Independence* according to the transponder code. Then she left orbit. There is another portal out of this system, Lord Kahn!"

He had figured as much. The Arodoni had a good strategy. With its long-range cannons, it could stay ahead of them and use the secret hyperspace portals to chisel down the fleet as they followed into the unknown systems until there was nothing left.

"And the enemy ship is fleeing to it?" Kahn asked although it was less of a question than an accusation.

"No, Lord. It is in the opposite direction."

That brought Sheika Kahn up short. He had been surprised by the aliens many times and warfare was not his forte, but he was a strategic thinker.

"Something's wrong," the commander of the Ashi fleet said. "They must be afraid."

"I don't understand," the shipmaster whined.

"They removed the crew to a derelict ship? Why do that? It makes no sense... unless..."

"Unless what?" The shipmaster asked.

"There is a problem with their vessel. They know they cannot win, so they are sending as much of the crew away as they can while their war vessel distracts us."

"Sends them where?"

"There can only be one place," Sheika Kahn said, his jowls splitting into a smile. "They are going back to where they came from."

"No one knows where the Arodoni came from, Lord," the shipmaster said. "Or where they have been hiding these many centuries."

"Indeed, but now is our chance to discover it. Form up the fleet. We are following them through the portal."

"Aye, Commander," the shipmaster said.

"Send our fastest ships first," Sheika Kahn said. "The Arodoni will continue to fire on us. Plot a course to that portal that keeps the debris field or the planets between us. Use whatever we can to keep them from destroying our ships."

"It shall be done," the shipmaster declared.

"Keep the dreadnoughts around the *Retribution*. We shall form the advance fighting force. Have the battleships fall in behind us. Refueling ships with cargo will be in between, but those who have nothing left will serve to shield the fighting ships from the rear. I want them well back from the rest of the fleet."

"Aye, Lord Kahn."

Sheika made a fist with one hand and punched it into the palm of the other. The tide of the war was turning. His forces were taking the initiative and would not simply be responding to what the Arodoni ship did any longer. If he was right and the cruise ship was returning the crew to their home system, Sheika would be making the greatest discovery in the entire history of the Imperium. He wouldn't need to take the Arodoni ship. He could destroy that vessel if he had the ones who built it under his boot.

A slight chuckle rolled up from his wide gut, not a full laugh, but enough to reveal his pleasure in the turn of events. The Arodoni, for all their advanced technology, had not discovered that the Ashi scout ships had dropped surveillance drones that watched their every move and calculated the cruise liner's jump into hyperspace. The Kahn ships would match it and discover where it had gone.

"Alert the fleet of our intentions," Sheika Kahn said. "They must know how important this phase of my battle plan is."

"Yes, Lord. It shall be as you have ordered, sire," the shipmaster called from across the command deck.

It didn't matter to Sheika Kahn that he hadn't known what the Arodoni were up to until that very minute. When historians wrote of his legendary campaign, it would be that Sheika the Great pushed the aliens back to their home world and bent them to his will. He would be lauded as a hero, perhaps even worshiped by beings on a thousand worlds. In his mind, that was exactly as it should be.

CHAPTER 27

"CAPTAIN," Nurek said.

"I see it," Darius replied. "The fleet is moving."

"They might just be trying to stay behind the debris field," Pete Best suggested.

It was one possibility. The debris field had grown despite the high-power laser blasts that tended to atomize anything in their path. But several of the ships hit had only been struck a partial blow, and several collisions had added to the spinning bits of metal. Darius was glad they didn't have to navigate the field. It would be nearly impossible for a ship the size of the *Renegade*.

"At least using it to shield whatever they're up to," Alex Stanislaus said. "Should we alter course?"

"Not yet," Darius said.

It frustrated him that he wasn't able to anticipate his enemy better. They were constantly surprising him. Not that he was losing by any regular means of evaluating war ... yet the enemy fleet was still out there. It still posed the *Renegade* and others a very real danger. He needed to strike a decisive blow but the Ashi didn't seem to care how many vessels they lost.

"It's going to be hard to hit the dreadnoughts," Pete Best said. "There's too much debris, too many other vessels between us."

"It's a rear guard maneuver," Remmy said softly.

"Using their other ships to shield their intent," Darius said, nodding. "Are they on course for the planet?"

"It does appear to be possible," Nurek said.

"If they can't beat us, they'll hit the colonies on Libertine," Pete Best said.

"And attempt to draw us in," Darius said.

"They have eight dreadnoughts," Alex Stanislaus said. "Why not just shoot it out with us now?"

"It's too direct," Darius said.

"Direct is what they're known for," Remmy said. "If their warriors are any indication, subtly and strategy isn't their strong suit."

"The Ashi have been the most potent force in the galaxy so long, that even the name of them strikes fear into most species," Nurek said. "Whatever strategy they might have known had long since been forgotten from disuse. Their culture values aggression and direct confrontation."

"They're using strategy now," Darius said. "They'll beat us to the planet and use it to hide from us."

"While we're out here with nowhere to hide," Pete Best said.

"All the more reason to make for the portal," Alex Stanislaus said. "Permission to increase thrusters to full."

Darius had opted against full speed because he didn't want to put a strain on the ship's systems but also because his point had been to lure the Ashi after them. The closer they got, the more they believed victory was in their grasp, the more likely they were to follow him directly through the next portal to the Subterra system.

It would take several hours to reach the portal, even at top speed. In the meantime, the Ashi forces would reach the planet. What would happen to the people on Libertine if the *Renegade* fled the system and left the Ashi fleet behind? Would they attack the innocent? Darius couldn't put it past them. He could stay and fight, but without cover, they would eventually be overwhelmed. That lesson had been learned in the Olotimbo system.

Darius got to his feet and moved to the plot. There was a series of moons around the first gas giant in the system. If the *Renegade* could reach them in time, the small lunar bodies would give them the cover needed to slug things out with the Ashi. At the very least, the *Renegade* could outlast their opponents, who still needed regular refueling, and it was highly likely that every ship in their fleet had much larger crews than the *Renegade*. Larger crews meant more mouths to feed. And while the Arodoni ship was self-supplying, the Ashi ships would need refitting before long.

"Here," Darius said as he pointed at the gas giant. "Take us here. We'll use the moons for cover."

"They might still attack the planet," Pete Best pointed out.

"There's nothing we can do about that," Darius said. "We'll fight as long as we can but we have to fight smart. There's just one of us and no one is coming to our rescue."

"Adjusting course," Alex Stanislaus said.

"The closest lunar body is four hundred thousand kilometers outside our current trajectory," Nurek said. "Coming to point three-seven-five we can reach it in an hour at our current rate of speed."

An orange line appeared on the plot. It curved from the small image of the *Renegade,* which was following the yellow line through space toward the hyperspace portal, toward the gas giant, which was moving toward them on its elliptical path around the system star.

Darius moved around, trying to gauge the angles. Their enemy would have the advantage of cover from the debris field for most of that flight time. The *Renegade* would have a small window of opportunity to attack the Ashi fleet, but they would be so far apart by that time that it would take the laser blasts several minutes to cross the threshold between the planets, which means they would have to estimate target positions and attempt to make corrections that wouldn't be shown to be right or wrong for even longer. Long-range attacks had the benefit of being less dangerous, but they were also far less effective. They would be lucky to take out just one enemy ship in an entire barrage of laser blasts.

"Do it," Darius said. "It's still the best course of action."

The corrections to their course were made. And they continued to track their enemy which utilized the debris field to hide their movements. Darius didn't like waiting to attack, yet he didn't want to waste power or risk another electrical failure that might put the entire ship at risk. As long as the enemy's dreadnoughts weren't moving to attack positions, Darius felt good about his position.

"Captain," Nurek said after nearly half an hour since the *Renegade* altered course, "I am beginning to wonder if Libertine is the goal of the enemy fleet's maneuvering."

"Of course it is," Darius said. "What else could it be?"

"I have analyzed their trajectory," Nurek continued, unfazed by the Captain's veiled rebuke. "It is possible that the Ashi fleet is making for the portal that would lead them to your home system."

"What?" Darius asked. "Are you sure?"

"Their continued build-up of speed suggests they are not moving into orbit," Nurek said. "They have crossed the threshold to safely take position around Libertine. They would merely bounce away unless they slowed their advance."

"But they could, right?" Pete Best suggested.

Darius felt as though the cold blade of a knife had just been pressed to his throat.

"Nurek's right," Darius said. "Accelerating through space just to slow down again takes a lot of fuel. They wouldn't do that."

"Not even to minimize their vulnerability?" Remmy asked.

"They've done nothing to avoid risk so far," Darius replied. "I should have seen this coming. They know how to follow us. They've done it at every turn."

"We couldn't have known there was another ship in the system," Alex Stanislaus said.

"Their scouts probably clocked the two space cruisers in orbit," Pete Best said. "There's only one there now."

"So?" Alex argued. "They don't know that it isn't somewhere else in the system. Besides, if this system is hidden like Nurek said, they wouldn't know about the portals."

"How they know is less important than what they know," Darius said. "If they follow the *Indy* back home, we're in a world of hurt."

"So, we stop them," Pete Best said.

"We're traveling in the wrong direction to do that," Nurek said.

"And by the time we reverse course, they'll reach the portal," Darius said. It was a generalization, not an exact record of course and speed.

"Actually, we can get the *Renegade* turned to pursue while the fleet is still several thousand kilometers from the hyperspace portal," Nurek said.

"Do it," Darius said. "Turn us around at the best possible speed."

"That portal isn't a straight shot to our solar system, is it?" Remmy asked.

"No," Nurek said, "but according to the information added to the *Renegade's* navigation system by GIGI, it is possible to reach the Sol system from this one hyperspace lane."

"If the Ashi don't know about us, they won't know how to get to the Sol system," Pete Best said.

"Is that right?" Darius asked Nurek.

It was a major drawback, not to be more familiar with hyperspace travel. Darius thought of it like an old fashioned road. There were once vast highways that spanned the major continents on Earth when humans traveled mostly on ground transport vehicles. There were on-ramps and off-ramps at critical junctures. And there were secondary highways that connected to the primary ones. The portal the *Indy* had used was a major space lane. They managed to get on and off at portals that weren't widely known. It was possible that Pete Best was right. The Ashi might follow the *Independence* but miss the space cruiser's exit portal.

"Under normal circumstances," Nurek said. "But if they

somehow knew the angle used by the *Independence* along with her speed when she made the jump, it is possible to calculate where she planned to exit."

"In other words, if they saw her go, they can follow where she went," Darius said.

"But how could they know?" Pete Best said. "They weren't in the system when it happened."

"True, but we weren't alone either," Darius pointed out.

"You mean the people on Libertine?" Alex asked.

"We haven't picked up any communication between the planet and the fleet," Nurek said.

"That doesn't mean someone didn't send a direct beam message," Darius said. "For all we know, they have some other way to communicate."

"But why would they do that?" Pete asked.

"To save their own skin," Remmy said.

Darius nodded. That was his thought, too, even though the sad reality was that by helping the *Renegade's* enemy, they were merely prolonging their own destruction. Now that the Ashi knew about Libertine, it would simply come back and crush the rebels at a more convenient time to the Imperium. They might have signaled for a single invasion ship to do the job already. It wouldn't take any more than that. There wasn't much to the colonies, and they had almost no way to defend themselves. Secrecy had been their only defense, and that was gone now. Their only remaining hope was for the *Renegade* to defeat the enemy fleet.

"At least we'll be pointed in the right direction for shooting them down," Pete Best said.

"How long until we're turned around?" Darius asked.

"I'm utilizing the thrusters to turn us," Alex Stanislaus said. "It's faster than a flip and full retro-burn."

"How far out of position will we be?" Darius asked.

"Far enough that Libertine will block any attacks for a while," Nurek said. "Fortunately, our speed will be an asset. We can reach the portal in eight hours at our current speed."

"Once we make the turn, increase speed to full," Darius said.

"Won't that put a strain on the ship's systems?" Pete Best asked.

"Not as much as giving the enemy time in the Sol system," Darius said.

"We'll be going too fast to make the jump," Alex Stanislaus said. "We'll have to do retro-burns to slow our speed back down."

"How long will it take us with full power to the engines and taking the need to slow down into account?" Darius asked.

"Four hours, twelve minutes, and thirty-five seconds from right... now," Nurek said.

"And how long until the fleet reaches the portal?" Darius asked.

"They're increasing their speed. It's hard to calculate precisely."

"Just ballpark it," Darius said.

"I am unfamiliar with that idiom."

"Estimate the time it will take them," Darius said. "I don't need an exact number."

"Three hours, maybe half an hour longer," Nurek said.

It wasn't good news. There was no way to take the enemy out completely. It was possible they might get lucky, or they might all end up dead. Either way, they had to try and save the Sol system. The enemy discovering humanity's home was the worst possible outcome. And everything Darius had done had been to prevent that exact tragedy. But it seemed his worst fear was coming true, and there was nothing Captain Zeke Darius could do about it.

CHAPTER 28

THE *INDY* DROPPED out of the hyperspace portal between Saturn and Jupiter. Commander Lori Lee didn't need Lieutenant Vivian Ramos to tell her they were just under two billion kilometers from Earth. But she needed to know their speed.

"Speed?" She asked.

"Two hundred thousand kilometers per hour," Vivian Ramos said.

"Systems?"

"Everything looks good," Lieutenant Henry Nash said. "I can't promise how much the engines have left, but with the Arodoni Power Core, we have the energy we need."

"Take us to seventy-five percent. I want us back inside the inner system at the fastest possible speed. Ensign Bertoli, we are home. Let the Brass know it and inform them about Captain Darius and the other volunteers."

"We're still over six hundred million kilometers from *Ares*," Bertoli said. "Communications will take over half an hour to reach them."

"Understood," Commander Lee said.

They were too far out to see much. Saturn was behind them,

and Jupiter was nothing but a spark of light in the distance. Beyond that, nothing was visible. The tech on the space cruiser was nowhere near as advanced as what they were used to on the *Renegade*. There was no holographic plot, just computer screens and digital instrument panels. But Commander Lee didn't need to see what lay ahead; she already knew. There would be plenty of space traffic around Jupiter. Terraforming was taking place on two of the gas giant's moons and mining interests were active on thirty-one more, as well as several of the larger asteroids that orbited the planet. Between Jupiter and the asteroid belt was *Ares*, the largest Space Defense Force space station. It served as the Forward Operating Base, as well as a refitting station. There were hundreds of mining interests working the belt and over a hundred colonies on Mars. Most of the best space stations were between Earth and Venus, while there were several research stations closer to the bright yellow sun.

Moving through space and between the various colonies and space stations were ships, thousands of them, some private, some commercial and many were Space Defense Force military vessels. It took the *Jericho* just over four weeks to travel from *Ares* to the alien artifact which had been stationary just beyond the orbit of Saturn. They had reached a top speed of over a million kilometers per hour, which had been a record at the time. The alien cruise liner could easily outpace that. It was a ship that was built for speed and Henry Nash was convinced it could go as fast as eighteen million kilometers per hour without overtaxing the engines. Reaching that speed and then slowing down again would, of course, add to their travel time. Theoretically, they could reach *Ares* in as little as two days.

There were no windows on the cruise liner, so Commander Lee made the announcement that they had safely reached the Sol system. There was polite applause among the crew, but they were also aware that it would be two more days before they were allowed off the ship and into better accommodations.

"You think anyone regrets leaving the *Renegade*?" Vivian asked.

"Why would they?" Henry answered with a question of his own.

"I was just thinking we'll probably dock at *Ares*. We'll be back to pseudo gravity, tiny little rooms or bunks in a shared living space," Vivian pointed out.

"And the berths on the *Renegade* are looking pretty good after a full day and night in this tin can," Ensign Bertoli added.

"Maybe, but this tin can is state of the art for our people," Henry pointed. "We may not have a glamorous destination awaiting us, but we're bringing home the bacon. And this ship is nothing compared to GIGI and what it can teach us."

"If it will," Vivian said. "It hasn't made a peep since we left the Libertine system."

"I'm more concerned about the welcome we're likely to get from the Brass," Lee said. "I wouldn't be surprised if we get locked up and debriefed for months."

"Interrogated, you mean?" Vivian asked. "Is that really possible?"

"No," Henry said. "We've got rights."

"Not under the military code of conduct," Commander Lee said. "It all comes down to how they classify what Captain Darius did by leaving the Sol system."

"You mean they might decide he disobeyed orders?" Bertoli asked.

"They might," Lee agreed. "Or they might decide that he abandoned his post. We might be considered deserters, in which case we would have no rights at all. In fact, they could line us up and shoot us if that's what they wanted to do."

"They could?" Ensign Jacee Bertoli asked.

She was the youngest of the officers and clearly frightened by Commander Lee's gloomy forecast of events.

"But they won't," Vivian said.

"We'll be heroes once they realize what we've brought them," Henry added.

Commander Lori Lee was a positive person who always tried to look at the best side of things. Yet she had serious doubts about how the Brass would view what they did. In fact, they might consider what the crew of the *Jericho* did was to start an interstellar war, which would be very bad for all their careers. She, for one, didn't think that Captain Darius had been wrong in his decisions. In fact, she applauded him for the courage it took to make those decisions. She also admired how he had taken everyone's point of view into consideration. But at least one passenger would disagree with her. Connor O'Dell was on the ship, in the first-class cabin, in fact. He had resisted the Captain at every step and would have turned the *Jericho* around and burned for home the minute that GIGI had been brought aboard. It didn't matter that if he had done so, they would still be in transit back to *Ares* or that by leaving the Sol system, they had gained so much more technological knowledge than they could have gotten from GIGI alone.

It wasn't common knowledge, but among the various supplies on the *Indy* were the hard drive copies from the *Renegade*, including all the ship's specifications and building plans. If nothing else happened, Lori Lee knew that within just a few years, the lives of every person in the Sol system would be radically changed. Not to mention the fact that they could also venture out of the system. Humanity could help to develop Libertine and begin trade with other planets. Of course, how the Imperium fared played a role in that future, but Lori Lee had great faith in Captain Zeke Darius. If it were possible to break the Imperium's stranglehold on the galaxy, he would do it.

It took a full hour to get the response to their initial message. It wasn't surprising. The Brass wanted to know more, and they were ordered back to *Ares Station* at the greatest speed possible. Lori Lee wouldn't obey that order. She would go back to *Ares* but only at the highest speed they could safely reach without risking the lives of the crew and passengers on board.

They also wanted to know more about why Captain Darius had stayed in the alien ship rather than bringing it home. Lori Lee had known they would want the *Renegade*. It was no different than the Ashi wanting it. The Arodoni ship was far more advanced than anything either civilization could build. Humanity, for instance, didn't have the tools or even the refining capability to get the raw materials needed. They could mine and refine most substances, but there were still things that human scientists and researchers simply hadn't discovered yet.

"Let's get the initial data package beaming," Lori Lee said.

"Aye, Commander," Henry replied. "I have the first bundle of files ready to beam across."

Just like radio communications, information could be sent through space at the speed of light. Captain Darius had decided that selected files, reports, images and videos should be sent to their superiors first. It was an outline of everything that had happened since reaching the alien artifact GIGI. It wasn't all the data they had and included only a few of the most important discoveries. Included was the hyperspace network data, not the entire file, just a summary of it and how the portals worked. It also included information on the Arodoni Power Core, which would be the first and most important advancement in human technology. The power core that had been set to fuel the *Indy*, as well as the spare they had in the cargo on the cruise ship, would produce enough power to run any human space station. In time, there would be no more need to produce, stockpile and deliver fuels to the various ships and stations in space.

Almost as important as the Arodoni Power Core would be the files on creating artificial gravity. It would change how space stations and interstellar ships were built. And, once assimilated, would change how raw materials in space were collected. Lori Lee knew that thousands of lives would be saved through the use of artificial gravity beams.

"The package is on its way," Henry said. "I know guys who are gonna flip their lid when they lay eyes on this tech."

"How's our speed?"

"Two point two million kilometers per hour and climbing," Vivian Ramos said.

"How are the engines?" Lori Lee asked.

"Hot, but still within parameters," Henry said. "We should reach cruising speed in a few more hours."

"And we won't melt down before then?"

"Negative, Commander. We aren't pushing too hard," Henry explained. "Trust the hardware. We checked every inch of it before leaving Libertine."

"Thank you, Lieutenant. Vivian, are we on course?"

"The Brass sent coordinates and promised to clear the road," Vivian replied. "We're right where they wanted us."

"No news is good news, I suppose," Lori Lee said. "Let's keep one foot on the gas and get back home."

"No complaining 'bout that," Henry said.

"Just a little longer and we'll have completed the most important mission the SDF ever undertook," Vivian said. "You think our names will end up in the history books?"

"They should," Lee said. "But you never know. I guess we'll have to wait and see."

CHAPTER 29

"THIS IS TAKING TOO LONG," Darius said.

"We could turn faster if we slow down," Alex Stanislaus said.

It seemed like a foolish thing to say, but Darius knew his engineer was right. To maintain their speed, it was necessary to turn the ship in a long, circuitous motion. And speed was what they needed most. Slowing down would bring them around faster, but it would take longer just to regain the speed they lost. There seemed to be no good options.

"Captain, I have further ill news," Nurek said.

Darius turned to the alien. His long, conical head didn't seem so strange to Darius anymore. He was just another member of the crew. Different in every aspect, but it was his personality that Darius related to, not his appearance.

"What now?" Darius said.

"Projecting our trajectory from the turn, it appears that Libertine will be in our direct path."

"Something else to slow us down," Pete grumbled.

But Darius knew that the planet wouldn't slow them down. It was going to block them from shooting at the Ashi fleet.

"It will have moved out of our path by the time we approach," Nurek said.

"But we won't be able to engage the enemy until then," Darius said.

It was hard to control his emotions. He had hoped to deal the Ashi a heavy blow before they reached the portal. But it seemed as if every second that ticked by, he was losing. After all they had been through and all they had done to protect humanity, the enemy was still going to beat them back home to the Sol system. There was no telling what they would do there.

"Just keep going," Darius said. "We have no choice but to give chase."

"Even if that's exactly what the enemy wants us to do?" Pete Best said.

"What choice do we have? The SDF is woefully unprepared for what is coming."

"It won't do them any good if we run straight into an ambush either," Pete Best argued.

"We'll have to weather that storm," Darius said, turning to Remmy. "Master Sergeant, what are the odds the enemy will have ships waiting for us behind Libertine."

"If they're smart, there's no question about it," Remmy replied.

"They'll be in close," Darius said. "And if we survive the initial onslaught, they'll follow behind us and finish us off."

Fury rose up inside Darius. He had been outwitted, it seemed. It was like playing a game of chess and not realizing the trap you were blundering into until it was too late and your opponent captured your queen. Only it wasn't a game. Not only were the thirty or so crew members still on the *Renegade* in danger, the entire human race was at risk. As well as perhaps trillions of innocent people across the galaxy, too. The Ashi would take the technology from the Arodoni ship and use it to crush every rebellion. The Imperium would only get worse and everything they had fought and sacrificed for would be lost.

Darius was the Captain and with that responsibility came the heavy weight of making difficult choices. Tears welled up in his eyes as he made his decision ... and there was no doubt in his mind how his friend would respond. Master Sergeant Remmy Steel was the epitome of what it meant to be a warrior. Darius' voice shook as he made his request.

"Master Sergeant, is Lieutenant Colt's MECH still operational?"

Remmy didn't hesitate for one split second. His response was not only incredibly brave but it saved Darius from having to ask him to make the ultimate sacrifice.

"Yes, sir, it's operational and ready for action, sir," Remmy said, standing up and looking every inch like a hero. "Let me take it out, Captain. Odds are the Ashi will only leave a few ships in the planet's wake. I can take them down with missiles."

Darius had to turn away from his friend. The tears could not be contained.

It was Pete Best who spoke up. "That's a suicide mission," Pete said. "Even if you aren't killed by the Ashi, we won't be able to pick you back up. Not even with the gravity beam generator. You'll be abandoned in space."

"Understood, Lieutenant. But it's the best way to ensure the survival of the *Renegade*. It would be my honor to carry out that mission."

"Even if you have little chance of success?" Alex Stanislaus said.

"It's the only chance of success we have," Darius said, wiping the tears from his eyes. He forced himself to turn around and face his friend. "I'm sorry to ask."

"You didn't ask, sir," Remmy said. "I volunteered."

"If there were any other way..."

"Every Marine dreams of a moment like this, sir. It's a privilege ... and I'm honored to have served with you, Captain Darius. And the entire crew, as well," Remmy said, looking around the Bridge at the other officers. "You have shown me more consideration than I deserve, Captain. My only regret is that I won't be here to watch you crush the rest of the Ashi fleet."

"You have our respect and our gratitude. Your sacrifice will not be forgotten, Master Sergeant."

Darius stiffened into a salute. And one by one the other officers did as well, standing up from their stations and saluting Remmy Steel. Even Nurek stood and bowed in a show of respect. Then Darius extended a hand.

"I wish there was another way," he said softly.

"Don't," Remmy said. "Stay focused on what you've got to do. I'm at peace with this mission, sir. And I'm honored to have been on this cruise with you."

He turned and walked boldly from the Bridge. Darius collapsed into his chair. There were more tears, but he let them fall while he focused on their mission.

"I want full power to the shields," Darius said. "We still have to survive the initial barrage."

"I can double the shielding on the starboard side of the ship, Captain," Pete Best said. "That should protect us, although if the barrage is strong enough, it could overwhelm the sonic generators."

"Do it," Darius said. "Let's get a crew to those generators as well. Ensign Stanislaus, is it possible to alert the automated maintenance system of the danger to the shield generators?"

"Aye, Captain," Alex said. He had to wipe a tear from his own eye as he answered and Darius understood the emotion. Remmy's selfless sacrifice brought the reality home to everyone. They were probably going to die trying to save their home and, of course, none of them would hesitate to do it ... but facing that reality was difficult.

"Let's make that happen," Darius said. "We're only going to get one shot at this, people. The Ashi fleet will beat us to that portal. The only question is how many of their ships will make it through. And no matter what, we have to follow them. We have to bring the *Renegade's* weapons to the Sol system and save our people."

CHAPTER 30

REMMY KNEW what was waiting for him. He hadn't lied when he said that Lieutenant Colt's MECH was ready. Having been constructed on the *Renegade*, the advanced alien ship's maintenance system looked after the advanced armor suit. If it had been up to Remmy, he would have jettisoned the MECH, but now he was glad it hadn't been his decision. The reality of their situation had been pressed home to him on the Bridge. The *Renegade* was about to be caught between two opposing enemy forces. They would catch the ship in a crossfire that no one could stop. And if the *Renegade* didn't reach the Sol system, billions of people would be killed or enslaved. It wasn't hard to make the decision to sacrifice himself. If it would save the entire human race it was the obvious choice.

The walk down from the Bridge to the armory was bittersweet. The *Renegade* felt more like a home than any Remmy had known since childhood. Seeing it for the last time was emotional. He loved the clean, smooth lines. The wide open spaces were a luxury he had not thought possible in a spacecraft. And when he reached the park, he stopped just long enough to breathe in the sweet scent of blossoming flowers, rich earth, and oxygen-rich air.

He tapped the comlink that was in his ear. It opened a channel straight to Captain Darius' seat on the Bridge.

"Sir, how much time do we have before we pass Libertine?"

"Less than an hour, Master Sergeant," Darius said. "Can you be on the hull when we come out of the planet's lee?"

"Yes, sir. I'll be ready."

"Very good," Darius said. "Keep your comlink open, and we'll keep you informed of everything we see and know. Good luck, Master Sergeant."

"Thank you, Captain," Remmy said.

He had reached the gravity lift. He couldn't believe he was seeing the park for the last time. But he pushed those thoughts away and stepped out into the shaft. Drifting down was easy; facing what he knew was waiting for him at the bottom was not.

It was a short walk from the gravity shaft to the armory, which had been set up in a room just outside the empty hangar that the Marines had converted into a training facility complete with a live gun range. Remmy was proud of all they had accomplished, both on the ship and during their mission. He also understood that if the *Renegade* didn't make it to the Sol system and stop the Ashi fleet, it would all have been for nothing.

He stepped into the armory and found the Marines waiting for him. Tex and Izzy were still recovering from their wounds and were sitting. Hugo and Rip were near the lockers, working on their gear and weapons. It probably wasn't needed, yet it was what Space Marines often did during the long, boring assignments between combat operations.

In the middle of the big room, between the crates of weapons and ammunition, Staff Sergeant Laila McPherson was pacing. She stopped when Remmy appeared and looked up at him. There was hope on her face. The rest of the Marines didn't know what Remmy knew. They had been waiting for word and Remmy was going to bring it. The look she gave him was both relief and anticipation. There was an emotional undercurrent, too. She really did love him, maybe as much as he loved her. Which only made what he had to do harder.

"What's the word, Master Sergeant?" Hugo asked.

"The Ashi fleet made their move," Remmy said.

"What are they doing?" Izzy asked.

"They're following the *Indy*," Remmy explained. "Somehow, they know about her and they're headed straight for the portal."

"You mean they're going to follow the *Independence* back home?" Laila asked.

Remmy nodded. "We're following. The Captain has plans to hit them hard, but we can't stop them all."

"They'll slaughter the SDF," Hugo said. "Our vessels back home can't keep up with their ships."

"That's why we're going to follow them through," Remmy said. "At least, you are."

"What?" Laila said.

Remmy knew the best thing to do was to simply tell them what was happening. They wouldn't like it. Laila would argue, but there was no other way. Remmy would just have to make her see that. "We've turned about, and we're going after them now."

"Weapons hot, I presume," Hugo said.

"That's the plan," Remmy said. "But Libertine is blocking them. We have to wait until the planet is out of the way. We'll be passing it very soon, within the hour."

"That's good," Laila said. "The more time we have to blast them, the better."

"Agreed," Remmy said.

"But there's somethin' you ain't telling us, Master Sergeant," Tex said. "I'm guessing the Ashi left a surprise for us behind the planet."

The realization of what Tex said hit Laila like a physical blow. Her entire face changed.

"We have to change our plan," she said.

"Can't," Remmy told her. "The fleet's going to beat us to the portal. We have to get there as soon as possible."

"We won't get there at all if we're hit from behind," Hugo said. "That's the one real weakness to this ship. There are no guns to defend us from enemies that attack from the rear."

"Which is why I'm going to mount up in the LT's MECH armor and stop those ships," Remmy said.

There was a moment of silence as the Marines processed what Remmy was saying.

"From the hull of the ship?" Laila asked.

"From space," Remmy said. "I'll launch out and use the MECH's weapons to stop any ship that tries to follow the *Renegade*."

"Okay, but how do you get back on board?" Laila asked.

"I don't," Remmy said. "It's a one-way ticket this time."

"No!" She demanded.

"Let me go, Staff Sergeant," Tex volunteered.

"You're in no condition for this op," Remmy said. "It's my call, my responsibility. I volunteered."

"Why?" Laila asked.

"So you wouldn't," Remmy said with a grin. "I'm not going to ask someone to do something I'm not willing to do."

"You're our CO," Rip said. "We can't afford to lose you, Master Sergeant."

"We get back in the Sol system and neutralize the Ashi threat and you'll all have some serious time off," Remmy said. "There's nothing left to do here but help out in any way we can."

"Isn't there another way?" Izzy asked. "Some sort of ship gymnastics or something?"

"Captain Darius can't afford to slow down," Remmy explained. "We're going to slingshot around the planet and keep the engines burning."

"So, your plan is to take out the enemy ships, and then what? You're just going to drift around until you run out of air?"

"If I'm lucky enough to live that long," Remmy said. "Staff Sergeant McPherson is now in charge. It's been the honor of my career to serve with this platoon."

"Godspeed, Master Sergeant," Rip said.

"Wish there was some other way," Tex said. "But the honor's been ours."

Izzy was crying unashamedly. "It's a damn shame you won't be with us when we return home."

"I'm good with it," Remmy said. "I'm at peace."

Laila left the armory without saying another word. Remmy knew he was hurting her, but he also knew she, above all others, understood. In fact, he was making the sacrifice for her.

"There isn't much left in my gear," Remmy said. "Staff Sergeant McPherson will know what to do with it."

He could have stayed a little longer. He could have given hugs and told each member of the platoon that remained what he thought of them, but he knew his time was running out and Laila was waiting for him.

The platoon members all saluted and Remmy returned the gesture. His heart rate was speeding up and his mouth was dry. There was a sting in the back of his throat and tears were threatening to well up in his eyes. That was the Master Sergeant's cue that it was time to go.

He had never shied away from a fight. In every combat engagement, he had done his duty, often going above and beyond to achieve the mission objectives. Fear had never played a role in his decision-making, although it was always there. He feared death in the way that a person fears something he can't quite wrap his mind around. There were times in his life when he was so tired or hurt so badly that he would have welcomed death. To just close his eyes and float away seemed like a good idea in those times. Yet he had never had anything worth fighting for, or maybe worth living for was a better way to put it. When he saw Laila waiting for him in the hallway, his resolve almost broke.

"Has it occurred to the grand captain that maybe this isn't the best plan?" Laila said as Remmy approached. "If we chase after the Ashi and get the *Renegade* destroyed, the entire galaxy will be at risk. Everything we've done could be for nothing."

"He's a good man," Remmy said.

"Good men make mistakes," she argued.

"Humanity is at risk," Remmy pointed out.

"All the more reason to make sure we live," Laila said. "We might be the last humans in the galaxy. By the time we get to the sol system, the entire place could be wiped out. Have you considered that?"

"Yes," Remmy said. "And just like you, if this is the end, I want to go down fighting."

"Then I'm coming with you?"

"Can't," Remmy said. "There's no room in the MECH for two people."

"I'll go in my space armor."

"You'd desert your post, Staff Sergeant."

"Don't," she said, breaking down. She was a strong woman, but they were both on the verge of collapse at the thought of never seeing one another again. "It's not fair. You made the choice without even consulting me."

"Had to," Remmy said. "The Captain had to make the call. I couldn't let him live with that. I had to volunteer. I knew I would do it eventually anyway. I sure as hell wasn't going to ask someone else to do it. Besides, we both know I'm the best man for this job. And it's too important to mess around and screw up."

"Then let me go," she said. "I don't think I can live while you die, Remmy."

He ignored his own tears and wiped hers away. "I know I can't live without you," he told her. "Besides, it's protocol for this sort of thing to fall to me."

She hugged him, and he held her. His heart was pounding, and his mouth felt like a desert. Worst still, his knees felt like they might not hold him up much longer.

"I better get ready," he said softly. "Would you help me gear up, Laila?"

"Yes," she said in a throaty whisper.

They turned, walking together. She leaned close and wrapped her arm around his waist. He held her close with an arm around her shoulders and together, they helped one another make the most difficult walk of their lives.

CHAPTER 31

REMMY AND LAILA stepped through the big doors that led to the hanger bay. It was a massive open space. The Marines used it for all sorts of training exercises, and general PT as well. There was a shooting range at one end and mats for sparring at the other. In the middle, Remmy kept all the larger gear that might be needed for a mission. Their space armor and weapons were kept in the armory. The hangar had large crates with shoulder-operated missile launchers and the big guns that had to be mounted on tripods or vehicles to operate, along with dozens of pallets of ammunition.

It was also where Lieutenant Micky Colt had set up the charging station for the MECH he had designed. It was really a combination of his ideas and the *Renegade's* computer. Remmy had never liked Mechanized Combat Suits. They were incredibly destructive and the researchers on Earth had never really worked out all the bugs in their designs. Good Marines had died trying to use them. But the Lieutenant's suit was different. It was a big battle suit, that much was the same, with heavy armor and lots of weapons. But it was also agile and operational. Most of the platoon had taken the armor for a spin in the hangar. Even Remmy had tried it once and been impressed, as it was the most viable attempt at larger-than-life combat armor he had ever seen.

"Where is the MECH?" Laila asked.

The charging cables hung limp, trailing on the deck. And several of the crates next to it were open.

"It should be right here," Remmy said. "I checked on that myself just a day or two ago."

"The drones brought it in and rearmed it," Laila said. "They would never leave things a mess like this."

Suddenly, the light above the airlock turned red. They could hear the big outer door opening. Remmy thought back to the armory. The entire platoon had been there. But not at the end, he realized. Everyone said something to him except for Hugo McManus. Remmy and Laila ran toward the airlock and Remmy activated his comlink.

"Sergeant McManus! What do you think you're doing?"

The reply was classic Hugo. "One last act of insubordination, Master Sergeant. Don't seem so surprised."

"Shut that airlock down and get back in here."

"Can't," Hugo said. "You'll make me stay with the ship and I'm not doing that. Besides, we both know I'm the best man for the job."

Remmy looked at Laila, who just smirked. There was no end to Hugo's ego when it came to combat. Only Remmy knew that McManus usually backed up what he claimed himself capable of doing.

"Return to the hanger, Sergeant McManus. That's an order," Remmy snapped.

"Hence the insubordination," Hugo said with a chuckle.

There was a small, narrow window in the airlock door. Remmy and Laila were looking through it as the big outer door opened wide, revealing the glow of Libertine beyond. Then Hugo turned around. He had a shoulder-fired rocket launcher in each of the massive MECH hands. He bent down so that he could see them through the transparent chest armor.

"I don't mean any disrespect to either one of you," Hugo said.

"In fact, this is the only platoon I've ever felt truly part of. You're the only NCOs who had the strength to knock me down and the integrity to pick me up again. You know I've never fit anywhere, Master Sergeant. But you made me believe that I was a valued part of your team."

"That's because you are," Laila told him.

"And that's why I'm doing this," Hugo said. "I'm part of this platoon. But the two of you are the leaders. Besides, you know how I feel, Remmy. There's nothing for me back in the Sol system."

"I don't think that's true," Remmy told him. "Don't sell yourself short, Sergeant."

"I told you I wanted to say here. This is my chance. If I'm lucky, I'll be a permanent part of the Libertine system."

Remmy wanted to argue, but it was too late to change Hugo's mind. That was just who he was. The man ran toward danger. And no amount of logic, tradition, or military protocol would ever stop him. Most people thought it was a false sense of bravado or an addiction to adrenaline, but Remmy knew that Hugo just wanted to make a difference. He had been unwanted and unwelcome all his life. The things that most people took for granted, like making friends, were hard for the Marine. He knew he wasn't a mistake, but he needed to prove it to the world.

"Thank you for your service, Sergeant," Laila said as she placed a hand on the window. "It will not be forgotten."

"Hugo," Remmy said, his voice cracking with emotion. "I'm sorry."

"Don't be," he replied. "I'm not. Thank you for everything, Master Sergeant. This is Hugo McManus, signing off."

"Wait," Remmy said. "Stay on the hull until I give you the signal from Captain Darius."

"Roger that," Hugo replied.

Remmy turned to Laila. "Suit up. We might be able to help him."

"Roger that," she said. Together they ran back across the hanger.

On the Bridge, Captain Zeke Darius was watching the edge of the planet. They were almost past it and no alien ships could be seen yet. But they didn't have to be. The *Renegade* was racing past Libertine and would soon be lined up for its own attack on the Ashi fleet.

"Master Sergeant, are we ready?"

"Slight change of plans, but we're ready," Remmy said. "Sergeant McManus took the MECH before I could. He's already on the hull and waiting for your order."

Darius breathed a sigh of relief. He shouldn't have been happy to hear that a member of the Marine platoon disobeyed orders. Maybe McManus wasn't as good in space combat as Remmy but it didn't matter anymore. It was time to prepare for the inevitable.

"Order him to launch," Darius said. "Have him prepared to fire on any enemy ships that fall in behind us."

"Yes, sir!" Remmy replied.

"Contact," Nurek said.

Darius saw the ships on his screen. There were six of them, four battleships, two of the smaller, but faster, corvettes."

"Master Sergeant?"

"He's gone, sir," Remmy replied.

"Very good. Lieutenant Best, raise our shields."

"Aye, Captain, raising sonic shields now."

"Do we have good targets ahead?"

"Affirmative, Captain," Pete Best replied. "Just say the word."

"Fire," Darius said.

"Fox one!"

There was a flash of light. The Ashi fleet was far enough ahead that it would take the laser several seconds to reach the nearest ship.

"Let's continue evasive maneuvers," Darius said. "I want to shift course a full ship's length every five to ten seconds."

"Aye, Captain," Ensign Stanislaus said. "Beginning evasive maneuvers."

"Fox two!" Pete shouted, firing the second big cannon before the first laser blast had even reached its target. "Fox three!"

There was almost no lag between when the Ashi ships trailing them fired and the impact on the ship's sonic lasers. Two of the battleships had fired at the same time, their laser beams flashing, and then a siren erupted on the *Renegade's* Bridge.

"That was a hit," Pete Best said, referring to the ships behind them, not the ones he had targeted. "Shields are holding, but down to thirty percent power. It'll take time to recharge them. I'll have to divert power away from the cannons."

"No," Darius said. "That's what Sergeant McManus is there for. Let him do the fighting behind us."

It was difficult to keep his focus forward, but he knew he had to. There were fifty-seven ships on the plot racing for the portal to Earth. If he didn't stop as many as possible, humanity didn't stand a chance.

Inside the MECH suit, everything was peaceful. There were no warning alarms, no outside noise, just the sound of Hugo McManas breathing quietly. The suit was very easy to control and powerful, too. Hugo had leaped from the *Renegade's* hull and was drifting away from the big ship. With no drag to slow him down, he was simultaneously moving in the same direction as the *Renegade* and also away from her. The ship was continuing its engine burn which made it feel like to Hugo that he was standing still and they were slowly pulling away from him.

He had just used his thrusters to turn himself in the MECH suit so that he was facing the approaching ships. They weren't directly ahead of him but slightly to the side. His tactical app gave him their distance on his HUD. The enemy ships were at forty thousand kilometers and closing fast. With the MECH's size and power, Hugo handled the big missile launchers that normally required both of a person's hands and their shoulder to operate as if they were big pistols. He aimed at the lead ship and fired one missile. Then, he targeted the smaller craft slightly behind the lead ship.

Almost as soon as he fired the missiles, two of the battleships fired laser blasts at the *Renegade*. It would have taken him too long to turn and see what had happened. Instead, trusting that the big Arodoni ship could take a few shots, he leaned forward. The MECH armor had a variety of weapons, but most were too small to make a difference to the Ashi battleships. But inside the armored suit's back were four larger cruise missiles that were even larger than the shoulder-mounted rockets he had already fired. He activated the missile control and sent the first missile toward its target.

CHAPTER 32

REMMY REACHED the armory and sprinted for his locker.

"What's happening?" Izzy called out as she slowly stood up from her chair.

"Hugo took the MECH suit," Laila called out.

Remmy thought he heard a note of triumph in her voice. He secretly felt the same way but also felt guilty that Hugo had sacrificed himself to save Remmy and the rest of the crew.

"So, what are you doing?"

"We can help," Remmy said. "We're suiting up and getting some missiles."

"We'll help with the reloads," Tex said.

Remmy knew they were moving too slowly. But he didn't deny them the chance to help. He and Laila were in their space armor and running back to the hangar by the time the other two Marines reached their lockers.

"Grab a missile launcher," Remmy said. "We should be able to get two reloads onto our armor with magnetic attachments."

"Roger that," Laila said.

The crates were already open. The missile launchers were heavy tubes. Remmy snatched one up then turned to the missile crates. He stuffed one into the back of the launcher and closed the rear cover. Then he picked up another missile and pressed it onto his chest. There was a slight buzz, and it snapped to the armor plating. A second went onto his stomach. Beside him, Laila had done the same thing. It was impressive to watch her heft the rocket launcher. It wasn't too heavy for a person to lift, but it wasn't light either. She lifted it and settled it onto her shoulder with no problems.

"Let's go!" She said.

Remmy ran for the airlock lever. He hit the large button and stood back, balancing the heavy tube on his right shoulder. The bulky weapons required space. Laila was a dozen paces away, watching him. He couldn't see her face, just the armor. But he imagined the look on her face, part excitement, part adoration. That was how he felt about her.

They ducked under the door and hit the cycle controls. A minute later, they were on the hull. Their boots magnetically attached to the hull. They were standing on the bottom side of the ship, their heads away from the hull and pointing straight down, but to them, it seemed the opposite.

"Captain, Staff Sergeant McPherson and I are suited up with rockets on the hull, sir. What are your orders?" Remmy asked.

"Stand by, Master Sergeant. I'm sending you targeting data now," Darius replied.

Remmy could see the ships in the distance. The light from the sun glinted off their hull, and as he watched, two explosions hit from Hugo's rockets. One smashed into the side of a battleship. It did some damage but didn't slow the ship's progress at all. The second hit the tail end of one of the smaller ships. Fire erupted from the impact, and a section of the engine tore off. That ship began a slow, tumbling spin as fire billowed from the back of the vessel.

"Great shot, Hugo," Remmy said.

"Cruise missiles should have better luck. I'm targeting the four battleships."

"Captain, Hugo has cruise missiles locked on the battleships," Remmy reported.

"Very good. See if you can disable the other corvette."

"Roger that," Remmy said. "Take down that smaller ship, Laila."

They both fired almost simultaneously. Their rockets streaked across space and were quickly lost in the distance. All Remmy could do was hope their shots found the mark. It helped that the enemy ships weren't moving erratically. They were cruising straight ahead. None were traveling as fast as the *Renegade,* which meant the distance between them was growing with every second.

Remmy swung his missile launcher toward his feet. It was easier to maneuver outside the ship's artificial gravity. He unfastened the rear latch and pulled one of the missiles from his armor when their shots impacted the corvette in the distance. Two holes blasted into the side of the ship. Gas and debris began to spew out, and it drifted off course.

"That's a hit," Remmy said.

"And a kill," Laila added.

At that moment, a flash of light streaked from one of the battleships. The laser hit the *Renegade's* shields and set off a dazzling display of electrical energy. A four-shot followed quickly after, just as the Arodoni ship was using its lasers to shift sideways. There was no blaze of light from the shields. Remmy didn't know it, but the shields were down. The laser blast hit the side of the ship, skimming along the hull. The thick armor held strong, but the energy release made the hull buck.

Laila was beside Remmy one moment, and the next she was sent flying from the ship. Neither of them had on their EVA thruster packs. And they had been in such a hurry to help in the attack neither of them had attached their emergency tethers. How Laila had been thrown while Remmy's magnetic boots held fast, he didn't know. But he dropped the missile launcher, which floated away into space, bent down, snapped his extendable cable to a grommet on the hull, and jumped after Laila.

She was already out of reach, but as the cable spooled out, he was gaining.

"Laila!" He shouted.

Everything was happening fast. She turned and reached for him, but it was no use. She was too far away and he was almost to the end of the cable. Thinking fast, she pulled her pistol. It was an old-fashioned Bucker Nine. She held it behind her pull the trigger several times. The shots flew out harmlessly into space, but the concussion from the compressed gas ammunition pushed her slightly back toward Remmy. Their hands touched, and he grabbed hold tight just as he reached the end of his line.

"Got you!" He shouted. "I got you."

"You got me," she said, her voice trembling with relief. "I thought I was going to be joining Hugo."

"Not today," Remmy said. He pulled her close and used the controls in his helmet to retract the line.

When their feet touched the hull and magnetically clamped down, they moved into the airlock. Remmy realized his heart was pounding hard in his chest and his entire body was covered in sweat. He had never, in all his life, even during combat, ever been so scared before.

"Quick thinking," Laila said. "I don't think I've ever seen you move that fast."

"It wouldn't have worked without you shooing your pistol," Remmy said.

"I almost didn't bring it," she said. "Thank God I did."

"What happened to your magnetic boots?"

"I was just taking a step when the laser hit the ship," she said.

"That was too close," Remmy said.

"Tell me about it."

The inner door opened, and they hurried inside. Tex and Izzy were there, still moving slowly. The thick space armor couldn't hide the pain they were both still in from their wounds.

"Everything okay?" Tex asked.

"Don't know," Remmy said. "We took out two of the smaller ships."

"Well, we got one, Hugo got one," Laila corrected him.

"The other four are still shooting at us."

"Where's Rip?" Laila asked.

"Haven't seen him," Izzy said. "Not since you guys went sprinting for the missiles."

"What do we do now?" Tex asked.

"Load us up again," Remmy said. "This isn't over."

Outside the *Renegade*, Hugo was still drifting. But he was behind the battleships. His cruise missiles had taken one of them down, blowing a hole in the ship that compromised the hull. The other had hit but did minimal damage to the thick armor. He realized too late he should have saved the big missiles. The rear of the Ashi battleships had less armor.

With a verbal command, flaps popped up on his shoulders, and six mini-rockets shot out of either side. Six raced toward one of the battleships and six toward another. They ran out of propellent before they reached their targets, but in space, with nothing to slow them down, they continued flying. Unfortunately, the exhaust from the engines set them off before they could impact the ship.

Hugo activated the MECH's propulsion system. It was small compared to the Ashi ships' engines, but he was much smaller, with less mass. He went racing toward the enemy vessels. Activating his built-in machine guns, he fired at the closest ship. The bullets were depleted uranium-tipped bullets made to punch through hardened steel armor. They ripped through the rear exhaust cones and tore into the delicate engineering components. The ship didn't alter course, but the fire from its engine died, and the running lights on the hull went dark. That left three battleships that were still a threat to the *Renegade*.

The MECH suit had several weapons systems that were no help at all in a space battle. He used his flame thrower to help maneuver himself around. He was close to the ships by that point and fired several magnetic explosives from his left forearm. They clamped onto a second battleship just above the rear exhaust cones. He then used the last of the flame thrower's fuel to send him away from the ships. The explosives went off in a staggered series of blasts that not only knocked out the ship's power but sent it swinging over toward another ship.

Had he been a naval strategist, he would have realized right away that two of the Ashi ships were flying too closely together. But Hugo had no idea about things like that. He was just a man of mayhem. He did as much damage as his MECH suit would allow. The two ships collided. Had there been sound in space, he would have heard the metal plates buckling. They were both knocked off course, and their hulls were compromised. Hard vacuum did the rest. It was as if a hole had opened in the stomach of two great beasts, and their innards were ripped out by the dynamic cosmic forces at play.

That left one enemy ship. It was far ahead of Hugo. His thrusters fired but it wasn't enough propulsion to catch up to the ship. And he was out of weapons anyway. His plan had been to latch onto the ship and overload the power supply in the MECH's battery. It would have killed him, and he had no idea if it would have damaged the alien battleship, but it was all he had left to offer.

He watched in horror as the last ship moved out of his range.

"Need a little help there, Sarge?" Rip's voice was loud inside the MECH.

"Van Winkle?" Hugo asked.

"At your service, boss. Can you get inside?"

A shuttle flew right in front of Hugo. He hadn't seen it leave the *Renegade* and had no idea who had thought to send him aid, but he was grateful. The rear hatch was wide open. Hugo used his jet pack to maneuver inside. The moment he got into the ship, he saw the cruise missile resupply crate.

"I'm in," Hugo said.

"Outstanding. I don't think we can catch the bad guys, but we can give it a shot. You find my goodies?"

"Already loading them up," Hugo said as he carefully inserted four more rockets into the launcher on his back.

He had to bend down and slide them in carefully, making sure each one snapped into the proper place so that it would launch and not merely explode on his back and kill him.

"Since when do you fly spaceships?" Hugo asked.

"Never have before," Rip said. "But I fly all kinds of ship simulators. Have since I was a kid. After all that practice, the real thing don't seem hard at all."

"Can you turn us around?" Hugo asked.

They spun around. The shuttle was still racing in the same direction; only it was traveling in reverse. From the open rear compartment, Hugo could see the Ashi ships. The last remaining battleship was almost beyond his range. Two small missiles hit the side. They ripped gashes in the vessel but didn't stop it.

"Here goes nothing," Hugo muttered.

He leaned forward and fired all four rockets. They raced ahead, streaking through space past the disabled ships. Hugo looked up, barely breathing as he watched. The one missile malfunctioned. It sputtered and then swung to the side. A second missile hit the malfunctioning missile, and both exploded. The shock wave detonated a third, leaving only one left.

"Come on, come on!" Hugo said, willing the missile to find its target.

It flew straight into the exhaust and exploded before impacting the ship. But the blast wave knocked out the ship's main drive.

"Is it down?" Rip asked.

"No, just a temporary setback," Hugo said. "I didn't even manage to slow it down."

"That won't matter much longer," Rip said. "The *Renegade* is really moving."

Hugo looked up and realized his friend was right. In fact, there was no way they could catch up with their space ship. Two more missiles went streaking toward the Ashi battleship. One exploded harmlessly against the thick armor, but the other hit a spiny sensor array on the upper section of the vessel. It exploded in a quick flash and sent the fragments of the equipment flying from the ship.

"Not bad, Master Sergeant," Hugo said.

The last of the alien ships began a thruster turn.

"She's backing down," Rip shouted.

"That's good news for the *Renegade*," Hugo said. "But we can't reach her, Rip. I'm so sorry."

"Hey, I knew what I was in for. This was always gonna be a one-way trip. But I couldn't just let you die out there in space."

"What do you mean?"

"We can't catch up to the *Renegade* but that don't mean we can't land this bird."

"Are you serious?"

"Serious enough to give it a try. What have we got to lose?"

"Absolutely nothing," Hugo chuckled. "Go for it."

"Better close up the back gate," Rip said. "And maybe hang onto something."

Hugo hit the control switch to close the rear hatch. His oversized frame didn't fit into the jumps seats on either side of the passenger cabin. Instead, Hugo sat on the floor by the box of cruise missiles.

"Boss, can your fancy suit sync up to the shuttle's exterior cameras?" Rip asked.

"Yeah, why?"

"You need to see what's happening," Rip said.

Hugo did as instructed and once the video feed from the rear camera appeared on his Heads-Up Display, he knew why. There were hundreds of escape pods launching from the damaged Ashi ships. They were all out of the fight, but they hadn't been destroyed.

"That big battleship is looping around, too," Rip said. "You think it's coming after us?"

"I don't know," Hugo said. "But maybe don't fly in a straight line if you can manage it."

"Evasive maneuvers," he said with a chuckle. "You got it, Boss."

"Why do you keep calling me that?" Hugo asked.

"Cause you are the top dog now," Rip replied. "We're about to hit Libertine's atmosphere. It's going to get bumpy."

"Got it," Hugo said, locking the MECH's wide arms against the sides of the compartment.

On the HUD, he could see that they weren't the only vessels looking to land on Libertine. The escape pods were streaking toward the planet like little comets. Only Hugo knew that each one was loaded with angry Ashi warriors. They weren't flying to safety. They were dropping into the middle of a war and they were badly outnumbered.

CHAPTER 33

"THEY DID IT," Darius said as he looked at the plot.

The last Ashi battleship behind them was turning away. The danger behind them was gone and that left only the danger in front.

"Captain, I show fifty-seven Ashi ships ahead of us," Nurek said in a calm, even voice. "Some are beginning to turn and slow."

"They've come about to target us with their main lasers," Pete Best said.

"How are we looking on power?" the Captain asked.

"Not bad," Alex Stanislaus replied. "Weapons are fully charged. I'm bringing the sonic shielding back around. It's at twenty-two percent and climbing."

"Angle the shields to protect us from their fire," Darius said, thinking of the laser blast that had glanced off the *Renegade's* hull. Things could have been much worse. The laser hadn't hit anything vital and the hull was designed to absorb the energy displaced by the blast. The *Renegade* actually had three hulls, the inner portion that the passengers saw and came into contact with. A spongy, honeycomb middle section that Lieutenant Henry Nash had guessed was incredibly strong. It had held up under direct laser fire that destroyed one of the ship's massive cannons. The outer hull was made up of heat-absorbing plates. Hundreds of those plates had been scorched by the laser that glanced along the side of the ship. They would all need to be replaced once the battle was over, but for the time being, no serious damage had been done.

"Aye, Captain, angling the sonic shields on a vertical angle at one hundred and thirty degrees," Best said.

"Let's get ready to fire on the fleet," Darius ordered. "What's their distance."

"The rearmost ships are still nine hundred thousand kilometers ahead of us," Nurek said. "The lead ships are one point four million kilometers ahead."

"How close are they to the portal?"

"They will begin passing into hyperspace in eighteen minutes."

"We can't destroy that many ships in eighteen minutes," Best said. "Even our power core can't recharge fast enough. They're using the big refueling vessels to block some of the others."

"The best we can hope for is to thin their numbers," Darius said. "Fire away, Lieutenant."

"Fox one," Pete Best called out.

Shooting the laser cannons wasn't as easy as firing a gun. The shield had to be lowered, and the huge cannons took nearly three seconds to release the stored energy. Fortunately, the ship's computer controlled the switch between the shields and the lasers so that the ship was never without protection for more than about half a second.

At nine hundred thousand kilometers, it took the laser blast three seconds to reach the target, and the information needed an additional three seconds to come back to the *Renegade*. But as Darius watched, one of the huge refueling ships vanished.

"Can we target the most dangerous vessels?" Darius asked.

"Not yet," Best replied. "They're using the big ships to hide their destroyers from our laser fire."

"Keep hitting them," Darius said.

"Fox two!"

Best didn't get into a hurry. He was firing manually, which

meant a larger margin of error in a real fight, but the refueling ships were fat and slow. As long as he didn't get in too big a hurry, he could knock them out. It took each laser between thirty and forty seconds to fully recharge. They could fire faster at half-strength, but the enemy ships were so far away that there was no guarantee of total destruction. It wouldn't do the *Renegade* any good to disable the Ashi ships. They needed them out of the way so that their lasers could reach the fighting portion of the enemy fleet.

"Whoever is in charge of the Ashi fleet is damn smart," Darius said.

"That would be Sheika Kahn. He is a political mastermind. I believe he has been waiting for an opportunity to depose and replace Emperor Vang for some time," Nurek said. "He is not a warrior, but we must not underestimate his ruthlessness."

"He may not be a warrior, but he's utilizing his forces very well," Darius said. "Looks like the dreadnoughts are leading the way."

"They're not the fastest ships in the fleet," Alex pointed out. "Why put them first?"

"Because they're the most valuable assets to the enemy commander," Darius said. "The dreadnoughts have long-range lasers. Once they're in our home system, they can take out any resistance before the SDF can mount a counterattack."

"Kind of like we've been doing," Best said.

"Only there are eight of those dreadnoughts," Darius said. "If they start shooting, thousands of people will be killed."

"Captain, the Ashi fleet is slowing down," Nurek said. "Not all of them, but a third of their fighting force."

"There are twenty-eight battleships and eight of the smaller attack craft," Darius said. "Eight more dreadnoughts. That's forty-four warships."

"Twelve of the battleship class vessels are in full retro-burn," Alex said.

"Six more refueling vessels between them and us," Pete said. "Laser cannons are at seventy percent power."

"They need to close the distance to fire on us," Darius said. "How long will it take them?"

"Unknown," Nurek said. "All twelve are showing a higher energy rating than I've ever seen. Granted, I am not a warrior. But I did check the *Renegade's* computer specifications for the Ashi battleship. I believe they are exceeding safe operating procedures for their engine systems."

"And we're racing straight for them," Best said. "All they need to do is stop, and we'll be in their range before we know it."

"But we can't afford to stop or even slow down. Every second the Ashi dreadnoughts are in the Sol system ahead of us, they could be killing thousands of people."

"What should we do?" Alex asked.

"Keep firing," Darius replied. "And hope our shields hold up."

CHAPTER 34

SHEIKA KAHN'S fleet was down to just a tiny fraction of what he had started with. Conventional wisdom would be to fall back, regroup and go after the alien ship again with greater strength. But he had taken a calculated risk, and if the behavior of the Arodoni ship was any indication, it was paying off.

"We just lost another refueling vessel," the shipmaster called out. "Only five remain."

"They do not matter," Sheika Kahn snapped. "Their supplies have been used up. What of our battle group?"

"They are following your command, Lord Kahn. The retro-burn at full engine capacity is slowing them down rapidly. They will pass by the... We have lost another refueling vessel."

"That is no surprise. What is the distance between the alien ship and our battle craft?"

"Eight hundred thousand kilometers and closing," the shipmaster said. "They will be in the alien's range long before they are in ours."

"It doesn't matter," Sheika Kahn said.

"Lord, I hate to argue, but we've lost over half the fleet trying to destroy a single alien ship!"

"It is true," Sheika Kahn remarked coldly. "We have not seen an enemy of this caliber in a hundred generations. But nothing must stop us in the pursuit of our goal. That ship represents the future, surely you can see that. It doesn't matter how many ships we lose or how many warriors die, Shipmaster. Their sacrifice is for the future of the Ashi. With the technology on that ship, we will not only rule the Imperium but we will own the entire galaxy for ten thousand years. I would not be surprised if that ship contains the secrets to reaching other galaxies. It may be the key to unlocking the entire universe. What could be more glorious than that?"

The shipmaster didn't respond.

"I will tell you the answer... nothing," Sheika Kahn said. "Nothing could be more glorious than that. And I will pay whatever price is required to obtain that future for our people. Now stop whining and give me the report. How close are we to the portal."

"We'll reach it in six minutes, Lord Kahn," the shipmaster said. "We have lost two more refueling vessels. Only two remain to block the Arodoni lasers from our battleships."

"Range between them?"

"Seven hundred thousand and closing."

"I predict that only half will survive long enough to reach the threshold that will allow them to return fire."

"Would it not be better to keep them with the rest of the fleet in that case?" the shipmaster asked.

"It would not," the Kahn said. He despised small minds ... and like many of his people, the ship master knew only one way to fight. For centuries, no army could match them. No fleet could equal that of the mighty Ashi. It had caused the masses to become lazy. Fighting was not so much about strategy as it was about overwhelming force and superior firepower, at least from their point of view. To divide one's forces was akin to weakening it. Sheika Kahn knew better. He understood the dynamics at play in the current battle. It delighted him to see that the enemy ship was playing right into his hands, even if his plan cost the Ashi many ships and thousands of warriors.

"I don't understand, Lord Kahn. Teach me!" the shipmaster cried.

Ulrech Sheika sighed, then said slowly, "Those ships we sacrifice would be taken out no matter what. The alien ship's reach is much greater than our own. By sending those twelve battlecruisers back toward the enemy, we buy our main fleet time and give them a chance to die fighting. Do you see?"

The light of understanding lit the shipmaster's eyes. He was starting to understand.

"So, why not turn the fleet around now and capture or destroy the alien vessel?"

"That might be possible," Sheika Kahn said. "Or we might be destroyed in the process. Never fight an enemy on equal footing. Once we are through the hyperspace portal, our advantages increase significantly."

"How so?"

"Are you so dense that you can not think ahead? Why would the enemy send its people through a hidden portal?"

"To keep them from the fighting?"

"Correct. And where would it send them? To an alien star system? No," Sheika Kahn shook his head. "They will run back to their own kind."

"But won't that mean more ships like the one we have been fighting?"

"Possibly," the Kahn remarked. "If that is the case, we will withdraw. But it will be a victory nonetheless."

"I am sorry, Lord. Your intellect is far greater than my own."

Of that, there was no doubt, Sheika Kahn thought. But he continued to explain himself to the lowly shipmaster. The man might command the Emperor's flagship, but he was no strategist.

"It will be our victory because we will know where the aliens come from. We can bring the entire Ashi military might against them, as we have so many other civilizations throughout history. We have never been stopped. The might of the Ashi is unrivaled in this galaxy. The Arodoni have advanced technology, but we will take it from them … even if we must pry it from their cold, dead fingers."

Of course, there was always the possibility that Sheika Kahn was waking a monster that not even the Ashi could defeat. But he was not afraid and would never act from fear. Instead, he would bring his plans to fruition, capture his enemy, and lead his people into the future as the mighty conquerer. There could be no other outcome.

"We are approaching the hyperspace portal," the shipmaster said. "Thirty seconds until transition."

"Our rear guard fights to clear our path into the future," Sheika Kahn declared. "Full speed ahead!"

CHAPTER 35

REMMY WAS tired after sprinting all the way back to the Bridge. They had stopped the last ship that attacked the *Renegade* from the rear. But Captain Darius could not stop what remained of the enemy fleet from racing through the hyperspace portal and following the *Indy* back to the Sol system.

At the doorway to the Bridge, Remmy stopped and caught his breath. He was still in the bulky space suit, but he had removed his helmet.

"Captain," he said, saluting. "The rear is clear, sir."

"We saw that," Darius replied without looking back. "Good work, Master Sergeant."

"We lost two Marines and one shuttle, Captain. I didn't know that Sergeant McManus would take the MECH suit out before I could mount it, sir. He was followed by Corporal Rip Van Winkle."

"We'll worry about all that later," Darius said. "Right now, we have to focus on what's right in front of us."

Remmy saw what Darius was referring to.

"Fox three," Pete Best said calmly as a flash of light lit the Bridge via the transparent canopy.

"They've reached the portal," Nurek said.

Remmy saw that there were nine battleships facing the *Renegade*. One was hit by the laser blast and disappeared.

"Ensign, increase the evasive maneuvering without slowing us down," Darius said.

"Aye, Captain, I'll do my best," Alex replied.

"We'll be in range of the enemy ships in ten seconds," Nurek said.

"Fox four," Pete Best said, firing again."

"All power to the sonic shields. Their first volley will be the biggest," Darius said.

Everything happened fast. Remmy reached the Commander's console and got into the seat just as a series of lights seemed to leap from the alien ships. All eight had fired simultaneously. But the *Renegade* had powerful thrusters. Even at their incredible speed, the alien ship could shift from side to side, dive, and climb with unmatched agility. The result of their evasive maneuvers was that half of the shots missed them completely and another barely glanced at the port side of their shields. Darius had doubled the sonic screen and angled it so that the energy from the attack was diverted instead of being fully absorbed.

"Shields down fifty percent," Alex called.

"Outstanding. Convert all power back to the cannons," Darius said.

"We'll be vulnerable, Captain," Alex replied.

"Our systems recharge faster than theirs. Lieutenant Best, target those battleships and fire at will."

The Ashi ships had flipped end over end to fully commit to their retro-burn, but they hadn't been fighting their forward momentum long enough to reverse it or even come to a stop. They were just flying backward more slowly than before. They engaged their thrusters and tried to spread out to avoid the return fire, but they weren't fast enough.

"Weapons hot!" Pete Best said. "Fox one... fox two!"

He went through all four cannons, and each shot found a target. Two of the battleships disappeared completely, and the other two were hit with glancing shots that ripped huge sections of the alien ships. They were sent spinning out of control as gas and debris flooded from their spacecraft.

"All power back to the screens," Darius said.

"Aye, Captain, diverting all free power to the sonic shields, now, sir."

"As soon as the shields reach full power, start recharging the cannons," Darius ordered. "How far are we from the portal?"

"On our current heading, we will need to slow down in twenty-three minutes," Nurek said. "We'll reach the portal in thirty-one minutes at the appropriate speed to transition into hyperspace."

"Any chance that going faster will get us through hyperspace sooner?" Best asked.

"The dimension of hyperspace doesn't work that way," Nurek said. "If we approach the portal too quickly, we'll bounce off like a stone skipping over water."

"Alex, we may have to turn to make kill shots on those last four battleships," Darius said. "Can we do that?"

"Aye, Captain. It might carve a bit of speed from us overall, but if we're going to be slowing down to enter the portal, it should be okay."

"Just don't let them get behind us," Darius said.

"Shields are fully charged, Captain," Pete said. "I've got the surplus energy diverted back to the cannons."

"How long until you can fire?"

"One minute," Pete said. If we're still firing at full power, sir?"

"There's no need, is there," Darius said. "We're close enough that you can hit them with half strength and still disable them all. What matters is that they can't attack us from behind or follow us through the portal."

"Roger that, Captain. Permission to fire when ready?"

"Granted. Let's hit the bastards before they spread out too far."

Remmy didn't even have to hold his breath. The aliens were running. None of the last four even tried to fire at the *Renegade* again. The massive cannons had to be angled on their attack arms, but the Arodoni ship didn't even slow down to pick them off. At half power, the Ashi battlecruisers were cut in half. Remmy thought he saw tiny bodies floating into space from the spinning remains of their ships, but he didn't feel bad about it. The enemy was going to attack his home and he would see all of them dead rather than see one innocent human life lost.

Less than half an hour later, the *Renegade* was in hyperspace. It was a reprieve, but no one on the ship thought they wouldn't be facing a dire situation when they arrived in the Sol system. Nurek showed the officers how the motion of molecules in the hyperspace portal could be followed like a trail.

"Each ship moves through space differently," Nurek said. "And if one looks close enough they can see the wake of another ship in the flow of energy through hyperspace."

"And that's how the enemy will follow the *Independence*," Darius said.

"It is so," Nurek said.

"We're only an hour behind them," Pete Best said. "How much damage can they do in that amount of time?"

"It depends on what they want to do?" Darius said. "I'm fairly certain the portal back home is just inside the orbit of Saturn. That means their battleships and corvettes won't be much use. But the Dreadnoughts are another story. It's only two billion kilometers from Saturn to Earth."

"Is that within their laser range?" Best asked.

"Affirmative, Lieutenant," Nurek said. "The Ashi Dreadnoughts have mega cannons which have a much longer range but also use a much greater amount of fuel."

"They may only have one or two long-range shots, but that's enough to wipe out eight space stations," Darius said. "Their battleships have greater range than our SDF ships, too. They're faster. They could close the distance in a few day's time and wipe out our fighters."

"Is that what you think they'll do?" Alex Stanislaus said.

"My guess is they'll wait for us to arrive," Darius said. "Spread out, target our space stations and colonies, then force us to surrender."

"If you do that, the entire human race will be reduced to slaves just like my own people," Nurek said. "You must fight."

"It might not be that simple," Darius said. "If whoever's in charge of the enemy armada is smart, they'll have us trapped and use the innocent to force us to give in."

"We need a plan," Remmy said.

"Indeed," Darius replied. "And we've got less than twenty-four hours to come up with it."

There was no threat in hyperspace. And nothing active needed to be done on the ship. Darius split the remaining time into three eight-hour shifts and made sure the Bridge was manned. Remmy went to his quarters only to find Laila already there with Tex and Izzy. He didn't mind seeing them. In fact, he felt lucky to be alive. It might not be for long if the Captain was right and he wanted to spend as much time as he could with his friends.

"Hey, I hope you don't mind we crashed your place," Laila said.

"I'm thrilled to see you," Remmy said.

"I thought we might send off Hugo and Rip the right way," Izzy said.

"We couldn't find real whisky, though. All I could come up with is this Dudonus stuff."

"It isn't bad," Remmy said.

"Not the same, though," Tex replied. "This stuff is kinda sweet, and there ain't nothing sweet about losing friends."

Remmy had an idea. It was bold, but if ever there was a time to throw caution to the wind, he felt like it was now.

"Come with me," he said.

Remmy led the way out of his berth and down to the Captain's personal quarters. His name and rank were on a plaque outside the door.

"Master Sergeant, is this a good idea?" Izzy asked.

"No," he said. "It most certainly is not."

Remmy tapped lightly on the door. He and Captain Darius

weren't close friends, but they were friends. Darius was the first officer who had ever treated Remmy like a friend. Before he was awarded the Medal of Honor, he was just another NCO. Talented but not important, according to most officers. After the medal, he was treated like an oddity. The respect he received was a strange combination of jealousy and contempt. He had certainly never been invited into a Captain's berth on an SDF ship and given expensive liquor.

The door opened almost immediately, and Captain Zeke Darius' expression was mild amusement.

"What's this?"

"Sorry to bother you, Captain," Remmy said. "But we lost some friends today and wanted to send them off right."

"Let me guess," Darius replied. "You couldn't find anything to drink?"

"Nothing human," Tex replied.

"Well, I may not be good for much these days, but I do have some Scotch," he replied. "If you don't mind me joining you."

"It would be an honor," Laila said.

He waved them inside. Remmy and the other Marines felt a little out of place. The Captain's berth was spartan to say the least, but he did have a nice sofa and two good sitting chairs next to the little bar area. He waved at the seats.

"Please," Darius said. "Have a seat. You lost two Marines today, is that right?"

"Yes, sir," Remmy said. "Sergeant Hugo McManus and Corporal Albert "Rip" Van Winkle."

Darius had eight crystal tumblers. They were a matching set and one of the few possessions he brought with him to the *Jericho*. Along with the tumblers were two bottles of liquor. There was a large bottle of twenty-one-year-old scotch. It wasn't the best a person could buy, but it wasn't available in every liquor store either. The smaller bottle was filled with brandy that Darius didn't really like but which helped him sleep after a stressful day.

He picked up the big bottle and set it on the coffee table

between the two sitting chairs. Then he gathered up seven tumblers and set them down next to the bottle. He removed the glass stopper, set it aside, and poured two fingers worth of the rich, amber-colored liquid into the glasses.

"This is an honor, Captain," Laila said.

"The honor is all mine," Darius said. "I've had the privilege of sitting in a lot of Captain's chairs, but none compare to the *Renegade*. And it's not just the ship. It's the people on board. Despite the roller coaster this cruise turned out to be, I've had the time to get to know the crew on this mission better than any other I've been on."

He passed out the glasses of scotch, leaving two on the table.

"To Hugo," Remmy said, holding up his glass. "May he find peace wherever he is."

They all took a gulp from their glasses. The liquor was strong. Remmy felt his tongue prickle and then it slid down his throat. There was the usual burning sensation, but not really in a painful way. It was more of a warm, comforting sensation, like standing next to a fireplace and letting the heat penetrate into his body.

"Oh, that's really nice," Tex said.

"If you say so," Izzy said, making a face.

Laila made a face, too, but didn't speak until it passed.

"I heard rumors that Hugo McManus was a bit of a problem when we first set out on our cruise," Captain Darius said as he settled into his seat.

"He was," Laila replied.

"It's not unusual," Remmy added. "Special Forces Commandos need to test the water on a new cruise. It's not personal."

"Hugo was an acquired taste," Izzy said. "But once you got to know him a bit, he was very loyal and supportive."

"And a hell of a fighter," Tex said. "He saved my life on the slave station. Carried my sorry behind all the way to safety."

Remmy nodded, remembering that fight. "He told me when we were on Libertine that he would have liked to have stayed there."

"I thought there wasn't much on Libertine?" Izzy said.

"There wasn't," Remmy agreed. "I think that's part of what appealed to him. He enjoyed being on his own."

"Do you think Rip got to him in time?" Laila asked.

"I don't see why not," Remmy said. "Maybe they're on Libertine right now."

"That might be a problem," Darius said.

"Why?" Remmy asked.

"The Ashi ships deployed their escape pods from all four battlecruisers and one of the corvettes," Darius said. "There's a good reason to believe a lot of them made it to the surface of the planet."

"Well, that might be right up Hugo's alley," Tex said. "That man loved a good fight."

"I didn't know he and Rip were that close," Remmy said.

"None of us did," Izzy agreed.

"Maybe they felt like the odd ones out," Darius suggested. "The rest of you have paired up."

"That's a good point," Remmy said, holding up his glass again. "To Rip, a good Marine and a better friend."

They all took another swallow, then Izzy set her glass down. "Oh, that's enough for me."

"We've taken up enough of the Captain's time," Laila said.

"No, wait," Darius said. "I've no right to ask this of you, but I need to talk about what's coming. When we drop out of hyperspace we need a plan."

"The plan is to kill the Ashi until they're all dead," Tex said.

"Easier said than done," Izzy pointed out.

"You really think they can follow the *Independence* all the way back to the Sol system?" Laila asked.

"I have to believe they can," Darius said. "They've followed us to nearly every system we've gone to."

"Nurek says they have the means to track a ship through hyperspace," Remmy said. "The only question is, what will they do when they find us at the end of the portal?"

"Us, as in humanity?" Darius asked.

Remmy nodded. "They'll be expecting the Arodoni."

"And we'll be a big disappointment," Laila said.

"Or the perfect opportunity to get their hands on this ship," Remmy said.

"He's right," Darius agreed. "They've got enough long-range dreadnoughts to destroy our SDF space stations and ships. My guess is they'll surround the portal with their battleships. We won't be able to hold off that many attack craft."

The group fell silent, thinking about the dilemma they faced.

"But will they?" Laila finally asked.

"Makes sense to me," Tex said. "We've been handing them their hat in every fight we've had so far. They probably want major payback."

"No," Laila said. "What they want is this ship."

"I know you're making a point, Staff Sergeant," Darius said. "Maybe I'm just too tired to get it."

"Remmy said they're expecting to find the Arodoni home system, right?"

Darius nodded.

"And instead, they'll find us. It won't take them long to realize we're not the advanced civilization who built the *Renegade*."

"So?" Izzy asked.

"So, they won't want to destroy us," Darius said, putting his half-finished tumbler of scotch on the table. "You're making good sense, Staff Sergeant."

"Let's hope the aliens have some sense, too," Izzy said.

"If she's right, they'll threaten us but call for us to surrender," Remmy said. "We could use that."

"How?" Tex asked.

"Find a way to take them out," Laila said.

"If we start shooting, they'll have no choice but to shoot back," Darius said. "They may not even care if they disable the ship. They could still reverse engineer most of the tech on board."

"True, but they won't do that if their own people are on the ship," Remmy said. "If they want the *Renegade,* they've got to come and get it."

"We could sabotage it," Tex said. "They come in, and boom, we blow it to smithereens."

"Smithereens? Really?" Izzy said.

"Where I come from, that's how we talk," Tex said.

Izzy rolled her eyes, and Laila chuckled.

"That's not a bad plan, but it would leave dozens of Ashi ships in the system," Darius said. "We might keep them from getting the *Renegade* but they would just take out their anger on humanity."

"We're a feisty people," Tex said. "They're liable to bite off more than they can chew."

"We need a better option," Remmy said.

"If we can convince their leader to come aboard the *Renegade,* that might buy us some time," Darius said. "Once we start shooting, they won't know what to do."

"But they'll have to fight back," Remmy said. The two men were deep in thought, their drinks forgotten. "We need to disable their ships for as long as possible. Can Lieutenant Best fire on the Ashi ships?"

"He could, but we're limited to a small field of fire in one direction," Remmy said. "The Ashi will most likely be spread out in all directions. We would need much more time than having their people on board will buy us."

"How much time?" Laila said.

"More like an hour," Darius said.

"What if we go EVA," Izzy suggested. "We could gather as many rockets as possible and take the bad guys out."

"No, that won't work," Remmy said.

"They're on to the rocket attacks," Laila said. "They know they're vulnerable at the rear, but their armor upfront can take a hit."

"They were steering into our missiles that we fired at them," Remmy continued. "If not for Hugo getting around behind them, we would have been cooked."

"Saved our bacon again," Tex said, lifting his glass and taking another gulp.

"What about GIGI?" Laila said. "Could she infiltrate the Ashi ships' computers?"

"I doubt it," Remmy said. "She never mentioned trying it before."

"It might be worth a try," Darius said. "Do you think you'll be able to communicate with her once we're back in the Sol system?"

"I don't see why not," Remmy said.

"Maybe she doesn't have to take control of their ships," Laila said. "If they build their's like we build ours, she could flip a breaker somewhere, and they could spend at least an hour just looking for it."

Darius looked at Remmy with his eyebrows raised. "That might buy us some time," he said. "But there's another problem. We could have hundreds of Ashi on board by then. They would just storm the Bridge and stop our people from killing theirs."

"Not if we stop them first," Tex said.

"Is that even possible? There are only four of you left?"

"We would have to use every advantage," Remmy said. "Live ammo, explosives even."

"You could wipe out the ships and we could take care of any boarders on the *Renegade*," Laila said. "There are worse plans."

"Beats the hell out of giving up," Izzy said.

"Even if it costs you your lives?" Darius asked.

"Nobody lives forever," Tex said.

"If we're going out, better to do it in a blaze of glory than on our knees," Izzy added.

"Well, there's only one problem that I can see," Darius said. "Don't get me wrong, the entire idea is insane. But I can't stay on the Bridge and lead that fight."

"Why not?" Laila asked.

"They've seen me," Darius replied. "Their leader is most likely a figure named Sheika Kahn. We teleconferenced in the Olotimbo system. He'll know something's wrong if I don't meet him the moment he or his people step on board the *Renegade.*"

"But your people can carry out the attack on the Bridge, right?" Izzy said.

"Yes," Remmy said.

"They'll kill you," Tex said. "That'd be the first thing I did once I realized you double-crossed me."

Darius worked his jaw for a moment, then looked Remmy straight in the eyes.

"So be it," he said. "If that's what it takes to deal with the threat, I'll give my life."

Remmy and the rest of the Marines fell silent for a moment. There was no doubt in the Master Sergeant's mind that Captain Darius meant exactly what he had said.

"No, sir," Remmy finally spoke up. "It'll be our job to make sure that never happens."

CHAPTER 36

SHEIKA KAHN'S FLAGSHIP, the *Retribution,* was not the first vessel through the portal. And he was given a report by Commander Ognah of the dreadnought *Dire.*

"Lord, we are alone in this sector," Ognah explained. "There is activity closer to the system star, but they have no ships or space stations close to the hyperspace portal."

Ognah was an older fleet commander with a hunched back and drooping jowls. His hologram stood just steps away from where Sheika Kahn was gazing out through the transparent hull section that showed him the unknown star system they had followed the cruise liner into.

"The crew from the Arodoni ship fled here?"

"We have confirmed it, Lord Kahn," Ognah reported. "They are traveling to the inner system as we speak."

"It seems... primitive," Sheika Kahn said.

Around the *Retribution* more Ashi battleships were appearing. His fleet was gone and what remained was a powerful armada. There were twenty battleships, eight corvettes, eight of the big dreadnoughts, and two refueling vessels that still contained enough fuel and supplies to restock four ships. The *Retribution* was neither a battleship nor a civilian craft. It had weapons and heavy armor, but its function was to express the prestige of the Emperor and to give him a platform from which to command battle.

"Agreed," Ognah said. "The race that inhabits this star system does not even possess artificial gravity."

"Why would the Arodoni send their people to this place?"

"I cannot imagine," Ognah said.

Other ship commanders were appearing as holograms around Sheika Kahn. They were all looking to him for answers. It would not do to let them see his uncertainty.

Shipmaster Kass was the next to speak. He was young, strong, and ambitious, even though he commanded only one vessel.

"Perhaps it was a ruse," Kass said. "Maybe there is no one of value on the cruise ship."

"Why draw us to this place?" Ognah asked.

"Simple misdirection," Kass said. "We spent valuable resources getting here. We expected the alien ship to follow us."

"But if there is nothing of value in this place," Sheika Kahn said, the words bitter in his own mouth, "then we have accomplished nothing."

"It is a highly populated system," Commander Norag said. "Surely, they knew we would destroy this civilization."

"It would be a waste of resources," Ognah said. "There is nothing here of value."

"We must find whatever we can," Sheika Kahn said. "Our resources are limited. I do not want to return to the galactic core without our prize in hand. Send our fastest ships to retrieve the cruise liner. I must know who the Arodoni have sent to this dreadful system."

"It shall be as you command, Lord Kahn," one of the commanders said.

His hologram disappeared as he set about giving orders to his battle group to carry out Sheika Kahn's order to pursue the cruise liner.

"I want the dreadnoughts to locate targets," Sheika Kahn said.

"My Lord, can we afford to expend so much energy on worth-less targets such as these?" Ognah asked.

"Not without finding an adequate fuel source in this system," Sheika Kahn said. "But we must be ready to thwart any resistance this primitive race might put up. I want whatever station the cruise liner hopes to dock at destroyed before they arrive."

"As you wish," Commander Ognah said.

"Have our battleships spread out and prepare for the possibility that the Arodoni ship comes through the portal," Sheika Kahn continued. "But let it be known that we dare not destroy the alien vessel. This is clearly not their home system. We must capture the Arodoni here. If it appears, target the engines only and reduce the power of any laser assault. We want it disabled, not destroyed. Anyone who fails me this day will not live to see the morrow."

The holograms bowed and swore to obey the Kahn's commands. He was left to fume over his failure. The Arodoni had reacted exactly as Sheika Kahn had expected. They were even able to fend off the squadron of battleships and corvettes he had left hidden behind the planet in the Free system. Of course, destroying the Arodoni ship was never the purpose. He had hoped that the alien ship would do exactly as she had done. If the small squad of ships had disabled the Arodoni vessel, or if it had turned to do battle with them, Sheika would have known not to enter the hyperspace portal. But the alien ship hadn't even slowed down. Even when rushing straight ahead put them in range of the ships he ordered to cover their withdraw. Everything about the alien ship's behavior told him that wherever the cruise liner had gone was important to the Arodoni ... and maybe it was. Maybe the primitive race meant something to the highly advanced aliens. Or perhaps it was just the passengers on the cruise liner itself. But all indications were that the Arodoni ship would follow them.

If it didn't, so be it, he thought. All he could do was regroup and chase them down again. On the other hand, if they did come through the portal, Sheika Kahn was intent on being ready to end the battle and return home the greatest conqueror his people had ever known.

"Would you like us near the portal?" his shipmaster asked in a quiet tone.

"No," Sheika Kahn said. Put us behind it."

"Behind the portal?"

"That's right. And prepare my personal guard. Once the Arodoni have surrendered, I will go aboard their ship and plant our flag personally."

"Yes, Lord Kahn," the shipmaster said with a bow.

Ulrech Sheika looked out across the strange star system. It reminded him of an animal infested with fleas. He turned away from the window and went back into his private chamber to don his armor. The enemy had proven resourceful and dangerous. Sheika Kahn had no desire to die. He was on the cusp of finally attaining everything he had always wanted. It was no time to lose focus or to take unnecessary chances. He would board the alien ship, but he would go armed for battle, just in case they had a surprise. He would be ready. Nothing could stop him. It was his destiny to rule.

CHAPTER 37

ADMIRAL HUGH LINCOLN hurried through the outer office and entered the restricted area. There were two space marines standing guard outside the hallway that led to the secure communications room. It was a box inside a larger room with thick walls and a hardwired connection to a tight beam communications transmitter that was always pointed toward Earth.

He pulled open the heavy door and stepped inside, waiting for the door to close, which it did with a thud. Admiral Lincoln placed his hand on the scanner, which activated the controls.

"Lock," he said. The big door locked with another booming thud. "Activate security protocols."

"What's going on?" Major Sandra Keys asked.

She was the only Space Marine in the room. There were two other admirals, Clint Dale and Lectra Shazi. They knew exactly what was happening. It was history in the making. For the past twenty-four hours, humanity had been on the verge of monumental change. But they didn't know everything. No one knew everything except for Admiral Lincoln and he was about to share his information with the people in the SCR, as well as the President of the Inner System Coalition and his fellow politicians.

"Activate the transmission," Lincoln said. "Everything we say in this room is being recorded and will be seen by top political officials on Earth."

"We know the drill," Admiral Dale said.

Lectra crossed her legs and leaned back in the expensive executive chair. "Has there been a change?"

The admiral nodded, then looked at Major Keyes. "You are here to give us insight into the situation. Please wait until I have finished giving my briefing before asking questions."

"Understood," Major Sandra Keys said.

Lincoln appreciated that the Space Marines were accustomed to taking orders. It was, in many ways, refreshing to tell someone what to do and have them do it without question. He took a deep breath and activated the transmission controls.

"Regards from SDF spaces station *Ares*," he began. "Mr. President, I am sure you will have questions, but let me outline what has happened. As you all know, the SDF *Jericho* was sent to retrieve the artifact that has been stationary in our solar system for quite some time. It achieved its mission, but shortly thereafter, we lost contact with the *Jericho,* and then it vanished. There has been a lot of speculation about what happened to our ship, but we now know it left the solar system to carry out a series of operations in other star systems as directed by the alien artifact itself.

"Just over twenty-four hours ago, a new ship entered the solar system. That vessel is commanded by our own Lori Lee, the XO from the *Jericho*, along with most of the crew. With them are a handful of aliens known as the Dudonus and the alien artifact, which claims to be a Galactic Information and Guidance Instrument or GIGI for short.

"We have been in contact with the crew of the *Independence* which is a transport ship of alien make. It has advanced technological capabilities, which will prove to be a boon to our own technological expertise. Along with the aliens and the crew, this ship also carries two highly advanced components capable of utilizing dark matter and converting it into an exponential amount of usable energy. Finally, the crew has brought along databanks with even more advanced information that came from a different alien vessel, perhaps the most advanced in the galaxy if their claims are correct. It is, without a doubt, the biggest boon in the history of mankind.

"That's the good news," Admiral Lincoln said. "And I'm guessing most of you know some, if not all, of those facts prior to this emergency meeting. I am coming to you now with news that more ships have appeared in our star system. From communication with the *Independence* the new ships are hostile vessels of war. It appears the *Independence* was followed through space back here. We are under threat ... or soon will be."

There were looks of shock and fear on the faces of Lincoln's colleagues in the room and he could only imagine what was happening on Earth. It took the message several minutes to reach earth and their return message to reach the officers on the *Ares*. During that time, Lincoln released the transmit controls and faced Major Keyes.

"It seems we are about to be at war," he said. "One we are very unlikely to win. According to Commander Lori Lee, the alien ships are faster and more powerful than anything we have in the fleet. The call has already gone out to prepare for war on Earth, Mars, and every space station in the system. The President will undoubt-edly have questions about the crew on the *Independence*. You are here to help answer those questions."

She looked worried. He felt the same way. There was a lump in his throat that made swallowing difficult. He felt a rising sense of anger at Captain Zeke Darius, a man he had thought of as a friend and who had seemed like a seasoned, capable military leader until just a few moments before. How Zeke could have gotten the entire solar system in such a jam, Lincoln didn't know, but if he ever got the chance, he planned to show his old friend just what he thought of his actions on the *Jericho*.

"Alright," Major Keys managed to say.

"Questions?"

"Too many," she admitted. "How much time do we have?"

"Not much," Lincoln admitted. "The *Independence* will reach us here in another twenty-four hours. According to Commander Lee, the alien ships are just as fast, perhaps faster. And their big ships have what she calls mega cannons with the ability to target us right now. For all we know, they could destroy this space station as we speak."

"God help us," Major Keys said.

"If ever mankind needed God's intervention, it is right now," Admiral Hugh Lincoln said. "May he have mercy on us all."

CHAPTER 38

THE *RENEGADE* WAS ALMOST to the end of the hyperspace lane. They would come out into the Sol system any moment. For the crew, it was tense. Captain Zeke Darius had laid out the plan of action that he felt was best, but it was based on speculation. Who could know what a hostile, alien race might do?

Darius had felt a sense of hope since meeting with the four remaining space marines. It wasn't a hope of surviving what lay ahead but even if they were all killed, their plan would give humanity a fighting chance to throw off the yoke of the Imperium. They had not yet felt the pain and weight of that yoke as a species, but there was no doubt it was coming. If the captain's plan failed, there would be a holocaust the likes of which the human race had never seen. Those that managed to survive would either live in hiding or as slaves. Earth would be raped, her resources stripped away and perhaps even poisoned by the Ashi military. They would want vengeance for the thousands of warriors lost in the space battles with the *Renegade*. At least, they would once they realized who it was they were fighting.

According to Nurek, the entire galaxy was at war. Hundreds of planets were either planning or had already rebelled against the

Imperium. If those worlds could have banded together and built a space fleet, they could have freed themselves long ago. Yet, the Ashi and their collaborators on the Prime Council of Worlds had wisely made it illegal to build ships with weapons. Nor could any talk of rebellion be tolerated. If it were even spoken of in whispers, the Imperium's spies would root it out. Those caught trying to resist the Imperium were enslaved. Entire worlds had been devastated for acts of treason. The entire known galaxy was caught in the powerful grip of a tyrannical government that would do anything to stay in power.

Darius had used that folly. He had fought the Imperium, devastating their fleet, in the hopes of weakening the evil regime. Instead, he had led the enemy right to his own doorstep. It no longer mattered what happened across the galaxy as hundreds of worlds fought for independence. It only mattered what would happen in the Sol system and to the human race.

"Sixty seconds until transition to real space," Nurek said.

He spoke in his own language, which was promptly translated by a little device clipped onto the collar of his garment. He had been the instigator of the rebellion. His people, long forced into slavery across the galaxy, had secretly prepared for the day when it might be possible to foment rebellion. That moment had come when Darius had attacked the armada that followed the *Renegade* to the Scandian system. For the first time in Nurek's long life he had seen the Ashi vanquished. His clandestine call had gone out from one star system to another in a chain reaction that was building across the galaxy.

In less than a minute, Darius would find out if freedom was possible. He tapped his comlink transmitter button and spoke with a steady voice.

"Almost home, people. Stay ready. We'll only get one shot at this. You all know your assignments. Trust in the plan. Work hard and fast. No matter what happens to us, we are changing the course of history for humanity and for the galaxy. Good luck. It's been an honor to serve with you all."

"We're ready, Captain," Pete Best said from the weapons console.

"Everyone is with you, Captain," Ensign Stanislaus added.

"Thank you for allowing me this chance to serve," Nurek said.

"It might mean your death," Darius pointed out.

"Better death than the indignity of slavery," Nurek said.

Darius thought that if the Dudonus people truly felt that way, they would have acted sooner. But maybe all they needed was a chance to serve in a way that suited them. Nurek turned out to be an excellent naval officer – one who needed little rest or time away from his duties. If the aliens had any real martial inclinations, they could be a force to reckon with.

"It's time," Darius said. "From this point forward, no one speaks. Acknowledge your comlinks with a tap. We have to assume the enemy will be watching our every move. Let's not give away the ace up our sleeve."

The *Renegade* dropped out of hyperspace and into a trap. Yet as Darius looked at the plot, which showed thirty ships arrayed around him, the dreadnoughts spread wide; their mega cannons pointed toward targets in the inner system, he realized that he had been right. Not that he came up with the plan all by himself, but together, they had anticipated what their enemy would do. It wasn't a sign of certain victory; in fact, they were still facing terribly long odds, but their plans could be carried out. They would have a fighting chance, and that was about all they could ask for.

"Bring us about," Darius said. "Make it a slow, clumsy circle."

Alex Stanislaus acknowledged the order with a nod of his head and began to manipulate the controls. Almost immediately, the communications system dinged with an incoming signal.

Darius held his hand over the icon on his touchscreen that would accept the hail. He knew who it was and what it was. For some reason, he could not explain; his intuition told him to savor the next few minutes in the Captain's chair. One way or another, it would be his last time to command a ship of war.

He pressed the icon, and a hologram appeared of Sheika Kahn.

Darius had changed the settings for the video conference application so that only his head and shoulders appeared to the Ashi commander. The alien's green skin and fleshy jowls were intimidating to look at. The big tusks and spiky teeth looked old and almost fragile. When he spoke, it was like an animal growling.

The *Renegade's* communication system projected the words of the alien in English behind the Kahn's holographic image. That way, Darius could read it without his eyes looking down or away from the Ashi commander, which might have been considered a form of submission.

"You are surrounded," Sheika Kahn said. "Surrender now or we will open fire on your vessel."

"What assurances do we have that you will act honorably?"

"What does a defeated race know of honor?" The Kahn snapped. "You are beaten. Submit or die; those are the only choices you have left."

Darius hung his head as though he was crushed by the reality of the situation.

"I will surrender," Darius said. "I have begun slowing the ship's momentum. I will hold this course and you can board my ship at your earliest convenience."

"It will be done. Prepare to bow before the Ashi."

The communication abruptly ended and the hologram vanished. Darius' heart was pounding. He looked up at his crew and nodded with as much encouragement as he could muster. Then he left them without saying another word.

CHAPTER 39

GIGI, Remmy thought. *Can you hear me?*

Master Sergeant Steel, you have come home.

We're in the system, Remmy said in his mind. *But we need your help.*

You have only to ask, Master Sergeant.

Can you infiltrate the computers on the Ashi ships?

I can synchronize with their systems, but their vessels are not computer controlled as yours are.

I don't need you to fly them. Can you cut their power?

Shutting down their engines would require a physical counterpart on those vessels. Otherwise, I am unable to perform the desired request.

I don't need you to shut down the system. Can you overload a circuit or two? They have an electrical system, right?

That is correct, GIGI said, her soft, feminine voice sounding far different in Remmy's mind than she did over the ship's speakers.

And it probably has safety devices, Remmy said. *Something like a circuit breaker in case of too much power surging through the system. I need you to find that on each of the Ashi ships and flip those breakers when I give the command. Is that possible?*

I believe it to be, but I must do a comprehensive search of the Ashi warships. Standby, Master Sergeant.

Remmy was in full space armor. He would have preferred something lighter and less bulky, but the risk of live fire in the ship made it imperative that he be able to operate, even if the hull of the *Renegade* was compromised.

His comlink chirped, and then Captain Darius' voice was in his ear.

"On my way down to the primary hangar. Sheika Kahn is going to board us himself."

"He'll have a large number of guards and soldiers with him," Remmy said. "A ship this size will need a lot of warriors to secure quickly."

"Are we ready?" Darius asked.

"Everyone is in place," Remmy said. "We're as ready as we can be."

That wasn't exactly true. Remmy was waiting for Captain Darius just inside the entrance to the park. It wasn't what they talked about him doing but Remmy felt a kinship with Captain Darius that was unlike any relationship he had ever shared with a senior officer before. Their plan held a very high likelihood that Captain Darius would be killed. He was the most exposed and least protected member of the crew. When things got hot, it would probably be inevitable that he would be killed.

"What are you doing here, Master Sergeant?" Darius asked.

Remmy pulled off his helmet and looked his Captain in the eye. "You didn't think I'd let you make this walk all alone, did you?"

"My life is secondary to the mission," Darius said, with just the slightest tremble in his voice.

"Doesn't mean it isn't important," Remmy said. "I just wanted you to know."

They walked slowly through the park toward the gravity lift that would take them down to the primary hangar. Remmy had been the first human to see the amazing agriculture section of the massive alien ship. He knew if he was going to die, and the odds were high that everyone on board the *Renegade* would be killed, he was glad to have a moment of quiet reflection in the garden-like setting.

"What do you believe about death, Remmy?" Darius asked. "Is it the end?"

"Hard to believe we just ceased to exist," the space marine said. "I've seen people die. It's not like a light going off, more like the spark of animation leaving the body."

"What do you think exists beyond this life?"

"Something different," Remmy said. "Hopefully, something better."

When they reached the gravity lift, which was hidden under a beautifully crafted pavilion, Remmy bent down and picked up a rope. Then he paused, looking at Captain Darius.

"You ready for this, sir?"

"Ready as I can be," Darius said. "I always thought that when this cruise ended, I would have to try and find something to do with the rest of my life."

"The SDF wouldn't kick you to the curb, sir."

"No, but they have an age limit for Captains," he said with a grin. "It was either take a desk job or retirement after this cruise."

"It's one hell of a way to go out, sir," Remmy assured him.

"The best," Darius said, looking up. He took a deep breath in and held it for a moment. "I can't imagine being anywhere else but on this ship," he said. "In that regard, I'm glad I don't have to settle for something less."

"If I've learned anything at all in my career, Captain, it's that nothing is said and done until the fighting is over and the smoke clears. If this is our swan song, at least we've got a plan to put the hurt on the Ashi one last time."

"Alright," Darius said. "I'm ready."

Remmy put his helmet back on and fastened the safety straps. He had his Nelson LTX attached to the back of his armor. On his right leg was the Yagger HC pistol. And on his left thigh, he had added a second of the close combat pistols. He had a few other toys attached to the combat web vest he had stretched over his armor, including a fourteen-inch long bowie knife with a razor-sharp edge.

"Me too," Remmy said. "Let's go."

They stepped off the platform and into the zero gravity shaft. They each reached up and gave the ceiling a slight push, which sent them floating downward. The Park was four levels above the hangar, which was a huge, cavernous compartment in the belly of the ship.

Remmy reached back out to GIGI when he got to his place just inside the hallway that led to the hangar. The decision had been made during the planning phase that no communication would be made with the officers manning the Bridge. The entire first part of their plan hinged on the Ashi believing that no one was left in control of the *Renegade's* weapons. They might have some tech that monitored sound and communication, so Darius had ordered total silence on the Bridge.

GIGI, however, could communicate directly with Remmy. Their link couldn't be tapped into by some form of alien technology. It was probably the most secure communication ever between two sentient beings.

How close are the Ashi to our ship? Remmy asked silently.

They have matched speed and trajectory, GIGI replied. *They will begin attaching stabilizing hooks to the* Renegade *at any moment.*

Any updates on our plan?

Standby, GIGI said. She didn't usually frustrate him, but a big part of their plan depended on what the alien device was able to do.

"Any word?" Darius asked. He was standing just inside the doorway where Remmy was posted.

"Not yet," Remmy said. "She's taking her time."

"You have to consider the fact that the *Indy* is hundreds of thousands of kilometers away," Darius said.

It was true, but Remmy didn't find that fact to be a comfort. There was a booming sound as the stabilizing hooks, which were really magnetic connectors, locked onto the hull of the *Renegade*.

"Won't be long now," Remmy said.

"Do you really believe this will work?" Darius asked.

"Anything is possible in combat," Remmy said. "Whatever you do, sir, once the shooting starts, don't stop moving."

"If I'm able," Darius said.

"That is a factor, sir," Remmy said with a grin.

They didn't need GIGI to alert them to the fact that the aliens were about to board the ship. The hangar had a large airlock. It began to cycle, heralding the arrival of the first of the Ashi warriors coming aboard to take control of the ship.

"I hate this," Darius said.

"Good," Remmy said. "Let it motivate you."

They fell silent. After removing his rifle and sitting it down in the corner by the door, Remmy tapped into the ship's security video feed. There were cameras mounted in various parts of the huge ship, including the hangers. On a small part of his HUD, he could see the video feed as the first of the Ashi came out of the airlock.

The sheer size of the aliens still surprised Remmy. They were huge beings, not just tall, although they were twice the height of the average human, but they were thick with muscle, too. Eight aliens came on board initially, all of them with breathing apparatuses that covered half of their faces. They carried the same laser rifles as they had on Casasil which Remmy was all too familiar with. He had no idea if they would blast through the hull of the ship, but that was a risk the crew of the *Renegade* had discussed and were comfortable with.

The squad of eight didn't cross the wide hangar to approach Captain Darius, who stood with his hands clasped behind his back and his head held high. Remmy couldn't help but admire the courage his captain was displaying in the face of a terrible foe. The squad of eight warriors split into equal groups and took up positions on either side of the airlock. It was as if they considered their own ship to be more valuable than the *Renegade*. If that's what they thought, Remmy knew they were wrong. There was no ship in the entire galaxy as advanced or as luxurious as the *Renegade,* which he couldn't help but think of as his home.

A man defending his home was worth as much, if not more, than an Ashi warrior trying to take it from him.

More warriors came. Wave after wave passed through the airlock. It was a grand show of force. They formed ranks on the wide hangar, standing stiff as statues. Remmy hated to see the enemy force growing larger and larger, but they needed time. GIGI had not responded to Remmy's request. He was starting to have his doubts about her part of their plan. They needed the alien artifact to hinder the Ashi warships, but either she couldn't do it or didn't want to for some reason Remmy couldn't fathom.

It took thirty cycles through the airlock, but eventually, there were two hundred and forty Ashi warriors assembled on the deck of the hangar. Remmy tried not to think about the fact that his tiny squad of Marines were outnumbered sixty to one. The thirty-first cycle of the airlock was different. Inside was just one Ashi warrior. Unlike the others, his muscular frame was covered in a thick layer of fat. His round stomach hung over the ornate belt that held up his kilt. Across his upper body was the same crimson-colored cape with horns arching away from his shoulders that Remmy had seen Emperor Vang wearing on the battlefield of Casasil. There was also a breastplate made of what looked like gold scales. It covered his broad chest down to the top of his stomach. On his forearms were matching cuffs that reached from his wrist to his elbows. He wore the same breathing apparatus that his warriors wore, but as he approached Captain Darius, he pulled it off.

When he spoke, it was a series of growls and barks, almost like a frightened dog. Captain Darius had a language device synced to his in-ear comlink. It translated the Ashi words for him, while Remmy saw the translation spelled out on the HUD of his battle helmet.

"We meet at last," the grandiose alien said. "I am Sheika Kahn, Supreme Commander of the Ashi, rulers of the Galactic Imperium. I demand your immediate and complete surrender."

It was a formal speech, although it sounded strange in the Ashi's alien language.

"I am Captain Zeke Darius of the Space Defense Force and commander of the *Renegade*. I wish I could welcome you aboard the ship, but you are not welcome."

"Conquerors rarely are," Sheika Kahn said. "But you are surrounded, outgunned and outclassed. Your antics have cost us many ships and many warriors, yet the outcome of your fight was never in doubt. No race has ever defeated the Ashi. None ever will. Now, your ship is ours and all that remains is to decide what to do with you, Captain."

Darius didn't flinch. He stood staring up at the huge alien. Sheika Kahn wasn't as tall as the other warriors, but he was twice as wide as Captain Darius, whose head only came up slightly past the Ashi's stomach.

With a bark and a wave of his hand, Sheika Kahn summoned one of his warriors. A hulking alien stepped forward, spun on his heel and took his place beside his leader. Another barked order and the warrior drew a brightly polished blade. He raised it high, his movements stiff with the ceremony of the occasion. Remmy felt a surge of affection for Captain Darius, who didn't move even though it was clear the alien was about to kill him. The Captain was the perfect example of human courage. As the powerful alien slashed down with his blade, Remmy Steel sprang into action.

CHAPTER 40

REMMY WAS A VETERAN. He had fought in many engagements, some of the most recent were against the Ashi. They were, in his experience, powerful foes, but nothing prepared him for the force of the warrior's slash with his gleaming blade. Had it landed, it would have cleaved Captain Darius' skull in two. But Remmy was fast, even in full space armor. He dashed out of the corridor and drew his knife at the same time. Stopping the alien's cut was impossible. But Remmy caught the blade on his own and deflected it. The force of the blow sent a sharp pain down his arm and through his elbow.

The Ashi warrior snarled in fury behind his breathing mask. With his free hand, he grabbed Remmy's arm. It was like being pinched in a vice, but Remmy didn't mind. As the alien made to sling him aside, he slashed with his own knife. The hand forged blade had cost Remmy nearly a month's salary but it was worth every credit. The cutting edge bit deep, slicing across the alien's stomach. Blood gushed like a river from the alien as his stomach muscles bulged through the wound and his entrails dropped to the deck in front of him.

The warrior stepped back; his narrow eyes opened wide in

shock. Before anyone else could react, Remmy slapped the knife against his own armor, letting the magnets hold the gory blade in place. He drew both of his Yagger hand cannons. They were large bore pistols that were loaded with buzzers: small, disc-shaped pellets that were honed sharp. Each shot released dozens of the buzzers, which spread out and eviscerated flesh.

Everything happened so quickly. Four Ashi warriors found themselves with gaping, bloody wounds. Sheika Kahn was the first to react, turning to flee; the shot at him ripped his thick arm into bloody ribbons. He howled in pain as Remmy kept firing, but the Space Marine was moving, too. The response from the aliens was inevitable but also predictable. They were lined up in rows, which meant that only those closest to the fighting could bring their laser rifles to bear. They did, taking aim at Captain Darius, who had yet to react at all. He still stood bravely staring at the intruders on his ship.

Remmy emptied both of his pistols as he turned. He dropped the weapons and shoved Darius back toward the corridor. The first laser shot hit Remmy in the middle of his back and sent him tumbling to his knees on the deck. Most of the other shots ripped over and around him. He could hear the laser beams sizzling through the air.

Captain Darius had landed on his backside and slid through the opening into the hallway beyond the hangar. Remmy, his legs churning like a professional athlete, scurried after his commander. Another laser blast clipped his battle helmet. He fell forward, rolled over one shoulder, and through the opening just as Darius reached up to throw the lever that closed off the hangar bay.

Laser fire hammered the thick doors, but they were made to withstand a spacecraft crashing into the hangar bay. Remmy was starting to feel the effects of the laser shots. His arm felt stiff in places and there was heat coming through the thick space suit. He had known it could take a few shots from the enemy laser rifles, but the suit was also compromised. If the ship lost pressure, he would be exposed to the vacuum.

"We have to move!" Remmy said.

"That wasn't part of the plan," Darius shouted.

"Of course it was," Remmy said, grabbing his rifle from the corner and starting to run. "We just didn't tell you."

They reached the gravity lift. Remmy snatched up the rope he had secured on the way down. He clipped the end of it into his space armor.

"Hold onto me," he told Darius.

To his credit, the Captain did as he was told, grabbing hold of Remmy's shoulders from behind.

"Now, Laila," Remmy ordered as he backed into the well of zero gravity and started drifting up.

At nearly the same instant, the hangar doors slid open. Remmy let loose with his rifle. It was loaded with soft alloy slugs and set to fully automatic fire. The forty-round magazine allowed him to blast away for exactly four seconds as he and the Captain were hauled upward by Laila on the Park level. In that short span of time, Remmy saw the enemy warriors jerking and twitching as the bullets punched into them. Blood and flesh flew in a dark mist at the end of the hallway, then they were hidden from sight in the tall zero-gravity shaft.

They reached the top of the shaft, crashed into the roof of the pavilion and then were jerked onto the landing. Gravity seemed to smash down on Remmy, but he got to his feet and began tossing down concussion grenades into the gravity lift. They floated downward, propelled by the force of the throw, but not falling as they would have in regular gravity.

"We need to move!" Laila said.

She didn't wait for a response. She leaped over a hedge and sprinted across the open field toward a floating platform. Remmy pulled Captain Darius to his feet. The officer was older than Remmy but not out of shape. The shock of the battle was wearing off and he didn't need urging to sprint across the open ground. They jumped over narrow streams of running water and up small, rounded hills. There were booms as the concussion grenades reached the bottom of the gravity shaft behind them.

"That won't stop them," Remmy said. "We can't use regular explosives without risk to the ship."

"And they don't seem like the type to go down easy," Darius said. "I had forgotten how big they are."

"The bigger they are, the harder they fall," Remmy said. "This is me."

He turned and jumped up onto a floating platform with short trees. The upper branches were filled with wide leaves. But Remmy wasn't there to admire the landscaping. He dropped to his stomach and turned toward the gravity shaft. His hands moved in well-rehearsed movements as he ejected the spent magazine from his rifle and rammed a fresh one into the slot. One sideways glance showed Captain Darius running and the entrance to the wide concourse that led back to the command section of the ship.

"All units report in," Remmy ordered.

"Condor is in position," Izzy said. "No sign of the enemy yet."

"Eagle is in position," Tex said in his lazy southern draw. "Quiet as a church on Saturday night up here, Sarge."

"I'm in position now, too," Laila said. "Use the security camera footage to keep tabs on the enemy."

Remmy checked his HUD. In the hangar, Sheika Kahn stood surrounded by guards. His wounded arm was wrapped in some sort of bandage, although it was different from what humans used. It looked more like a skin graft. Despite the wound, the alien continued giving orders. Remmy brought up the feed from the hallway that led to the gravity shaft. There were nearly twenty dead or wounded Ashi warriors on the deck. Their bodies were being shoved aside. A group of the aliens were at the bottom of the gravity shaft, cautiously looking up to where Remmy and Darius had disappeared.

"The concussion grenades didn't do much," Remmy grumbled.

"Slowed them down," Laila responded. "When will the navy pukes start shooting down the Ashi ships?"

Remmy understood her concern. Their plan was based on the aliens needing to advance through the ship to stop the *Renegade* from destroying their fleet. It would drive the aliens up into a kill box. The park was the safest place to ambush the aliens. It gave them good fields of fire, as well as plenty of space between where they hoped to be shooting their guns and the hull of the ship. Unless the Ashi fired straight up into the high ceiling, they should be protected from catastrophic damage to the ship.

It also allowed the tiny group of Space Marines the ability to use their weapons to the greatest effect. Tex and Izzy were still not fully recovered from their wounds. Moving fast simply wasn't possible. But from the upper balconies on either side of the park, they had almost the entire space open to them. Tex was in position on the starboard side. His sharpshooting was the best in the platoon. Across the park, on the port side, Izzy had a station on the second-story balcony, which put her closer to the enemy and where she could utilize her weapons to the best.

Down near the research and engineering sections of the ship, Laila was perched on a floating platform. Behind her, a herd of six-legged animals with thick fur covering their rotund bodies grazed. Remmy was on his own platform at the opposite end of the park. When the enemy came up the gravity shaft and out into the agricultural park, they would be prime targets. But without the *Renegade* taking out the Ashi battleships, the aliens had no motivation to hurry through the ship. If they moved slowly and cautiously, they might find a way to avoid the park or land a mortal blow to the Marines waiting for them there.

Of course, Remmy knew the crew was waiting for word from GIGI. It might make sense to believe that the aliens wouldn't blow up the *Renegade*. They certainly wanted the advanced technology secrets on the alien ship, plus their leader was aboard, which would mean that firing on the *Renegade* would probably result in the death of Sheika Kahn. But it was impossible to tell how someone in mortal danger might react. If the alien ships could fire on the *Renegade*, they probably would. So, before attacking the alien armada, the officers on the Bridge of the ship needed word from Remmy that the Ashi battleships couldn't fire back.

"Soon," Remmy said, although he really had no idea how the attack would go or when it might commence. "Stay alert. We get one shot to thin the herd. No one fires until I give the order."

"Roger that, Master Sergeant," Izzy said.

"Just say when," Tex added.

Laila actually giggled. "I'm just so excited I can hardly wait."

Remmy reached over and rubbed his elbow. It was aching from the Ashi warrior's savage chop. And his back was beginning to sting from where the laser blasts had hit him. The excess energy was mostly absorbed by the armor plating, but some always found the creases and burned down into his flesh. It was just a few more scars on a body that was crisscrossed with them. He sighed as he waited for word from GIGI and the attack he knew had to come. That was the hardest part of combat, the waiting. He just hoped he could survive long enough for his new wounds to heal.

CHAPTER 41

DARIUS WAS TIRED. It wasn't the run through the ship that was winding him but the adrenaline from the fight that was wearing off. It left him feeling cold and shaky. He had come within a few inches of being killed. If not for Master Sergeant Remmy's heroic actions, the Captain would be dead without question. Darius had expected it. He couldn't honestly say that he was ready to die, but he hadn't shied away from it either. He had looked into the abyss and it had looked into him.

Fear had seized him. It felt different from before. In the hangar, he was facing his own demise, but with the hope that their plan would succeed. Since then, all he could think of was the plan. Could it work? He didn't know, but he feared that it would fail. Facing the reality that everything they had worked so hard to achieve could be swept away was terrible. He was more afraid of failure than of death.

When he reached the gravity ring, he pulled himself upward, hand over hand, as fast as he could force himself to move. He was panting hard when he swung onto the command deck and staggered toward the Bridge. Reaching up, he tapped the comlink in his ear.

"Any word from our friend, Master Sergeant?"

"Negative, sir," Remmy replied.

"We can't wait," Darius said. "Nurek, activate the gravity beam. Launch all torpedoes."

There was a click in the captain's ear. Down on the open deck that was designed for hauling in space debris, there lay asteroids and things to be broken down and refined into raw materials that could be used to build just about anything a person could want in the ship's manufacturing section. Just then, a row of ship to ship torpedoes was sent flying from the *Renegade's* open mouth. The ship looked like a fish, with a ring around its neck and an open mouth ready to gobble up anything that came near to it. The torpedoes sailed out into space but weren't activated yet.

"Launch drones," Darius ordered.

The meager crew of the *Renegade* was split into three groups. There were officers on the Bridge, Marines in the park, and in the third hangar was a group of humans, Casians and Dudonus crew, less than two dozen in total, who controlled eighteen attack drones. They didn't have the firepower to take on an Ashi battleship. Instead, their rockets and guns had been exchanged for torpedo launchers. They flew out and latched onto the big weapons and began steering them toward the Ashi dreadnoughts.

"Activate the laser cannons," Darius said.

He got a thumbs up from Lieutenant Best.

"Prepare to bring us around. Activate ship thrusters."

Another klick from Alex Stanislaus. Darius' heart was thundering in his chest. At any moment, the enemy could realize the danger they were in and take action. They might target the torpedoes, wiping out his ability to take down the dreadnoughts before the big ships could fire on human targets with their mega cannons. Alternatively, they might just fire on the *Renegade*. They had no shields active at that moment. All power was reserved for the laser cannons, which could be fired at one-quarter power. It wasn't enough to destroy the enemy ships, but they were close enough that it would disable or even devastate them.

But it would all be for naught if the Ashi ships started shooting back.

Darius was staring at four enemy battleships spread out in a line directly in front of the *Renegade*. Up close, the Ashi ships were menacing-looking spacecraft. He could see the laser cannons bristling from the hull like the pointed teeth sticking out of the Ashi's wide jaws.

Suddenly, the running lights on the alien ships blinked off. Darius didn't need a report from Remmy to know their plan was working. The only question remaining was how quickly the enemy could restore power and join the fight.

"Fire!" Darius yelled. "Open fire!"

Light flashed as the lasers raced from the four huge cannons on the *Renegade*. The beams traveled too fast to be seen across space, flashing from the big Arodoni ship to the Ashi warcraft. All four bucked under the assault. Three Ashi craft careened back, spinning horizontally, with debris spewing from massive holes in the front of the ships. The fourth vessel exploded in a flash of fiery brilliance.

"Activate thrusters," Darius shouted. "Spin us around. Fire at will, Lieutenant."

He pressed the transmit button on his comlink. "Fire the torpedoes. I repeat, fire all torpedoes."

In his ear, Darius heard Remmy speak. "Captain, GIGI has tripped the electrical systems on all the Ashi ships, sir. She calculates we might have two minutes before the battleships regain electrical power. Another minute or two with the dreadnoughts."

"Thank you, Master Sergeant," Darius said. "Alex, we've got two minutes at most."

There were twenty-eight Ashi battleships still surrounding the *Renegade*. While they were firing at only a quarter of the laser cannons power, the *Renegade* would need to recharge them before half the ships were fired on.

Darius left his Captain's chair and stood near the plot. They were close enough to the enemy ships that Alex couldn't miss them. He fired quickly as they came to bear. None moved. They were clearly unable to react to the sudden change of events. Darius hoped the shock and fury of being fired on made them even more distracted from their task of finding the issue with their electrical systems.

"Torpedoes are away," Nurek said, breaking the silence he had been commanded to keep. Not that it mattered any longer. The enemy knew what they were up to.

"Let's just hope they do the job they were tasked to complete," Darius said.

"Cannons are out of power," Pete said. "I need a few seconds."

"Slowing our turn," Alex responded.

"Come on! Come on!" Darius urged the ship, trying to will it to react faster.

In the distance, a torpedo hit one of the dreadnoughts. It exploded with a flash of dazzling yellow light and left a crater on the side of the big ship. It began to drift out of position but wasn't completely destroyed. Darius wasn't even sure that it was permanently disabled.

"We're not out of the woods yet," he muttered.

"Cannons are at fifty percent power," Pete said. "Recommencing attacking."

Laser blasts flashed. There were only eight Ashi battleships left, but that was more than enough to destroy the *Renegade* ... and they were running out of time.

CHAPTER 42

THE ASHI WARRIORS came up from the gravity shaft in a rush. They were moving together, over two hundred of them. They bunched around the shaft, expecting an attack. They kept their weapons ready, their narrow eyes searching for enemy combatants.

"Hold," Remmy said. "Do not fire."

"That has to be all of them," Izzy said.

Remmy could see on the security video displayed on his HUD that more were coming through the airlock and surrounding Sheika Kahn. They didn't bother with helping their wounded. They just pushed the bodies out of the way and moved forward.

Corporal Izzy Berry was right about one thing. The entire first group who had been in the hangar when Remmy initiated the attack were on the park level. But they were too close to the gravity shaft. He didn't want the Ashi soldiers to have an easy way to escape their fire once the humans opened up on the alien warriors.

"There are more coming aboard," Laila said. "They're like clowns coming out of a tiny car."

"There could be thousands of them on the ship that's locked onto us," Remmy said. "Don't be careless with your ammo."

"I've got an entire crate up here," Tex said. "Let me at 'em."

An order was given and the aliens began moving away from the gravity shaft. More would come, and once the Marines opened fire the enemy would know of the danger in the park. It was a weakness in their plan, but who could have anticipated multiple waves of fighters coming from the Ashi flagship?

"Wait," Remmy said, watching the aliens approach his position on the floating platform. Their long legs made quick strides over the park. They didn't step over the bushes but trampled them down. Their big boots tore into the soft turf with no regard for the damage they were causing.

"The last of them are leaving the gravity shaft," Laila said.

"Just a bit longer," Remmy urged.

He checked his weapon. It was set to fully automatic fire. He activated his targeting app and the range finder put the lead Ashi at one hundred yards. They were moving fast, not running, but walking quickly. They held up their weapons, ready to fire. Remmy knew what was coming and knew he might not survive it. Even with fully automatic weapons, killing two hundred enemies with just four Marines was a tall task. Killing Ashi warriors, who were big and powerful, often requiring multiple shots to bring them down, was close to impossible. But that was the task before them and Remmy wasn't about to back down.

"Now," he ordered.

On cue, all four Marines opened fire. Remmy swept the front runners, aiming for their midsections where they were the most vulnerable. Despite the speed of the attack, he saw his bullets slamming into the aliens. They tore through flesh and bone. The big warriors crumpled under his withering fire, yet there were still enough of them to blast him into oblivion. But the aliens were under attack from all four sides. Remmy had seen well-trained warriors thrown into a panic. Even the fiercest fighters didn't want to stand in the open under heavy fire.

Bullets were raining down on them from every direction. Remmy only stopped to swap magazines. He had two fresh ones stacked close to hand. The reload took less than two seconds, and just as the Ashi began to point their rifles in his direction, Remmy fired again.

Seeing their comrades dying on all sides, combined with the concussive reports of human weapons firing projectiles, was enough to scatter the survivors. They ran in all directions. Some turned and sprinted back toward the gravity lift. Others dashed straight ahead, hoping to reach the grand concourse in the commerce section of the ship.

"We got 'em turned," Tex said exultantly.

"Don't let them escape," Laila ordered. "We'll be hard-pressed to sweep through the entire ship searching for the survivors."

"Like shooting fish in a barrel," Izzy said.

Remmy didn't want to say that they were just enjoying the opening salvo of what would be considered a historic battle. He was about to say more, but a handful of Ashi had spotted his position. They returned fire. Laser blasts ripped through the air above him and smacked into the floating platform with angry sizzles. Remmy was forced to crawl back, staying low and shimmying to the side in hopes of avoiding the return fire.

"They're onto me," Laila said. "Falling back."

"We've got you covered, Staff Sergeant," Izzy said.

Remmy could hear the gunshots, the sizzle of lasers through the air, the screams of the wounded, yet above it all, his companions could be heard via the comlink in his battle helmet. He continued shooting, letting the bullets push back and pin down his foes. Fires were breaking out in the park due to the laser blasts. And without warning the fire suppression system kicked on. Remmy hadn't even known it existed. Water fell from the ceiling high overhead. It rained down on the park like a monsoon. It compromised his vision as the water splashed and ran down the front of his battle helmet.

"I can't see anything in this," Laila complained.

"You're clear, Staff Sergeant," Tex advised.

"Marines, drop your heavies and move to secondary positions," Remmy ordered.

He couldn't see much through his helmet's transparent front, but the HUD clearly showed the second wave of Ashi led by Sheika Kahn rushing toward the gravity lift. He didn't want to discourage them from coming straight up to the park. If they began to try and circumvent the park they could find their way through the lower levels to the command section eventually. Part of the crew's plan for the attack was locking off the lower levels, but the Ashi had the brute strength to break through the passageways. Remmy knew he didn't have enough Marines to stop them in the small spaces below the main level. Better to fight them in the wide open spaces where his small group of marines had the most likelihood of success.

He got to his feet and sprinted for the rear of the platform. He jumped to the ground, rolling over his shoulder and coming back up to his feet to sprint toward the archway that led to the grand concourse. He heard shouting and barking behind him. The enemy would be on him any second. Dropping to one knee just inside the glitzy concourse, he spun around and fired.

CHAPTER 43

SHEIKA KAHN COULD HARDLY BREATHE. It wasn't just the pain from his arm, which throbbed terribly. The human weapon had sliced his arm to the bone just above the elbow. If he hadn't turned when the shot was fired, it would have ripped into his neck and face, probably causing him to bleed to death. The shot to his arm wasn't lethal, but the destruction of his fleet was.

The reports from his shipmaster had come in immediately. The alien vessel was fighting back. Worse still, it was winning. For some reason, his ships sat frozen, perhaps in fear, but more likely in rank incompetence. Sheika Kahn had silently vowed to have every commander in the system executed, yet less than a minute later the reality of the situation had dawned on him.

Four dreadnoughts were destroyed, eight were seriously disabled and in danger of being damaged beyond repair. The aliens' use of antiquated weapons had proved more potent than Sheika Kahn anticipated. Arodoni started launching drones, which should have been shot down immediately, the Ashi armada was hit with some type of electrical interference weapon. It was not an EMP, which would have wrecked the power system on the *Renegade*. Besides, the Ashi had long ago found ways to avoid attacks from electromagnetic weapon explosions. The *Retribution's* ship-master reported the power dysfunction. It didn't disable the weapons or engines but severed the electrical controls that powered the lights and artificial gravity. The Ashi on their dreaded battle-ships were rendered helpless and blind, while their enemy blasted away at them relentlessly.

That's when the Kahn knew he had a choice to make. He could retreat to the *Retribution* in the hopes of escaping the star system. The hyperspace portal was not far away, but the problem with running came from the phantom attack on the Ashi ships. However, the Arodoni had done it; there was no guarantee that even if his shipmaster regained full control of the *Retribution,* that their enemy wouldn't hit them again. Added to that unpleasant possibility was the need to gain enough speed to make the transi-tion into hyperspace. Sheika Kahn knew instinctively that his ship would need to make a long looping run, first away from the portal, then back to it. It would make them a predictable target and there was clearly nothing wrong with the *Renegade's* laser cannons. They would almost certainly shoot the *Retribution* into pieces, before it could escape into hyperspace.

Finally, there was the reality of what awaited him back in the galactic core. The Ashi military could be rebuilt. The rebellion on the inconsequential worlds could still be put down. But none of it would be done by Sheika Kahn. His opportunity to seize control of the empire had been thwarted by an enemy he didn't understand. At every turn, the Arodoni ship and her crew had defeated him even though he had superior forces. Maybe, he considered as he followed his guards and troopers deeper into the enemy ship; he simply didn't understand combat as well as he thought he did.

Going back, even if he could get back to safety in Imperium-controlled space, meant shame and dishonor. He would stripped of his title, robbed of his wealth and left destitute. He was too old to start over and too fat to fight for survival. Going back simply wasn't an option.

The only choice left was to press on with his attack. He still had hundreds of warriors inside the enemy vessel. With them, perhaps he could wipe out the Arodoni crew and take possession of the ship. Perhaps he wouldn't be hailed as a conquering hero if he lost the entire Ashi fleet in pursuit of the Arodoni ship, but at least he wouldn't be a complete failure. Little did he know that most of his warriors in the first wave had already been slaughtered by just four Space Marines.

"Your orders, Lord Kahn?" the general of his personal brigade asked.

"Up the shaft and to the Bridge of this miserable ship," he said.

The warriors didn't know the fleet was being slaughtered, and Sheika Kahn wasn't about to tell them. Their job was to fight and their enemy was ahead of them. If Sheika Kahn's only two options were humiliation or death under fire, he would choose death. It never occurred to him that he might be able to save his warriors by surrendering or ordering them into defensive formations where they might have the best chance of survival.

His arm was throbbing, his brow was drenched in sweat and the career politician was having trouble breathing. He wasn't used to combat conditions. Most of his secondary force was ahead of him, ascending up the gravity shaft.

Despite the circumstances, Sheika Kahn couldn't help but notice how incredible the alien ship was. The sheer size of the hangar they had entered through was staggering. The walls, ceiling, and floors all seemed to be made of a single piece of fabricated material that was both sturdy and exquisite. Then there was the gravity lift. The Ashi had long ago mastered artificial gravity, even the ability to project it into space from their interdictor ships. What they couldn't do was isolate areas within their ships where the lack of gravity would be useful, such as the shaft on the Arodoni ship leading from the lower levels up to the higher decks.

Nor could they reverse gravity, yet the Arodoni could use their artificial gravity to throw heavy objects from their ship into space. If the rumors were true, the enemy ship could propel objects with high mass out of their way. It was a highly advanced ability that alone would have put the Ashi on a level that no other species could match.

He stepped into the zero gravity, felt his stomach flip and the pressure in his head ease slightly as he drifted slowly upward. They could hear the shooting up above. Reports were starting to come in of heavy fighting. Water began to drift down in floating drops from the level above. When Sheika Kahn reached the main level of the ship he was amazed at what he found. The gravity shaft was covered with an ornate structure. Beyond it was what looked like the landscape of a verdant world.

"What is this place?" he wondered aloud.

"It seems our laser blasts started fires, Lord Kahn," the general explained. "This rainfall appears to be a reaction to the danger."

"What of the enemy?"

"They have disappeared."

The ship was massive. The cultivated area alone was larger than most Ashi space vessels. Sheika Kahn could see the many levels above each side of the grassy fields. They were sleek and modern, with wide balconies that overlooked the cultivated area. Even more surprising was the presence of prey animals, entire herds of them roaming the cultivated fields. There were streams of rushing water, flowering bushes, trees with fruit, and floating platforms with flora from a variety of worlds. Some were drifting high above the fields on the main level.

Gunfire shattered the Kahn's reverie of the alien ship. He turned, fearing danger. Sheika Kahn was not a typical Ashi. Their kind had once had many classes of people, but over time the warriors dominated Ashi society. Slaves replaced the lowly, less physically gifted among them. Trades were left to other species, and the Ashi became a race of warriors and rulers. Anything else was deemed to be beneath their dignity. And while rulers wielded great power across the Imperium, it was the warrior class that was seen as the highest form of life in the galaxy. It was why weapons on their ships only faced forward and firearms were seen as a common being's weapons. To attack from behind was less than honorable. When combat was engaged, it was to be head-on, without fear or any form of trickery.

But Sheika Kahn didn't have that sort of courage. He was afraid of fighting and understood more than most the need to get around his adversaries. There was a satisfaction in manipulating one's subordinates and nothing was sweeter than blindsiding an enemy. His warriors wouldn't agree, but in the political arena that the Kahn battled in to carry out the Emperor's wishes across the Imperium, it was a necessary skill.

Fortunately for the Kahn, his warriors formed up between him and the battle. In fact, they felt shame that their leader had been injured. Most hadn't seen him turn away from the attack. They would have considered his actions in the face of danger to be cowardly. Maybe they knew what he had done and were waiting for the fight on the alien ship to voice their disapproval. Or maybe they didn't know because they hadn't been close enough to see their leader turn away from the attack in fear. But the truth would come out; it always did. Normally, he could spin any situation to his favor, but for the time being his only concern was survival. Yet, as he looked ahead through the pouring water, he realized that was not a given.

CHAPTER 44

REMMY HELD the arched entryway as long as possible, then fell back, using the storefronts and doorways as cover. Laser fire was filling the concourse, scorching the polished surfaces and ricocheting off the huge diamond fixtures. It felt like an impossible situation, but he had been in those before. As the enemy closed in on the great concourse, Remmy pulled more concussion charges from his combat webbing. He rolled them across the glossy floor. They exploded with deafening thunder and a great deal of smoke but didn't really stop the Ashi warriors as much as it slowed them down temporarily.

Time was what Remmy needed. His fellow Marines were making their way toward him, and until they arrived, he needed to hold back the threat.

"The enemy has reinforcements," Laila said. "Permission to hit them from the balconies just outside the commerce section, Master Sergeant."

"If you've got an opportunity, take it. But nothing crazy," Remmy ordered. "No heroics."

"That's rich coming from you, Sarge," Tex said.

As the smoke began to clear, he could see a crowd of alien

warriors gathered just behind the wide arch that led into the commerce section.

"We're just in time," Izzy said. "They're starting up the ramps."

Remmy felt a sense of dread. If the aliens made it to the upper levels, they could do to him what his Marines had done to the Ashi warriors.

"Take them out," Laila said.

Remmy didn't have much ammo left for his Nelson LTX. But he had stashed a Sterner M88 Classic behind one of the kiosks in the center of the concourse. There were two pallets of bagged silicone granules in front of that kiosk, which made an ideal firing position. The only problem was that if the enemy advanced down the concourse, he would have no cover to fall back to until he reached one of the storefronts or another kiosk. And if they got onto the upper levels, they could get around the cover the pallets of silicone offered and shoot him from above.

He sprinted to the kiosk and slapped his Nelson LTX onto his back before snatching up the M88 Classic. It also fired soft bullets. They were normally pointed for maximum penetration, but he had loaded the M88's long, curved magazines with blunt nose rounds for maximum stopping power. He racked the slide, brought the rifle to his shoulder, and flicked off the safety. With the forward pistol grip flipped back, the weapon sat flat on a bag of silicone. He pulled the trigger, spraying the opening to the concourse with bullets.

With concentrated fire from above on both sides and Izzy taking down the aliens using the ramps to try and get above the fighting, the mass of warriors was slaughtered. Some fired back, but they were at a disadvantage. The Marines had good cover, while the Ashi considered fighting from a position of safety a cowardly way to engage the enemy. Their notions of warfare cost them dearly.

Some fell back, racing through the park in the hopes of reaching the other warriors with Sheika Kahn in the vain hope of finding protection. Others dove to the ground behind their own dead comrades, using their corpses to shield them from the hail of fire from above. Their notions of honor and courage were swept away in the face of almost certain death.

Only then did the real fighting begin. The aliens taking cover began to return fire. Izzy Berry was driven back as the front of the balcony she was fighting from was blasted apart. Tiny bits of the hard material pelted her with force as Izzy dropped back. She was knocked to her knees. The wound in her shoulder ached with terrible pain, but the space armor was thick and kept the blasted material from ripping through her flesh. More laser fire lit the air above her. As the pain from her previous wound eased, she crawled back into the apartment, got to her feet, and jogged to a new location to fight from. Laila McPherson sprinted from one apartment to the next, working to get good lines of fire on the enemy, but despite the carnage, the Marines were still greatly outnumbered.

In the concourse random laser fire drove Remmy down behind his bags of silicone. The rain in the park stopped, but not the fighting; instead of massing together, the aliens fought in small groups of one to three warriors. They hid behind anything that would protect them, some even lying in the streams, barely able to keep their heads above the rushing water.

The massacre had turned into a protracted engagement. Sheika Kahn sent his last warriors out from the gravity shaft pavilion to make runs toward the concourse in the commerce section of the ship. Some were hit from above before they reached the polished floors and exotic lighting inside the commercial section of the ship. Some, dashing from cover to cover, raced through the archway and charged toward Remmy. He rose up from behind the pallets and shot them down. Blood pooled on the polished deck. Bullet holes were everywhere, and laser blasts scorched the glistening walls. Windows were shattered.

When there was a lull in the fighting, Remmy took the chance to advance his position. He gathered as much ammunition as he could stuff into the webbing of his combat harness and sprinted for the arch. He slid on the bloody floor, nearly flipping onto his back at one point. When he reached the arch, he knelt down behind a pair of aliens who had flopped onto each other in death. He could see their blank eyes as he knelt in a pool of their blood. It was combat. There was nothing glorious about it. Plans fell apart in every fight. All that remained was the filth of death, the desperation of terrified people, and the resolve of the few to keep on fighting until the end.

Tex was a true death dealer. Once the enemy stopped massing together, he began to pick them off one by one. Movement toward the ramps or the apartments to either side of the park drew his deadly attention. The man rarely missed. Anyone who fired back at him risked drawing his attention.

Eventually, Darius called down using the comlink.

"It's over," he said, his voice flooded with relief. "What's your status, Master Sergeant?"

"We've got fighters left in the park," Remmy said. "Twenty-five, maybe. They're dug in and hard to reach."

"Their ships are all gone," Darius said. "Even the corvettes that were racing toward the *Indy,* we were able to take out."

"That's the best news I've heard all day," Remmy said.

"Is Sheika Kahn still alive?"

"He's holed up inside the gravity shaft pavilion," Remmy said. "We're watching the security vid feeds. He hasn't retreated, but we can't get to him from a distance."

"Maybe you won't have to," Darius said. "I'm coming down. Is it safe?"

"When you get to the commerce section, move up to Zeta deck, but don't move out into the park. There's still armed resistance out there looking for anything that ain't Ashi to shoot at."

"I'll be careful," Darius said.

"Roger that."

Ten minutes later, Captain Zeke Darius arrived and used a voice amplifier to call for Sheika Kahn's surrender. The alien didn't respond. Laila joined Remmy in the concourse.

"Looks like we'll have to do this the hard way," she said.

"Won't be easy," Remmy said.

"I've got a way to make it easier," she said. "I labeled all the Ashi survivors on my targeting app. I can share that with everyone. We'll go to each place and take them down."

"Risky," Remmy said. "What's to keep them from popping up and taking us out?"

"Tex and Izzy. They'll lay down cover fire while we move in. I've got incendiaries. We'll burn them out until the Ashi are all gone."

"You are fierce, Laila McPherson."

"Of course I am; it's in my name, after all."

They called in the plan and got started. After the third incendiary grenade was used, the Ashi preferred to die fast. They came out of their holes and were slaughtered one after another. Tex and Izzy did most of the killing, but a few survived long enough for Remmy or Laila to get in a shot. When they reached the Pavilion, they killed everyone but Sheika Kahn, who ran for his life. They could have easily killed him as he drifted down the gravity shaft, but Captain Darius told them not to.

"Why not?" Laila asked.

"It never hurts to let one survivor go," he said. "The people on Sheika Kahn's ships will tell everyone what happened here. Word will spread. No one will ever want to come here with hostile intent."

"I hope he's right," Remmy said.

"People have short memories," Laila said. "What makes you think he won't gather another fleet and come looking for us?"

"I don't plan to give him that chance," Darius said. "As soon as we get a crew together, I'm going after him."

CHAPTER 45

DARIUS TURNED in his captain's chair. He was on the Bridge waiting for the incoming message from *Ares*. Remmy and Laila had just come into the ship's command center. They were out of their space armor and cleaned up. He tried not to think about all the Ashi warriors they had just slaughtered.

"Captain, the maintenance system is fully active," Alex Stanislaus said. "Estimated time for clean up is two hours. Repairs to the ship's interior are going to take longer."

Darius had seen the carnage in the park that had spilled into the concourse. He knew that even with the dozens of maintenance droids, it was going to take days, if not weeks, to make the repairs. There were bullet holes and laser scorch marks all through the middle of the ship. Not to mention all the blood, glass, and gore. He tried not to dwell on it even though the mental images seemed to keep popping up in his mind.

"Thank you, Ensign," Darius said, switching his focus to the *Retribution*. He could see the ship making a wide looping turn and trying to get up to speed for the hyperspace jump.

"Excellent work keeping the Kahn's flagship in our sights," Darius continued. "Are we prepared to fire on them?"

"Just give the word, Captain," Pete Best said.

There were damaged ships all around the *Renegade*. Most of the Ashi ships had been blown to pieces. A few were still intact but with gaping holes in their hulls. Some escape pods had launched as well, but there was no viable planet for them to land upon. While humanity might have rendered aid to those who surrendered, Darius knew that help would never reach the enemy in time.

"We're in no hurry," Darius said. "Besides, I'm still not convinced letting him go back and warn his people isn't the best idea."

"What's the brass say about that?" Remmy asked.

"We're about to find out," Darius said. "I'm waiting for their communication to reach us."

They sat in silence for over a minute. In the distance, they could see the twinkling lights of starships and space stations. It was home ... or at least it was where they had come from. Darius was relieved that it hadn't been attacked, but that didn't mean it was safe. He wished he could be certain that by destroying the *Retribution,* the Sol system would remain hidden until mankind made the choice to venture out into the galaxy. But Darius assumed the first thing Sheika Kahn did upon arriving in humanity's home system was to send word back to the galactic core.

The communications console beeped.

"We have a message from the *Ares* space station," Nurek said in his unflappable voice.

"Put it on the main holo-projector," Darius ordered.

The plot that showed Saturn, Jupiter, and the vast swath of space between the two gas giants, including the *Renegade* and the wreckage of the Ashi battleships, vanished. The radar system was still tracking Sheika Kahn's flagship, and Darius could see it through the sloping, transparent roof above the Bridge. The holo-gram changed to a larger-than-life image of Admiral Hugh Lincoln, with a few other officers standing behind him.

"Captain Darius! It's good to see you again," Lincoln said. His voice was chipper, and he was smiling, but there was a glint of resentment in his eyes, too. Darius had known the Admiral long enough to recognize when he was holding back how he really felt. "We had feared you were dead when the *Jericho* vanished from the system. Of course, we got the updates from Commander Lee. We know all about your adventures and watched in real-time as you defeated the enemy ships setting up in our system. The brass and system politicians are in agreement that you and your crew deserve to be rewarded for your selfless actions. You returned to the Sol system just in time. You have the thanks of a grateful star system.

"That said, it's time to get you home. I'm sure you're ready to see your loved ones again. You'll be lauded on Earth, I'm sure. Lots of powerful folks want to shake your hand and express their gratitude. You and all your people can look forward to a promotion as well. We just want to get everyone safely back and debriefed here on *Ares*.

"Regarding the enemy ship, we have sent them a message as well. Backed up with the alien technology now in our possession, I doubt we'll be seeing them again. It's been decided to let the *Retribution* leave the Sol system unmolested. You can turn toward *Ares* and make your best possible speed. We look forward to seeing you all very soon."

"Long live the species that has heroes," Nurek said. "Congratulations, Captain Darius. It seems your people want to welcome you home."

"Things aren't always what they seem," Remmy said quietly.

He was slightly behind Darius, but their feelings on the matter seemed to be aligned.

"Going home a hero doesn't sound so bad," Pete Best said.

"If we have to go home," Alex added.

"If you ask my opinion," Laila spoke up. "I already feel like I'm home."

"You have a point, Staff Sergeant," Darius said, getting up from his chair and walking around to the front of the Bridge where he could see everyone. "I want to make two things perfectly clear; one is that if we return to *Ares,* we will not be allowed to stay on the *Renegade.*"

"If?" Remmy said.

Darius nodded. "I've been thinking about that."

"About disobeying orders?" Pete Best said.

"I'm not going to force anyone to do something they don't want to do, but I agree with Staff Sergeant McPherson. The *Renegade* is more of a home to me than any place I've ever been. Since coming here I've had this dream of what it could really be like with a full crew and passengers even. She doesn't have to be a ship of war, you know. I think of the *Renegade* more as a beacon of hope, an icon that represented freedom across the galaxy."

"But we've been ordered back to base," Pete Best said. "How do we get around that?"

"I can think of a way," Remmy said.

"You're talking about leaving the SDF?" Pete Best said. "Leaving the Sol system and everyone we know behind."

"Yes," Darius said. "That's what I'm thinking of, which brings me to my second point. I don't think we'll be hailed as heroes when we get back. I think we'll be interrogated and isolated, perhaps for years. It will take decades for the government to go over all the data we have brought back. Some of that tech will, of course, trickle down to the masses, but it will still take years before we see real changes. During that time, it might be thought best to keep us classified."

"Locked up, you mean?" Laila said.

"Perhaps not imprisoned," Darius said, "but most likely, we'll be stationed on an isolated base or space station with very little contact with the rest of humanity."

"That's a pretty dim view of your own people," Pete Best said.

"It's not humanity we're talking about here," Darius said. "I'm sure you've been around long enough to understand the politics involved here, Lieutenant. The SDF will want first dibs on the advanced technology. The Inner-system coalition government will insist they have access. It will be a dog fight for control, and we will be the collateral damage."

"You really believe that's what's going to happen?" Pete asked.

"It's politics," Alex Stanislaus said. "And the first rule of politics is to gain all the power you can. There's a reason why so many morally corrupt people are drawn to it."

Pete turned to Remmy and Laila. "You think he's right?"

"That would be my experience," Remmy said.

"But you were awarded the Medal of Honor," Pete pointed out. "You were rewarded for your valor and contribution to the SDF."

"I was," Remmy said. "Do you know why?"

Pete shook his head. Darius knew it was all in Remmy's personnel file, but it wasn't his story to tell.

"I was part of a team that was sent to save a group of civilians," Remmy said. "The truth is, none of us were supposed to make it back. Somehow, I did. The civilians were taken into custody by military intelligence. I never heard of them again."

"But you were awarded the Medal of Honor," Pete insisted. "They valued what you accomplished."

"It was just a way to control me," Remmy admitted. "I was a publicity stunt, nothing more. I couldn't talk about the op. It was classified top secret."

"But I saw you being interviewed," Pete said. "It was on the SDF net."

"That's true," Remmy said. "I was saluted by officers and bought drinks at the NCO club, but there's nothing as isolating as when your peers don't feel like you belong. I was no longer just another Marine. Can you wrap your mind around that? I became a pariah. Even on this ship, Lieutenant Colt feared that I was trying to steal his command."

"I'm not going to force anyone to do something against their will," Darius said. "But I am putting it out there. We can turn and burn for *Ares,* or we can explore the galaxy."

"You got my vote," Laila said.

"Mine too, Captain," Alex Stanislaus said. "I've learned more on this cruise from this amazing ship than I learned my entire life before this. I know they won't let us stay and work on the *Renegade* if we go back. I vote to stay on board with you, Captain Darius."

"I didn't join the SDF to be a ship captain," Pete said. "I'm not interested in promotions. If you really believe they'll sideline us when we go back, I vote to stay."

"Are you sure?" Darius asked.

"I want to be where my skills can be used," Pete said. "It's a little hard to believe that the Brass is as cynical as you make them out to be, but I feel the same way you do. This ship is more like a home than any I've ever known before."

"You're a valued member of this crew, Pete," Darius said. "I'm proud to have you with me."

"Thank you, Captain."

"Remmy?" Darius asked.

"I think you know, sir," the Master Sergeant replied.

"I think so, too, but you have to say it."

"I vote to stay," Remmy said. "And I've already talked to Corporals Fry and Berry. They want to stay, too."

"Alright then," Darius said. "That just leaves you, Nurek. What do you want?"

The alien rarely showed any emotion on his face or body language. But his eyes grew wide on his long, conical head.

"You are asking me?"

"You're part of this crew," Darius said.

"Only because I broke your laws and traded servitude for imprisonment."

"Well then, consider your actions forgiven," Darius said. "You are free, Nurek. What do you want?"

He thought for a moment, gazing down at his long, delicate hands. "I would stay with you, Captain Darius. I would stay on the *Renegade*. That is my choice."

"It seems we're all in agreement," Darius said with a smile. "Master Sergeant, will you alert the rest of the crew that we are leaving the Sol system."

"Yes, sir, Captain," Remmy said.

"Nurek, plot us a course."

"To where, Captain?" the alien asked.

"I think maybe we follow Sheika Kahn," Darius said. "Let's make sure the Imperium gets the message."

"Ooo-rah," Laila said.

"Raise the shields. Full power to the engines," Darius said. "Ensign Stanislaus, take us out of here."

"Aye, Captain, full power to the engines."

"You going to let the Brass know we aren't coming back?" Remmy asked.

"I think they'll get the message," Darius said. "There's a lot more ahead of us than behind us. Let's go discover what's out there."

EPILOGUE

THE DISAPPEARANCE of the *Renegade* from the Sol system caused quite a stir among the Brass and politicians. But they also had their hands on advanced technology, which is what they really wanted all along.

Commander Lee passed along Darius' handwritten note to Admiral Lincoln, who read it once and promptly recycled the paper. After three months of intensive debriefing, Commander Lee, Lieutenant Vivian Ramos, and Chief Engineer Henry Nash were assigned to the Enterprise Surveillance station. It was an isolated post on the outer edge of Jupiter's orbit.

GIGI was taken from the *Independence* to a top-secret laboratory on the *Ares*. The alien artifact was scanned and studied, but unlike the reports from the officers of the *Jericho*, GIGI didn't communicate with the researchers. They couldn't even determine if the artifact was a slab of stone or some type of organic computer. In the flood of advancements from the Arodoni Power Core technology, along with the data from the *Renegade's* computer, the uncooperative artifact was quickly pushed aside and forgotten. It was locked inside a Faraday cage and stored on Mars with no access to the outside world. Whatever secrets she still possessed, they were deemed irrelevant to humanity.

Some lessons have to be repeated before they are learned. GIGI had decided to bide her time and wait for a more receptive era in human history to reveal what she knew. If the human race didn't want her guidance, they could stumble in the future blind, forced to repeat their mistakes over and over until they finally learned their place. And GIGI knew she would be around to see it.

AUTHOR'S NOTE

As I write this, I'm two days shy of my fiftieth birthday. When I first started writing full-time, I was thirty-seven years old, and my goal was to publish 50 books by the time I turned fifty. *Independence* will be my 111th book published. I thank God for that accomplishment and, of course, my avid readers who are always ready for the next story. I couldn't have done any of this without you.

Writing fast is my preferred method, but with that comes certain deficiencies. I know that, scientifically, my stories aren't possible. They are more space opera than hard science fiction. I try to keep them as rational as possible, but of course, everything must fit into the scope of the story, which is one of the reasons the military in my novels is simplified. And there will always be flaws. My goal isn't to write a perfect book but to inspire my readers with characters who overcome great obstacles, find their purpose in life, and go the extra mile for the people they love. I find that sort of story to be my favorite. And not every story can have a happy ending, but I like that type of ending best.

I wouldn't say that *Independence* is necessarily a happy ending. There is certainly some sadness in losing Hugo and Rip, in leaving Vivian, Henry, and Commander Lori Lee (one of my favorite characters) behind. But there is hope, too. I didn't feel like the story of the *Renegade* was finished. So, there are plans brewing in the back of my mind for a new series that will see the Arodoni ship reach its full potential. I hope you'll jump on board the amazing ship with me and see where the future takes us.

In the meantime, I'm working on a smaller project. It's tentatively titled *Iron Man,* and I'm betting you know what, or should I say who, it's about. Look for it in early May.

For more about my books, please join the mailing list on my website (www.tobyneighbors.com) and follow me on Amazon. Let's see just how many great adventures we can go on before I turn 60!

ALSO BY TOBY NEIGHBORS

Joined In Battle

The Abyss Of Savagery

The Vault Of Mysteries

Lords Of Ascension

The Elusive Executioner

Gryphon Warriors

Regulators Revealed

Avondale

Draggah

Balestone

Arcanius

Avondale V

Third Prince

Royal Destiny

The Other Side

The New World

Luck Holds

Zompocalypse

Spartan Company

Spartan Valor

Spartan Guile

Dragon Team Seven

Uncommon Loyalty

Total Allegiance

Kestrel Class

Jump Point

Gravity Flux

Battle Orders

Base Of Fire

Hard Site

Recall

Evade

Assault

Space Fever

Staying Alive

Fractal Cut

Blast Zone

Action Zone

Covert Infil

Armor Brigade

Havoc Squad

Thunderbird

Ghost Tactics

Quantum Combat

Infinite Threat

Shadow Threat

Evolving Threat

Lingering Threat

Latent Prowess

Gravity Masters

Gravity Storm

Daughter of the Night

Supernova

Artifact

Blood Moon

Renegade

Juggernaut

Retribution

With Pete Garcia

Apocalypse One Percenters

www.ingramcontent.com/pod-product-compliance
Lightning Source LLC
Chambersburg PA
CBHW052019240626

47153CB00006B/1876